SEVEN RULES FOR A PERFECT MARRIAGE

SEVEN RULES FOR A PERFECT MARRIAGE

REBECCA REID

BLOOMSBURY PUBLISHING
LONDON • OXFORD • NEW YORK • NEW DELHI • SYDNEY

BLOOMSBURY PUBLISHING
Bloomsbury Publishing Plc
50 Bedford Square, London, WC1B 3DP, UK
29 Earlsfort Terrace, Dublin 2, Ireland
29 Earlsfort Terrace, Dublin 2, D02 AY28, Ireland

BLOOMSBURY, BLOOMSBURY PUBLISHING and the Diana logo
are trademarks of Bloomsbury Publishing Plc

First published in Great Britain 2025

Copyright © Rebecca Reid, 2025

Rebecca Reid is identified as the author of this work in accordance with the
Copyright, Designs and Patents Act 1988.

This advance reading copy is printed from uncorrected proof pages and is not for resale. This
does not represent the final text and should not be quoted without
reference to the final printed book

This is a work of fiction. Names and characters are the product of the author's imagination
and any resemblance to actual persons, living or dead, is entirely coincidental

All rights reserved. No part of this publication may be: i) reproduced or transmitted in any form,
electronic or mechanical, including photocopying, recording or by means of any information
storage or retrieval system without prior permission in writing from the publishers; or ii) used
or reproduced in any way for the training, development or operation of artificial intelligence
(AI) technologies, including generative AI technologies. The rights holders expressly reserve this
publication from the text and data mining exception as per Article 4(3) of the Digital Single
Market Directive (EU) 2019/790

A catalogue record for this book is available from the British Library

ISBN: PB: 978-1-5266-8137-9; EBOOK: 978-1-5266-8134-8; EPDF: 978-1-5266-8133-1

2 4 6 8 10 9 7 5 3 1

Typeset by Integra Software Services Pvt. Ltd.
Printed and bound in Great Britain by CPI Group (UK) Ltd, Croydon CR0 4YY

To find out more about our authors and books visit www.bloomsbury.com
and sign up for our newsletters.

For product safety related questions contact productsafety@bloomsbury.com

For M

A Note on the Content

This story contains discussion of fertility issues, miscarriage and abortion.

The Launch Party

Jessica

Before I was a little bit famous, I used to find private dining rooms fascinating. On the rare occasion I'd end up at a restaurant fancy enough to have one, I'd spend the evening straining my neck, trying to work out who's inside and why they're special. Only it turns out, now that I spend quite a lot of time in them, dining rooms are usually a disappointment. Cold, boring even. Sometimes I've found myself in one for a work event and I spend the evening feeling left out, missing the hustle and bustle of the restaurant. But tonight is different. This is where the party is. The room is filled with thirty of our favourite influencers; it is loud and warm and wonderful. Each time the door opens, as the waiters bring in another bottle of wine, I can see people out there trying to look inside, trying to work out who we are and what we're doing. For the first time in my entire life – and even though my imposter syndrome is never gone for long – I feel like I've made it.

Anyone who catches a glimpse will see the carefully decorated table, laden with fat white pillar candles and out-of-season flowers. And they'll see me, hair blow-dried, make-up professionally applied, wearing two sets of shapewear under the dress lent to me by some designer I can't pronounce, sitting next to my handsome dark-haired husband who has rolled up the sleeves on his shirt and slung his perfectly tailored (also borrowed) jacket over the back of his chair.

I'm trying very hard to drink in every detail of it, to stay completely present, because I don't know if I'll ever get to feel like this much of a big deal again. As I scan the room, Clay stands up, tanned and beaming. In fairness to him, even if he had been lying on a sunbed somewhere for the last couple of weeks, you'd never have known it. He's an absolute shark of a manager, replies to every single one of my emails within seconds. And in the run up to this, there have been a *lot* of emails. Clay clinks a knife against his glass and the table falls silent.

'I've known Jessica and Jack for a while now.' He smiles, looking at us. 'And I have to say, being around them is absolutely –' he pauses for dramatic effect – 'sickening.'

Everyone laughs.

'Seriously,' he says, after he's waited for the laughter to subside. 'When you're in the same room as them, you feel it. There's an energy, a sort of force field. I've never known two people who are so much in love, let alone after so long together. In fact –' he pauses again, clearly very much enjoying the spotlight – 'they're perfect. But unlike most perfect couples, these two have something very special and very unusual. They are willing to tell the rest of us how we can make our own relationships just as successful as theirs.' He picks up a book. It's the same book that's dotted all over the room. A pale purple hardback with embossed blue letters. He holds it up triumphantly.

'Fifty thousand pre-orders,' he announces. 'Due to be published in fifteen countries. Film companies are making offers as we speak. And all because Jack and Jessica have found the secret to a perfect marriage. Or rather, the Seven Rules which make a perfect marriage.' Applause breaks out and Clay waits for it to subside before he goes on. 'Even I might be able to make a relationship last longer than two weeks with their help. Anyway, we brought you all here tonight to celebrate, so I will just say, I've never been so proud to represent anyone.' He raises his glass. 'To Jessica and Jack.'

Everyone else choruses, 'To Jessica and Jack.' There's a little pause as Suze, who works for our agency, gets up and wrestles with an enormous gift-wrapped box. Jack and I look at each other in surprise. We rip the paper off like excited children and reveal a beautiful framed print.

Seven Rules for a Perfect Marriage

1. *Ignore the old advice, and go to bed on an argument – staying up fighting never helps.*
2. *You are your partner's greatest cheerleader, act like it.*
3. *100% honesty, 100% of the time.*
4. *Sex and intimacy have to be a priority, even when life gets in the way.*
5. *Self-care isn't selfish; make time to make yourself the best possible person.*
6. *Your parents are your family and your responsibility.*
7. *Always leave the party together.*

'Something to hang over the marital bed,' Clay jokes. We both laugh and I lean over the mess of wrapping paper to kiss Jack while someone snaps a photo of us.

'Thank you,' I say, beaming. Someone calls 'Speech', and while I wasn't really intending to say anything, they've all made such a fuss of us, this is so much more than we deserve, I feel like I sort of have to. So I get to my feet, a little unsteady on the shoes that the stylist convinced me to wear.

'Thank you, Clay,' I say, giving him a grateful look. 'You've been the most fantastic manager imaginable. You've changed our lives. Jack and I are so, so grateful. And while I would hesitate to describe our marriage as perfect ... I know we both agree that our relationship is the most important thing in our lives. And we really hope that by sharing what works for us, we might be able to help other people. Putting those rules together took years, and lots of mistakes. I just hope we might be able to help some other people get there quicker than we did!'

Everyone claps and takes pictures as I raise my glass.

'Was that okay?' I murmur into Jack's ear as I sit back down.

Jack slips his hand in mine. 'Perfect.'

Rule One

*Ignore the old advice, and go to bed on an argument —
staying up fighting never helps*

Jessica

My cheeks are aching as I say goodbye to the last of our guests. Clay takes yet another picture of me hugging a woman whose posts I comment on every week but who I had never actually met until tonight. Eventually, everyone is gone. I ease the shoes off my feet and drink in the aftermath of our party. The table is strewn with glasses and bottles, the tablecloth ringed with red wine stains, and the room is softly quiet.

'I think we can call that a resounding success.' Clay smiles.

'Do you think so?' I ask. 'I really hope everyone enjoyed it — did you hear that one of the girls was saying she posted this afternoon and she'd had more people clicking through to the book than any of the cleaning products she's shared?'

'I did, but I do not hate hearing it twice.' Clay laughs. 'It's like lightning in a bottle. I'm telling you, this just doesn't happen.'

Jack picks up a glass from the table, a glass that I'm not entirely sure was his, and drains it. 'Do you need anything else from us?'

'No, no, you're free to go,' Clay says. 'Unless anyone wants a nightcap?'

'No thanks,' Jack replies. He takes my hand. 'We've got a hotel room to make the most of. Thanks for the print, very thoughtful,' he gestures, about to pick it up.

'No need to take it now, I'll have it shipped.' Clay kisses me on the cheek. 'Try to get some sleep, superstar. Big day tomorrow.'

He turns to Jack. 'The car is booked for six a.m.'

'I could have driven us,' Jack says.

'Don't be daft,' Clay says. 'You're selling books in the kinds of numbers we usually see from wizards or kinky billionaires. The least they can do is arrange a car.'

They shake hands, I gather my things, and we head through the cavernous lobby to the lifts.

'That went well,' I say.

As we step inside, Jack drops my hand. 'I think we put on a decent show.'

'Show?' I ask, rolling my eyes and pressing the 'P' button for penthouse. Nothing happens until I scan our key card.

'You know what I mean,' he replies. I look at his strong, gorgeous profile against the backdrop of London splayed out beneath us. The skyline is rambling, messy and beautiful, studded with lights. The lift is glass and it slides effortlessly up all twenty-five floors, leaving my stomach behind and doubling the effects of the champagne I've been drinking all evening. I can't help feeling sort of giddy. We are here. We've done it.

'I still don't really understand why we need to stay in a hotel when our house is less than half an hour away,' Jack mutters as the doors swoosh open, right into the room.

'Oh, come on. You're really telling me you'd rather be at home than here? Looking at all of this? We're in the penthouse, Jack. The *penthouse.*'

Weirdly, me repeating the word penthouse over again doesn't seem to convince him that this is exciting. He shrugs. 'I'd just like my own bed.'

'Poor darling. No one has ever known such suffering,' I tease. 'Forced to stay in a five-star hotel on the night of his book launch.' Am I teasing? I think I am. We both gaze out at the view again and I wonder if people pay extra for expansive hotel room views because they're a conversation piece for couples who've already said millions of words to each other.

'So, we've got a hotel room to make the most of?' I ask, repeating his comment to Clay and trying very hard to sound sexy rather than sarcastic.

'Don't worry,' he says, half smiling. 'I know we're already covered for this month.'

He means the perfunctory sex we had earlier this week, which he only initiated because I'd put it in our shared diary. Given how painfully unsuccessful our attempts have been for months on end, it probably won't make any difference anyway. We've been trying for a year now, without so much as a late period.

'We can have sex when I'm not ovulating,' I say, irritated by the entirely accurate assessment of our once brilliant, now depressing sex life. We can. We don't, but we *can.*

Jack takes a whiskey from the minibar and pours it into a glass. 'I'm knackered,' he says. 'I'd be no use to you.'

It's funny how his vehement disapproval of minibar drinks has disappeared now that the hotel is giving us a free stay in exchange for coverage. Years ago, on a cheap package holiday to Greece, I actually cried because I was so hungover and I wanted a Diet Coke but he insisted on walking to the local shop in 35-degree heat rather than pay the inflated price for the one already in the room. He called it a 'matter of principle'. I am tempted to point this out, to remind him how far we've come. But I sense he won't see it that way, and it will lead to an argument. And he did put on a good show this evening. He's never liked big groups of people he doesn't know, but you would never have been able to tell; I am grateful to him for that. So I sit, cross-legged, looking out across the sky. The bed is half the size of our first flat, covered in a huge blue silk and velvet cover. I breathe out, trying to exhale the tension from the day – the worry that the party would be a disaster, that Jack would make some intellectual joke that no one would get, that half the guest list wouldn't turn up or my dress wouldn't fit.

'You know, I read somewhere once that hotel eiderdowns are one of the most heavily bacteria-saturated surfaces in the world,' Jack tells me, opening the minibar and rifling for snacks. I get up. Not that I especially care about the idea of E. coli lurking on my bedding, but because he's ruined the moment. 'Are you going to shower before bed?' I ask.

'I wasn't planning to, no,' he responds without looking up.

'Fine.'

'Do you want me to shower?'

'I don't care if you shower or not.'

'Then why did you ask?'

'Because I wanted to know if you wanted the bathroom first,' I explain, increasingly irritated. I'm tired; we've been in performance mode all day – longer than that if you count the weeks of press. I just want to wash the evening off me and get into bed.

'Okay, fine, I'll have a shower,' he says.

I roll my eyes at his back as he retreats into the bathroom. I realise that I am relieved to hear the door lock and the shower run. It means five minutes where we don't have to talk to each other, look at each other, be together, after a two-week prepublication press tour where we've spent literally every second of our time together. It would be weird if we weren't sick of each other, I tell myself. I wrap myself in the enormous towelling robe they've left on the bed and then lie in blissful peace, watching videos on my phone with the volume turned up. Eventually, while I'm watching a French chef make an éclair which looks like a sausage dog, he surfaces from the bathroom wrapped in a towel, and then pulls on a T-shirt and pair of boxers. I turn the volume off on my phone and we nod at each other like colleagues who've bumped into each other on the train platform, and then I go into the bathroom, taking my clothes off behind the closed door. I can't work out how to make the huge complicated shower, clad in marble and brass, work. I could go and ask Jack how he did it. But I won't.

I pull at various knobs and levers, patience wearing thin, and somehow I make the thing turn on. The warm water feels glorious, washing off the layers of make-up applied earlier this evening by a professional make-up artist whose fingers smelled comfortingly of cigarettes – a pleasant memory of when I used to be fun. There's something sort of pleasing about rubbing it all away with cleanser after an evening spent not touching my own face lest I smudge her work. I reach for the shampoo on autopilot and tip it into my hands. Nothing comes out. I inspect the small brown bottle, holding it up to the light and looking closer to see that it's empty. How is that possible? I decanted my shampoo and conditioner into these little bottles, exactly enough for one hair wash. After years of fighting with my hair, which really wants to have a sort of wire-wool consistency, I have finally found something that works, and I never travel anywhere without it. I smack the bottom of the bottle with the palm of my hand, as if I can magic more shampoo out of it, but obviously I can't. It is completely empty.

Jack looks surprised to see me standing, wrapped in a towel, hair soaking, mascara under my eyes.

'What?' he asks as I stand there, brandishing the bottle.

'You finished my shampoo,' I accuse him, like I'm trichology Poirot.

'I don't think I did.'

'I see. So, someone else broke in here, used my shampoo and left everything else untouched?' I ask. 'A shampoo-focused hotel thief?'

'Are we really about to have a row over shampoo?' The way he says 'shampoo' drips with disdain, like I'm being utterly mad.

'Yes, we are, because you used all of mine and I've got to look half decent tomorrow morning.'

Jack gets to his feet wearily. He walks to the bathroom with the gait of a sullen teenager and picks up the bottles of hotel shampoo. 'There's loads of shampoo in here.'

'I can't use that.'

He looks at me like I'm deranged. 'Obviously you can use it,' he says.

'My hair will look like shit if I use that.'

'Don't be ridiculous.'

'I'm not being ridiculous.'

He looks at me and, for a moment, I wonder if I might hate him.

'Oh come on, this is like Coke and Pepsi; if I took the labels off there's no way you'd know the difference.'

'I would,' I say, restraining from stamping my foot, or pointing out that I could totally tell the difference between Coke and Pepsi. 'Jack, I grew up with curly ginger hair, I know almost everything there is to know about shampoo.'

I lean forward and sniff at his damp hair. It smells unmistakably of my £54-a-bottle shampoo.

'You did use it!' I say, my anger taking root.

'Sorry.' He shrugs. 'I thought it was the free stuff that came with the room.'

I take a deep breath. Not really because I want to, but because our book tells people to and I've learned that if I ignore our advice, then I feel like a hypocrite and that makes me even more annoyed. What I'd really like to do is tell him that he's a selfish arsehole and he's spoiling what was supposed to be a treat to celebrate the genuinely massive achievement of our first book launching straight on to the bestseller charts.

Instead I hear myself saying, 'I understand that it wasn't your intention to upset me by finishing the shampoo, but it has frustrated me. I don't feel that you respect how important this issue is to me in this moment.'

Jack glances at the ceiling and then – and I can tell it's taking superhuman effort – he replies, 'I apologise for using your shampoo. I didn't understand how important it was to you. I will endeavour not to use your shampoo again.'

He picks up his book and retreats into his own world. I don't feel any better and I would bet every penny our followers have spent on pre-orders for the book that he doesn't either. I miss the catharsis of snapping at him. But the rules work for everyone else, so they tell me constantly in our DMs. The issue here, clearly, is me.

As I retreat into the bathroom, I try not to curse Jack while washing my hair with the crap shampoo the hotel has provided, wondering why, even in really fancy places, the toiletries are always so useless. Then I blow-dry my hair, unpacking the very complicated science kit of a hairdryer, clipping my hair up into sections, smoothing each of those sections with a cool blast of air to 'seal' it. As I work, I think about what it must be like for Jack to wake up literally every day looking perfectly rumpled and actively more attractive for having made no effort. The unfairness of it burns so hot that I almost burn a section of hair.

It takes almost an hour to finish, and by the end, my arms feel like they're about to fall off. I lean forward to admire my handiwork in the mirror, but realise that this entire thing has been a waste of time – my hair looks like it was drawn on by a small child.

'See?' Jack says, when I eventually come to bed. 'It looks fine.'

'It does not,' I grind through my teeth. It looks frizzy and hideous, and it will look even worse tomorrow morning. His hair, on the other hand, looks better than ever.

'Could you turn the bathroom light off?' I ask. He doesn't look pleased about it, but gets up without objecting. While he's gone, I lean over to his side of the bed and, without pausing to think about what I'm doing, I pull his bookmark out and move it forward about ten pages. He gets back into bed and we turn the light off, half a mile of Egyptian cotton between our bodies, lying on a mattress which must have seen a thousand fucks. I smile into the dark at my own tiny, malicious little triumph and try not to wonder what it means that moving his bookmark has given me more satisfaction than the mature, sensible discussion I attempted earlier.

Jack

Jessica's fancy alarm clock allegedly senses when she's in the lightest part of her sleep cycle and then gently wakes her up with the sound of birds and waves. My alarm clock is on my phone. It doesn't sense anything, but when it reaches the time I've set, it makes a loud beeping noise to ensure that I wake up. So, while I'm up ten minutes before we need to leave, she is not.

This is, apparently, my fault.

'For fuck's sake!' she shouts as she runs around the room throwing things into her suitcase. 'How can this have happened? Why didn't you wake me?'

I sense that my opinion on her choice of alarm clock will not be well-received, nor will my observation that she didn't have to unpack as if on a two-week holiday for a nine-hour hotel stay. So I say nothing. Instead, I try to be helpful and pick up a pair of shoes. 'Shall I pack these?'

'No, I'm going to wear those.'

'Okay.' I pick up another pair. 'These?'

'I might wear those.'

'You're going to wear four shoes?' I ask, attempting to add some levity to the situation.

'Just let me do it!' she shouts. So, I do. I get my book out and settle in one of the many armchairs scattered around this comically large room.

'The cab's downstairs!' I shout at the closed bathroom door. I know hurrying her up will anger her further, but my phone now has three texts from Addison Lee.

'I'm nearly ready!' she shouts back.

'I think the driver gets a fine or something if we're late,' I try to reason. 'Can't you do some of this in the car?'

She pulls the door open, looking absolutely fine – beautiful, actually, because she always looks beautiful – but she seems to be on the brink of tears. 'No. I can't. And I'm sorry about that. I'll get his number and I'll pay him. But I can't go to a meet-and-greet looking like shit, otherwise people will take pictures and put them online and then discuss why I look so shit.'

'I look rough as a badger's arse,' I say, because if I make enough jokes, or half jokes, then eventually one of them has got to land. 'The event's about the book, not about what we look like.'

She gives me a look, which says 'are you fucking thick?' without having to say anything. I take her point. We might have written the book (and unlike most 'influencers', we did actually write our own book) but we're not exactly going to a literary enclave. The people who buy our books will very much care what we look like, which is presumably why Jessica never stops working out and mostly eats tenderstem broccoli these days. I try a different tact.

'Maybe they'll think that we were up all night shagging?'

'Well, then they'd be wrong, wouldn't they?' She sighs, and closes the door between us. I am more hurt than I have any right to be, given that her comment is completely true.

When the publishers first mooted the idea of a book tour, we were delighted. We'd never spent more than a week together on holiday, because we'd always spent most of our annual leave on other people's weddings and hen dos. The idea of two weeks going from hotel to hotel, just the two of us, sounded like a dream. Stupid as it sounds – especially from two people who are allegedly experts in this stuff – I don't think it occurred to either of us that we might start to find each other annoying.

Eventually we emerge from the warm yellow glow of the hotel lobby on to the freezing, dark street. Cold air goes straight down every gap in my jacket and I wince. The driver jumps out of the huge black van he's been waiting in patiently for half an hour and takes our bags, shivering in his suit. We slide into the warmth of the car and I feel myself relax. For everything I said to Clay last night, I'm pleased that I don't have to drive.

'It'll be about four hours,' the driver tells us.

I take a jumper from my bag and scrunch it up, putting it into the gap between my head and the car door, ready for another four hours of kip before we arrive. We're on the home straight now, almost done being show ponies. I've just got to do a decent job on this, and the breakfast TV show slot tomorrow, and then we're done.

'I think we need to go over some talking points,' Jessica says.

'We can do that,' I say, without opening my eyes. 'But I promise I will not remember anything you say to me before a cup of coffee.'

If she replies I don't hear it, as my head sinks into its makeshift pillow.

When Jessica first mentioned this event, I will admit, I was sceptical. I worked as a news producer for over ten years, so half the people I know have written a book, and they all say the same thing: book tours don't happen anymore. Big, famous authors do talks. Normal people don't. It's the classic lament that they give at dinner parties so that they don't sound up themselves while talking about work – 'Oh, I did a reading and three people came' – 'Oh, I went on a book tour and it was empty shop after empty shop'. Privately I've always thought that talking to a small group of people about a novel you've written sounded like the best thing imaginable, but that's neither here nor there. Anyway, when Jessica told me we were doing this, I nodded and said yes without objection, even though it was miles away and the day after the launch party, because I assumed it would be cancelled closer to the time due to lack of interest. But apparently the people who follow us (mainly her) actually want to spend their morning at a bookshop in the centre of Leeds so that they can talk to us. We've already done four of these in different places and every time I've been shocked by the attendance. Today is no different. As I nurse a cup of coffee like it's a dying lover, I'm feeling rather ill-equipped for this crowd. There was an email detailing everything about it, but it's on our shared email account, which I don't have on my phone, because I told Jessica I did, but I didn't, then I didn't really want to admit that I didn't, so I couldn't ask her for the password. I could have asked her, obviously. But for the majority of our relationship, I've been the sorted one, the one who prints out the tickets, returns her clothes to the post office so she gets a refund, fills out the RSVPs to weddings. But when it comes to Seven Rules, that's her role. I miss being the competent one, and I don't like disappointing her. But somehow lately all of my efforts not to disappoint her seem to directly result in me disappointing her.

The hangover I had when I woke up at the hotel was apparently only the John the Baptist of hangovers. The three-and-a-half hours of sleep I enjoyed in the car were supposed to leave me refreshed and ready to work, but very unfairly they have instead left me with a blinding headache and the feeling that my brain is a liquid, easily slopped around if I move my head too much.

'You understand what you're doing, right?' asks Suze, who is holding a clipboard and a Starbucks the length of her forearm. It occurs to me that she must either have driven up last night when the party ended, or got a monstrously early train, when she could easily have got in the car with us. My best guess is that now we're being treated like celebrities, they don't expect us to share our car with 'the staff'. I make a mental note to make sure she can get a lift home with us afterwards if she wants one.

'Yes,' I lie. I have got no idea, and I can't remember whether or not Jessica told me. Presumably it'll be the same drill as ever – people asking us questions I'd rather not answer. 'But let's just go over it one more time,' I say, because I've worked in radio long enough to know that only an idiot turns down a briefing on offer.

I can see Jessica rolling her eyes from the other side of the room. She knows I don't know what we're doing here. God, I hope it's a Q & A so we can just answer the questions thought up by the audience – that I can do.

'I'll introduce you, then we'll have questions.' My relief is extremely short-lived because she pauses for a breath and then continues, 'Jessica will speak, then you'll speak, then we'll have the signing. Keep it quick with people; don't let them tell you their whole life stories, otherwise the queue will get too long. Don't sign anything other than your own book, otherwise people won't buy them. Got it? There are just over three hundred for the talk and then you'll have about a hundred for the signing.'

The first piece of terrible news is that I'm supposed to be making a speech, which I definitely haven't prepared. The second is that I know without a shadow of a doubt that Jessica will have told me this, probably three or four times in the last month, and I will have told her that I'm listening and that I've got it sorted, all the while planning to write it in the car on the way up. I swallow some more coffee and feel the reassuring swell of anxiety which means the caffeine is kicking in.

They've filled the bottom level of this very large book-shop with chairs. Every single one is taken and there are more people standing at the back. I'm honestly not sure how this is going to go, but one look at Jessica, in a black polo neck and skirt, her legs endless in sort of see-through black tights and ankle boots with spikes on them, tells me I have to pull myself together because it's happening. We step out on to the stage to raucous applause. And I allow myself a moment of amazement at what Jessica has created. All of these people are here because of her. I still sometimes find myself shocked that I'm allowed to sleep next to her with my arm between her and her pillow or slip my hand down the back of her jeans while I kiss her neck. That I'm the one who gets to hold her hair back when she's sick or refill her wine glass over dinner. She's magic. I know that. But it still takes me by surprise that her magic has become ... a revenue stream.

I tried to compliment her on it, a few months ago. The fact that she has such a head for this business. But it came out wrong, and somehow it turned into a weird, uncom-fortable conversation about her monetising our marriage. Neither of us has mentioned it since. Anyway. Once the press tour is over, we can enjoy the money and hopefully I can gently fade back into semi-obscurity.

'I can't believe how many of you are here!' Jessica says, standing at the podium, her weight more on one foot than the other. I know she's nervous – that's defi-nitely one of her tells – but no one else would realise. I catch her eye and shoot her an asinine thumbs up. 'Thank you all so much for being here. Jack and I could never have dreamed that starting an Instagram account could have changed our lives like this, and we really do owe all of that to you.'

She talks a little while longer about marriage, about relationships, about wanting things to last. On the face of it, she says nothing new. There's probably very little in there you couldn't get from other self-help books. But she's charming and she means what she says. You can really feel how much she means it, and her earnest cheerfulness is contagious. I can see every face in the room trained towards her, absorbing her energy, radiating it back at her. When she's finished, the audience eagerly applauds. She sits back down and there's an excited flush along her cheekbones. She is so very, very good at this. Which makes me feel even more like a fraud.

I get to my feet and look out at the crowd. As ever, it's almost entirely women. After all, this is the gender that puts in the effort to save the marriage rather than looking surprised when someone leaves fifteen years into a 'happy' relationship.

'Hi,' I say. My voice echoes over the speakers. 'Thanks for coming. As Jessica says, it means a lot.'

The audience starts shifting in their seats. They can see that I'm not confident in this position, and it's making them uncomfortable. I sense that I've only got a matter of minutes before I lose them entirely. I wish, not for the first time, that I were better at this. The irony is, I used to dream of doing this. Giving a talk in front of a packed audience in a bookshop. Only, in that dream it's a novel, written by me, and I'm there as a bona fide author. Not an accessory.

If that sounds self-pitying, it's not supposed to. I'm very aware of how lucky we are. I'm just also aware of my own limitations. Jessica does the legwork on Instagram. She does the videos and the 'ask me anything' stories. I smile in photos and write one weekly caption. I'm not the reason they're here. She is. I'm the Charles to her Diana. Though, hopefully not in any more meaningful sense than that people are more excited to see her than me. This is not a helpful train of thought. They're all looking at me, waiting for me to speak, to say anything.

To my enormous relief, I think of something I can say, something I still know off by heart. 'The first time I met Jessica, we were queuing up to take our last exam at university. We'd both been there for three years, and we'd never crossed paths before. She was standing behind me, she tapped me on the shoulder and she asked if she could borrow a pen. And the first thing I thought was, how have you come to an exam without a pen, you absolute psycho.'

Everyone laughs. Thank Christ.

'But the second thing I thought was, how weird that the most beautiful person on the face of the planet is in the same exam hall as me. I chased her out into the street after the exam, asked for her email address, and to my absolute shock, actually got it. And from then on, it was easy. But I think it was easy because we kept choosing each other over and over again. And that's the thing about marriage.' I pause for a moment in an attempt to try and sound profound, giving my words more gravitas. 'It's not just a choice you make when you propose, or when you walk down the aisle. But a choice that you make every single day. When I wake up in the morning, the first choice I make is to try to make Jessica happy. And she does the same. Everything we do is aimed at being better, kinder, funnier, sexier, just generally an improved version of ourselves, for each other. And that's easy for Jessica. You all follow her – you know. She's the perfect woman. I don't think she even really has to try to be that beautiful, that funny, that kind. But me, I'm not perfect. I'm grumpy. My hair grows in four different directions. I don't like sharing the crossword in case someone solves a clue I can't get. And that's why I need Jessica. She's the reason I don't lean into all my bad behaviours, all my worst choices. I want to be the kind of person who deserves to be in a relationship with her. And I spend my life trying to make that happen. Even if I did miss out on getting a first, because I spent the whole of that exam staring at her, wondering if I'd ever get to talk to her again.'

I pause and look around. They're smiling. I look to Jessica, hoping for a thumbs up or a nod, but she's looking at Beatrix, gauging her reaction.

'I can't believe that any of this has happened to me – that we have a book, that you're all here to speak to me. But I can believe that it happened to Jessica. She's just too special a person for it not to turn out this way. And that's why I plan to keep choosing her, keep choosing to make her happy for as long as she'll have me.'

I sit back down and try not to feel pleased that their applause for me is as loud as it was for Jessica.

We spend the next couple of hours sitting behind a long table with stacks and stacks of books between us.

'I loved your speech,' says a middle-aged woman. 'Your account saved my marriage.'

'I'm sure you saved it,' I reply, signing the book and passing it to Jessica. 'You did the hard work.'

'Where do you find one this lovely?' another woman asks Jessica, gesturing towards me as she hands over her book to be signed.

'I got very, very lucky.' Jessica smiles back. 'And we work hard at it. Sometimes we work really hard!'

A pretty blonde woman with a baby comes to the front of the line. 'Your advice works,' she says conspiratorially as I sign her book.

'Oh?' I ask.

'When I found your account, my marriage was on dialysis. But we followed the advice and, well ...' She holds the baby up, like a rubber stamp of approval that she and her partner have worked it out.

I laugh. 'I'm glad to hear it. Did you name the baby after either of us?'

She giggles and Jessica shoots me an appreciative glance from her end of the table. I hadn't realised she was so worried I wouldn't make the effort to chat with all the fans who've queued up.

My wrist is cramping and my signature starting to look comical by the time we finally finish up. They take photos of us outside the shop and with various local influencers, and then we're bundled into a waiting Addison Lee. In the car Jessica neatly eats exactly half of the sushi Beatrix brought her and then puts the rest of it away. It's the only thing I've seen her eat all day, whereas I've eaten three plates of the free biscuits they provided, and the very large BLT Beatrix got me from Pret. Jessica is on her phone, editing photos from the event and drafting captions. I reach out to touch her hand, but she pulls away.

'What's wrong?' I say, stung. I can't remember her ever having done that before. 'I thought that went quite well.'

She doesn't reply.

'You didn't?' I ask, trying to work out how she could possibly be upset with me when we've just put on a storming performance.

'The only thing I asked you to do for today was to write a speech.'

'I did write a speech.'

She gives me an icy look. 'No. You repeated your speech from our wedding.'

'People seemed to like it,' I protest.

'But that was supposed to be special. Private. Not something you trot out at events.'

I can't hide my look of surprise. For some reason, I couldn't say why, this irks me. Actually, it does more than irk me. It makes me angry, something that whenever possible I try to repress, lest I give into it and never stop shouting. If I get it wrong even when I get it right, then honestly, what's the point in trying?

'You've got quite a nerve talking about integrity, let alone lecturing me about trying to keep things private,' I snap.

'What's that supposed to mean?'

'You'd share our bowel movements if it was going to get us more followers.'

She gives me a look which I think is supposed to convey disappointment. Time was, I would have done anything to make that look disappear, to have her approve of me again. But since we've been in full Seven Rules territory, spending every day together writing, editing, rewriting, and then every minute together promoting the thing, it seems like her disappointment has become an increasingly constant companion of mine. We do an event and I answer a question wrong. She asks me to take a picture of her and then groans at the image. I turn the air con up too much at the hotels we stay in or I pack the wrong things to wear. I hum too loudly when I'm getting ready, fall asleep reading and leave the light on, have holes in my socks, still wear a pair of pants with Scottie dogs on them that I bought in 2008, the list goes on. And on. And on. And the volume of the criticism is such that I'm increasingly less inclined to care. She picks her phone back up and returns to editing the picture of us, my arm around her waist, her eyes cast lovingly up at me. We don't speak for the rest of the journey.

When we get home, Jess puts a sheet mask on her face which makes her look like a burn victim. She spends the evening watching something brain-rotting on the massive TV while I wander around the kitchen looking for something I can meaningfully contribute. But it's all clean and ordered by the sweet Eastern European woman who comes twice a week. I pick up books and try reading them, I scan the *New York Times*, and eventually, when the silence and the boredom and the atmosphere in the house is too much for me to tolerate, I retreat to bed on the pretence of wanting an early night.

'Good idea,' Jessica says, clearly pleased that I'm going to piss off and stop wandering aimlessly around the house. 'The car's coming at five-fifteen tomorrow morning. It's literally just the breakfast TV show, and then the residential retreat, and then we're done with publicity for the book and we can go back to our normal life. Okay?'

I pause for a fraction of a second, wondering if this might be the moment to tell her that I've been thinking about emailing my old boss and asking about getting my old job back. She notes my hesitation and misreads it. 'It's *Morning Chat* tomorrow,' she tells me.

'I know,' I snap, harsher than intended. I don't want to snap at her, I've just never been tired like this. Back when I worked as a producer, I'd happily work the night shift and then stay into the morning to work on the show for the next day. Maybe it's getting older, but I've never felt drained like this before. Obviously I can't tell Jess this, because she'll make some comment about this not exactly being another day down the coal mines.

'You didn't know about the bookshop today, so forgive me for assuming—'

'I'm going to bed, I really don't feel like doing this,' I explain.

'I don't think just walking out—'

'Rule one.' I cut her off, realising that I've got a trump card to play. 'Don't stay up arguing.' And before she can mount a calm and reasonable complaint about me pettily citing the rules, I've closed the door behind me and I'm standing in the hall, wondering why I spend so much of my time being pretty bloody horrible to someone I love. In a couple of weeks' time all this book stuff will be over, and we'll be able to get back on an even keel, and honestly it won't be a moment too soon. I've been living for the moment that this mad good fortune, and the not-insubstantial money it brought with it, can buy us some peace. A morning drinking coffee in bed with Jess, a long walk and a pub lunch at the expensive place with the decent roast, a shared crossword and a bottle of wine. All the stuff which makes us perfect together.

The First Fight

Jack

From the moment that Jessica gave me her email address, I haven't stopped thinking about her. Every time my mind isn't occupied by something else, and often when it should be, my imagination drifts to her standing in the street outside the exam room, a halo of red-gold frizz against the sun, agonisingly beautiful in a short silk skirt printed with little elephants and a white T-shirt which left a band of skin exposed below her navel. Fortunately this fixation is just about permissible, because Jessica Richards is still very much in my life.

I've spent the last eleven months living in Oxford. She's been home in Surrey. So we've emailed each other every single day for a year. We've tried to meet up before, but her mum has been so ill that leaving her wasn't an option. A few weeks ago, I walked over to the college IT room to start on an essay and I had an email from her, telling me that she wanted to come and see me. I'd like a change of scene, she wrote. I just want to do something fun. I want to feel normal.

So it has become my sole mission in life to make sure that I deliver something fun, and something normal. But I've already hit a stumbling block: the sleeping arrangements.

Because I'm doing my master's, I don't live in one of the colleges – instead I've got a double bed in a shared house on Ship

Street. It's nice. Central. But it's not huge, and there isn't a sofa. In films, whenever a man and a woman are forced to share a bedroom, the man gallantly says 'I'll take the sofa' and then somehow their sexual tension is so magically palpable that they just end up having sex anyway. I don't have a sofa, not in my room and not in the house – the landlord sacrificed the living room to make more money off another bedroom. So, I'm going to have to sleep on the floor. But if I'm going to sleep on the floor, then really I need an air mattress because the floor is covered with that sort of hard plastic carpet that they put down in primary schools, presumably because while it is technically a carpet, it's very easy to clean if someone is sick on it. To be honest, it's probably on the floor of this student house for the same reason. So in a non-bed-sharing timeline, the air mattress is essential. The question is when to inflate it.

Blowing up the aforementioned air mattress means plugging in the pump, and then waiting what would inevitably feel like thirty-five minutes for it to inflate. It's about as awkward of a moment as you can create, and if I've screwed up the date so badly that she definitely doesn't want to have sex with me, I think watching this air mattress inflate might actually finish me off.

I could pre-inflate it, of course. But then when she arrives, she'll see it, and either think that I don't want to have sex with her (about which she would be very, very wrong) or that I'm such a colossal loser I couldn't even bet on myself persuading her to sleep with me.

There's also another minor detail, which is that I haven't actually fully, technically, completely, had sex before. So it's possible that I'm using the air mattress as a bit of a distraction from my embarrassing status as a 22-year-old virgin.

I'm standing over the uninflated mattress when the doorbell rings. I don't move; it'll just be Claude's Amazon delivery of protein powder. When I'd told him that I thought Amazon only did books, he'd laughed for about half an hour. The bell rings again and I sigh in frustration. Clearly, no one in this house realises that I am wrestling with the single most important decision anyone has ever made. I go downstairs, still in my school PE shorts and KONY 2012 T-shirt, and throw the door open. But standing on the doorstep isn't a delivery driver. It's a girl. A woman. A person somewhere between girl and woman. She's got green eyes and red hair and she looks so beautiful, so glamorous and so familiar that for a second I think she must be famous.

'I got an earlier train,' she says. 'And then I realised that was probably really inconvenient and really rude, but I was already on my way here, so I just—'

I drink her in for a moment and she's so beautiful that I stop thinking about the fact that I'm wearing a pair of shorts that say St Aloysius Boys Rugby VIII team, or that there's a half-unwrapped air mattress on my bedroom floor. Instead I do the first genuinely cool thing that I've ever done. I reach forward, I wrap my arms around her waist, and I kiss her. I finally understand why other people think that this objectively slightly disgusting activity is a good idea. Because they're right. It's a really good idea. The best idea.

'Hi.' She smiles.

'Hi.'

For some reason, and I really can't fathom what that reason would have been, I told a girl named Calliope that we'd come to a party she's throwing tonight. I only agreed to it casually on the way out of a seminar, but since then she's asked me three times and sent me an inbox message on Facebook to confirm.

So when Jessica and I emerge from between the sheets after the best two hours of my life, during which I dispose of my virginity without completely embarrassing myself, and all I want to do is lie there and count her freckles, instead I have to tell her that we're going out. 'It's just down the road,' I say apologetically. 'And we can leave after an hour.'

'Cool,' she says, getting up and finding her knickers from the bottom of the duvet. 'A party sounds fun.'

A party does sound fun. This is, by that metric, not going to be a party because it is almost certainly not going to be fun. Parties around here, at least the ones I get invited to, are people standing in each other's rooms without any music, talking about their essays.

I want to warn Jessica, as she puts on a pair of denim hot pants and a pink floral crop top, that she's going to be overdressed, but she looks beautiful and I'm worried it'll come across like I'm complaining, or worse, judging. So I say nothing as she draws a massive wing of eyeliner on each eye and then laces up the highest heeled boots I've ever seen in my life. We walk, hand in hand, my feelings for her a slight sunburn after a day on the beach, warming my skin. It's going to be a crap party because they always are, but if I'm totally honest, there's a prickle of excitement about showing off that I'm with Jessica.

'I'm really glad you came,' I say eventually.

'Me too.'

'How is she?'

She winces at the question. 'Not good. I felt like I shouldn't leave her. I keep thinking, if anything happened ...'

'If anything happened, I'd get you back there as quickly as humanly possible.'

She gives me a weak smile. 'Thanks.'

'I know I don't know your mum,' I say, very aware of what delicate ground I'm walking, but determined not to ignore the thing that has dominated Jessica's life for the last year. 'But she raised you, and you're the most single-minded person I've ever known. So I don't think she'd have told you to come unless she meant it.'

There's a smile at the edges of her lips.

'How did you two meet?' Calliope asks when we arrive. She's wearing a jumper with END APARTHEID knitted into it. There is no music, and only a handful of people leaning against the walls. I cringe for her, but she doesn't seem worried about it.

'It's quite a funny story,' I begin. 'We were queueing up to take our final exams at Bristol, and Jessica was in front of me, and she asked me if she could borrow a pen.'

'You went to your finals without a pen?' Calliope is very tall and slender with bright blonde hair and a lot of opinions about wealth distribution for someone who went to Benenden.

'I figured it was a fair bet someone would have one.' Jessica smiles. 'And this nerd had one of those foot-long plastic pencil cases with like, twenty.'

'WHSmith's sells them in twenty-packs,' I say defensively. 'It would be arbitrary not to bring them all.'

'And how long have you been together?' Calliope asks.

'Oh, no, we're not officially together,' I say quickly. The last thing I want is Jess to assume that I've been walking around Oxford talking about my stunning girlfriend who 'doesn't go here'. She's taken great pains to use the words 'seeing each other' and 'hanging out' in our emails. Obviously, one day I'm going to have to have a big drink and then man up and ask her if she's willing to consider being my girlfriend, but the fact she's turned up in Oxford and consented to come to this embarrassing attempt at a party is enough of a win for now.

'I'm going to get another drink,' Jessica says, tapping the mug that Calliope had poured two fingers of red wine into when we arrived.

I watch as she disappears through the dozen people standing around the kitchen and goes outside to light a cigarette on the pavement. I want to follow her but Calliope is talking at me about a guy on our course who doesn't know the difference between illusion and allusion, and I've never understood how you're supposed to leave a conversation in a social setting. Through the window, I can see Jessica talking to two broad-shouldered boys in rugby shirts who seem to have stopped on the way somewhere. The windows are open because the air is warm; I can catch the scent of smoke but not what they're saying. My phone buzzes, and I look down to read the message: met some guys outside, going to follow them to another party and see if it's fun, catch up later?

By the time I look up from reading it, she's gone. I stay at the party, furious, for another hour. I listen to boring stories from boring people, and I simmer with confusion and hurt. Eventually I make my excuses to Calliope.

'Where did your friend go?' she asks.

'She met some meaty sports blokes and went off with them,' I reply, surprised at the vitriol in my voice.

'Seems more her speed,' she replies.

'What?'

'Well. She's not exactly — you know. She looks like more of a party girl than a reader.'

I fix her with what I hope is a look of disdain. 'You know, for someone who talks a lot about the patriarchy, you've made a pretty lazy judgement about another woman.' And then I walk out.

Three hours later, back at the flat and having received exactly zero messages from her, I call Jessica.

'Hi!' she shouts when she picks up. 'Where are you?'

'I'm at home,' I say, like a Victorian father. 'Where are you?'

'Some club, it's really shit. Do you want to come join?'

'No,' I say.

There's a change in background noise and I can tell she's gone somewhere quieter so we can talk. 'What's the problem?'

'I thought you were here to see me,' I say, hating the childish whine to my voice. 'Not random blokes from the street.'

'It was quite clear you needed some space with that girl,' she snaps.

'What girl? Look, do you want me to come and find you? Or do you want to come home? I mean back. To mine.'

We have a long, irritating discussion where neither of us can decide what to do and eventually it's agreed that I'll meet her and we'll go home. So I trudge over to the Purple Turtle and collect her, once again feeling like the most enormous loser. We walk home, no longer hand in hand. How did this go from the absolute best day to the absolute worst?

We stop at a kebab van at Jessica's insistence. She orders something complicated involving extra halloumi, and then we arrive back at mine, still in total silence. Creep up the stairs. Get to my bedroom. And sit in more silence.

'Jack,' Jessica says.

'Yes?'

'I know you're upset, but I really want to eat my kebab.'

I can't stop myself from laughing. 'I think it's very important that you eat your kebab,' I say.

She does eat it. And then, once she's licked the mayonnaise off the inside of the foil, she looks at me. 'Right. What's the problem here?'

'I don't understand why you left?' I say eventually, because someone needs to say something.

'*What?*' *she snaps. 'How could you not understand?*'

And then it starts. We go around and around and around. She talks about how Calliope was rude and snooty, I inexplicably try to defend her despite completely agreeing. I say that it was poor form of her to go off with other blokes hours after we'd had sex and she accuses me of being a puritan. At some point I start trying to defend the party Calliope threw and I realise that I'm fighting for the sake of fighting. I need to stop it. She's been caring for her mum non-stop, of course she wanted to blow off steam. I should have thought to take us to a club instead of the worst party in human history.

'*I'm sorry,*' *I say, trying to form a sentence which is apologetic without being weak. I look over. She's fallen asleep, lying on her front, on the bed. I consider waking her up so we can go back for round five thousand of this argument. You're not supposed to let the sun go down on an argument, everyone always says that.*

I go and start to try to inflate the air mattress, but the pump is too loud and it'll wake Jessica, so I sort of lie on the half-deflated shell.

'*Jack,*' *Jessica murmurs, half asleep.*

'*Yes?*'

'*Come and sleep with me even though I smell of onions.*'

I lie next to her and fall asleep almost instantly.

'*I'm sorry about last night,*' *she says, as she rolls over and stretches. I look at her stomach under the white pyjama T-shirt she changed into at some point during our row.*

'*Me too,*' *I add.*

'*I just wish you'd told me that you didn't think we were dating.*' *She sighs, getting up. 'I'm going to be honest. I was starting to have feelings for you.*'

I sit bolt up, like a cartoon character. 'When did I say that?'

'At that party last night.Your friend asked how long we'd been together and you like, sprained a muscle trying to tell her that we weren't dating.'

'What?!' I say in disbelief. 'I didn't want you to think I was being presumptuous. I thought you'd be embarrassed if I said we were together.'

She looks at me in confusion. 'Why?'

'Many, many years of being a massive loser?'

Jessica rolls her eyes. 'Okay, well, I came halfway across the country, we had sex and then you told me to get dressed so we could go to a party with a girl who clearly fancies you, and then rushed to tell her that I'm not your girlfriend. That's not loser behaviour, that's horrible fuck-boy behaviour.'

I'm aghast. 'But that's not what happened! I was trying to show you that I've got a fun life here so you might want to come back. I didn't think I was supposed to want you to be my girlfriend.'

She smiles and comes to sit back down. 'Are you telling me that we wasted four hours arguing about this last night, when actually you want us to be together, and I want us to be together?'

I nod.

'Why didn't you just say that? Last night?'

I sigh. 'Honestly? I didn't really know what we were arguing about. We'd been going for like, hours. I'd completely lost track of where we'd started.'

'And of how much we like each other.'

'Exactly.'

'We're idiots,' she says, leaning in for a kiss. 'Let's never stay up arguing like that ever, ever again.'

Jessica

It's half six in the morning and I'm sitting in a well-worn leather chair while a make-up artist makes it look like I had more than four hours of broken sleep. The room smells comfortingly of hairspray and coconut. There are hundreds of neatly organised products arranged on a black towel in front of me, lipsticks and palettes glinting under the huge lights, my coffee cup wedged in among a row of rose-gold-cased lipsticks.

'You've got such beautiful hair,' says the make-up artist, as she dusts powder over my nose. 'I like it this length. What made you go for the chop?'

I look at myself in the mirror and wonder if it's time to go from two areas of Botox to three. I consider telling her that despite captioning my recent pictures #BeautyHasNoAge, I felt having waist-length hair in my mid-thirties was running the risk of looking like someone who homeschools nine children on a farm in Utah. So, the day after my last birthday, I booked an appointment with a snooty French hairdresser who charged an eye-watering sum to take my hair from my mid-back to my shoulders.

'I'd always had it long and I just fancied a change,' I tell her. 'And honestly it's so much less work.' I am lying through my teeth – it's way, way more work to make this perfect cut look half decent. 'Jack was heartbroken, weren't you?' I look over at Jack, who is slumped in his chair, reading a battered Penguin paperback, not listening. 'Darling?'

'What?'

'I was just saying that you were upset when I cut my hair.'

'Oh. Yes. I liked it long. It's still nice, though.' He drains the last of his coffee and then goes back to his book.

'He's terrible in the mornings. Not human until after his first coffee!' I joke. Why am I talking like this? I sound like an embarrassing millennial cliché.

'You wait until you've got kids,' the make-up artist says, as she takes a bottle of hairspray from a shelf. I hear that comment, or a version of it, at least once a week and every single time it's like someone's tipped a glass of cold water over my lap. 'Close your eyes and hold your breath.' I'm not sure why she's going to spray my hair – there's no chance the glossy curls she created will drop between now and my making it on set. I try to brush off her comment, glad of an excuse to squeeze my eyes shut.

I look at Jack, but he's too engrossed in whichever dead Russian he's currently reading to have heard anything. I know he's tired, and I know it's been a lot of press, but God, I wish he could just look a bit happier to be here and maybe even try to enjoy it. We're so unbelievably lucky to have landed this interview, the publishers literally rang us to tell us what a win it was. It could really change things for us, and if we seem like we don't want to be here, then we might not get asked back. Yes, *Morning Chat* is a slightly tacky morning programme, and yes, the studio is a long way from our house. But everyone we know has to get up early and wrestle their kids into school uniforms, or drag themselves on to the train to get to an office, and then spend the day sitting at a desk, being told what to do. We get to sit in a chauffeur-driven car, have our hair and make-up done, and then perch on a sofa for ten minutes and have a quick chat with people about their problems. Clay said we'll sell at least five hundred books from the exposure, and they're paying us £400 each for doing it. It's the easiest, most privileged job a person could do. But Jack is just moping. I'm pretty sure, I think, my outrage mounting, that if this was something like going on Radio 4 to talk about some complicated political crisis, he'd pull it together even if he was tired.

'Are we nearly ready?' a runner asks, putting her head around the door. The first time we did the show, I hadn't been able to believe that they really ran around with headsets and clipboards, just like in a drama. This must be the fourth or fifth time we've been here, but I've never stopped feeling like a tourist. I know better than to ask for selfies with the other guests but inside I'm still squealing. I have a last look in the mirror, checking that everything is as smooth as it can be. I didn't used to be vain about it, but HD television is not kind, and if there's a single bump on my skin, I'll have people all over Twitter talking about how old I'm looking. I don't blame them. We're claiming to have a perfect marriage, we can't be surprised if that makes people want to pick holes in everything we do. Clay warned me when we started that I was making a tricky bed for myself. And he's right. I am professionally smug and there are plenty of people on the internet who hate me for it. If I wasn't me then I would probably hate me for it. I have an easy, fun, lucrative job and a lot of really expensive stuff I don't pay for, of course people are going to start threads speculating that a spot near my top lip is a cold sore. But I'd take that a million times over going back to the miserable marketing job I had before all of this.

They shepherd us from the make-up room, along the dark corridors and down to the sound stage, where the hosts, Graham and Lily, are sitting on a pink sofa, staring at their phones. It's a strange place. The studio itself is huge, with triple-height ceilings and these enormous doors that slide open so you can move bits of furniture around. It's dark and there are props and random bits of wood leaning against the walls. And then in the middle of it, brightly lit, sort of like a doll's house, is the set. It's a perfect fake living room, with sofas and a kitchen table, even a little breakfast bar with a stove. The backdrop is a TV screen showing a cityscape of Central London, with boats gliding up the river. The first time I came here, I was shocked. All the times I'd had the show on in the background of a morning, I'd always thought it was a real window.

Graham has been on telly for decades, originally in politics, but now soft and fluffy for the morning audience. He used to do the show with a woman named Cate, who was equally smiley and about his age. As of last year, Lily has been her replacement, brought in to appeal to a younger, yummier-mummy audience. She's beautiful, even more so in real life than she is on telly. Rail-thin, with an enormous diamond engagement ring on her left hand and lips which are very definitely not her own. Last week, the papers were saying that her husband has been sexting someone from *Love Island*. I've got no idea if it's true, and I really hope she won't try to talk to me about it. People do that sometimes. I had an MP come up to me in the bathroom at a restaurant once and ask me how she could get her husband to listen to her properly. I wanted to tell her that I had no bloody idea, and that if she found something that works, to tell me what it was. I didn't say that, of course. I told her to assess her communication style and mimic the way that he speaks to her. They haven't announced a split since then, so I guess that's something.

A voice from somewhere in the studio starts a count-down, and Graham and Lily's phones disappear into their laps, replaced by glowing expressions, warm smiles towards the people at home. 'Good morning, good morning to all of you out there. What a show we've got for you today. Later, we'll be meeting a puppy who was born with two tails, and just after nine a.m., we'll be joined in the studio by a choir of single dads who are also drag queens.'

Lily leans forward. She's still nervous, clearly. I don't blame her. One of the broadsheets called her Pinocchio the other day, suggesting that she's unacceptably wooden. 'And in a moment we've got the UK's happiest married couple here with us. It's the authors of new book *Seven Rules for a Perfect Marriage*, Jack and Jessica Rhodes. They've been together for fifteen years, they're still head over heels for each other, and they're going to be answering your questions and helping you fix any little niggles in your relationship.'

Jack is leaning against the wall, staring up at the cavern-ous studio ceiling and looking like he'd rather be anywhere but here.

'Are you okay?' I hiss.

'Just tired.'

'Please try to look a bit happier,' I whisper.

'I'll smile when we're on.'

'It's not just about acting happy when we get on set. Everyone is watching us. All the fucking time.' I smile through gritted teeth as I say it, brushing my hand against his arm. I hate myself for doing it, for putting on a show like this. It's completely mad. I know that. It probably doesn't really matter if the runner who gets our coffee sees us bickering. But we've got a suffocating mortgage and a pretty empty pension fund, and the publishers have poured staggering amounts of money into advertising and marketing. If we can make at least some of it back for them, then they might want to publish more books with us. It would just take one credible comment about our marriage being under strain and the whole premise of our brand falls apart. Surely one more morning of pretending to be cheerful isn't that much to ask in exchange for financial security?

'Touch-ups?' The make-up artist dashes back on set, her kit packed into a plastic bag around her waist. 'Jack, love, can I pop a bit of powder on you?'

'Yes, please,' he says agreeably. 'As much as possible, I want to look as beautiful as my wife.'

My shoulders relax by about half a millimetre. I try to catch his eye, to silently thank him. But his gaze is straight ahead, at the set.

'Time to go!' announces the runner. 'You'll be amazing!'

The lights on the set are always brighter than is entirely comfortable. I settle on to the sofa, trying to look relaxed while sitting up straight so that I don't look bigger than I actually am. The whole thing about the camera adding ten pounds is more than true for me. Even as my body has shrunk over the last months, from the various (probably not very scientific) fertility-enhancing diets I've read about online, I always wince when I look at the screenshots afterwards, painfully aware of the softness of my upper arms. Jack always seems to look exactly the same as he does in real life, handsome and lean and perfect.

He slides his arm around my waist, and my heart rate steadies. I feel a little wave of gratitude towards him. He's always so warm. I can feel the heat radiating through his jumper, through my dress, to my skin.

'Thanks for joining us.' Graham beams before introducing us. 'With us in the studio now, we have Jessica and Jack, relationship influencers and marriage experts. They've taken the internet by storm, with over a million followers on social media, and now they've got a new book to share the secrets to making a relationship work.'

'It's called *Seven Rules for a Perfect Marriage*,' Lily reads, slightly stilted. 'Wow, a perfect marriage, that sounds pretty amazing! Is it actually perfect?' She laughs. The cameras all move around and I can see myself on the screens. I try very hard not to look. Jack and I both do a sort of half laugh.

'We do our best,' I say.

'Well, I think a lot of us could do with some tips!' Graham smiles. 'Shall we get started with some questions?'

'Yes, please.' I nod.

Lily stares at her cue cards. 'First up, we've got Sandra from Barry in Wales. Hi Sandra!'

Sandra's voice is piped in over the speakers.

'Hi Jack and Jessica,' the voice crackles. 'I love your posts and I can't wait to read your book. But my question is: how do you avoid arguing?'

Jack laughs. 'We're not superhuman, Sandra!'

She says she loves our account but I'm pretty sure that she hasn't read any of my posts because we've got an entire highlights section about positive arguments – a very good theory which I realise, as I consider my answer, we've been ignoring ourselves lately. Shit. That's probably not good.

'We absolutely don't avoid arguments,' I add, leaning into Jack's body a little. 'No one does! Show me a couple who say they never disagree and I'll show you two people who aren't telling the truth – or who are repressing their feelings a lot of the time.'

'Research shows that it's actually far healthier for a couple to express their frustrations with each other than to bottle it up,' Jack adds.

'The important thing,' I say, 'is to make sure that you're arguing in a positive, proactive way. See the problem as the enemy, and you both as a team. It's not you versus your partner, it's you versus the issue at hand. And remember – one of our *Seven Rules for a Perfect Marriage* – go to bed on an argument. Our first rule is actually that you should never stay up arguing – get some sleep and come back to the issue fresh in the morning.' Someone in the gallery cuts Sandra off before she can ask any follow-up questions, leaving viewers to assume that she was satisfied with our answer. I hope she was. I wonder if we can make sure that everyone who called in gets a follow-up. Or at least a signed copy of the book?

'Well, I have to say, I'm relieved to hear that a bit of marital argy-bargy is normal!' Graham chuckles. Everyone knows that he's a complete shit. He keeps his wife at their country pile so that he can entertain a series of twenty-something mistresses at his enormous London house. A few months ago Jack and I went to his Christmas party, with five hundred of his closest friends. It was our first big showbiz invitation and I was more shocked than I wanted to admit that we'd been asked (in fact, I made Clay check it wasn't an accident). Jack kept telling people that my best Christmas present was seeing celebrities getting drunk and doing coke off every single shiny surface, and he was 100 per cent right.

The next call comes from a very sweet-sounding older lady. 'I'm Janice,' she says, her voice crackling, 'and I'd like to know what you'd recommend for dating apps for older people, and if you think it's ever too late?'

Jack and I exchange impressed looks. 'I have to admit,' Jack says, 'Jessica and I met in the bad old days when you had to just approach people in person, so we're not app experts.'

I simultaneously love how charming he is and want to pinch him for forgetting the media training where Clay told us never to remind people that we've been together so long we know nothing about modern dating.

'Well, first up, great on you,' I chime in. 'It's absolutely never too late, and I think you'll be inspiring a lot of other older people to take that leap. Maybe we can fix you up with someone who's watching at home right now – what's your type?'

'Channing Tatum,' she replies, and we all laugh. 'I'm not fussy,' she goes on, in her husky smoker's voice. 'But I do prefer a man with a bigger—'

Someone in the gallery cuts Janice off in case she's about to say what we all think she's about to say on morning television. We all laugh and resettle ourselves while they find someone else to bring in.

'Our next caller is Willa from West London. Hi Willa!'

'Hi Lily, hi Graham. My question for Jessica and Jack is this: how do you keep your marriage fresh and exciting when you've decided not to have children? My partner and I have decided that we're going to be child-free, but as all of our friends start their families, we're feeling a bit left behind.'

I pick up my water glass, trying to unstick my throat, praying that in the seconds of silence, Jack will pick up the question. But he doesn't. And now he's silent, and the silence isn't getting any less silent. Graham leans forward, waiting for one of us to say something. Lily is checking her cue cards again as if there's going to be any kind of answer on there. Why weren't we offered the chance to vet these questions? I try to pick the glass up again but my fingers slip and it clatters, wobbling. I grasp for it and set it right. Surely someone was supposed to check? There's no way Clay and Suze would have allowed them to ask that without at least telling me first. And why the fuck isn't Jack saying anything? Of all the questions in the world to leave me to answer, how could he possibly leave me to answer this one?

'That's a really good question,' I say, my voice too high as I break the world's longest silence. 'In our book, *Seven Rules for a Perfect Marriage,* which came out, uh, last week...' I move my hair forward over my shoulder, looking at the camera, and wonder if this is one of those moments where only I can tell how badly this is going, or if people at home are cringing for me, noticing the tear in my left eye, the fact that I'm digging my fingernails into the palm of my hand. 'In our book, we, uh, we talk about the importance

SEVEN RULES FOR A PERFECT MARRIAGE

of shared hobbies, goals and interests. Perhaps you and your husband could look at trying a new activity together, which might provide a new focus for your life. All marriages go through different stages, whether you're having children or not, and it's important to make sure that you've got a shared goal throughout.'

I try to fix a smile on my face but I can feel my thighs sweating. And if there weren't tears in my eyes, and my voice wasn't so high, that would have been a decent answer. I hope against hope that someone in the gallery will realise that I have nothing else to say on the topic. The woman's voice starts again, asking something else, but it's cut off almost straight away. I catch sight of myself in the giant monitor, my own face displayed three times its actual size, as is Jack's. He's smiling away. Has he even noticed that I'm having a nervous fucking breakdown next to him?

'Some really great questions,' says Graham. 'We'll be back shortly, but if you'd like to win ten thousand pounds and a brand-new Ford Fiesta, stay put and listen to this ...'

I can't tell if our section was supposed to run longer, or we've taken the appropriate amount of time, and obviously I can't ask them. We get up and do hugs and kisses before having our microphones taken off us. Then we're walked to the exit by an enthusiastic posh boy doing work experience as a runner, and finally, waiting for our car to arrive, Jack and I are alone.

'I'm sorry,' Jack says quietly, as we stand in the dark corridor, even darker after the blazing lights of the studio.

'Sure,' I say. It would be a lot easier to be forgiving towards him if this was the first time he'd left me to fend for myself when it comes to fertility.

Jack

The show booked us a return car – generally speaking, the 'talent' doesn't like to take the Tube. We're in stationary traffic, because apparently the 'talent' prefers privacy to expediency. Jessica, sitting on the other side of the people carrier, has put her earphones in, wireless ones, which means that she loses them about six times a day, and most of the time when she wants to use them, they haven't got any charge. I pointed out once that the old headphones we all used to have, the kind with wires, were far harder to lose and couldn't get a dead battery. She looked at me like I was pissing on her bonfire, which I suppose I was. I feel like I do that a lot these days and I really don't mean to; it's the same sarky humour I've always been able to charm her with in the past. Apparently it's not charming anymore.

The headphones are very clearly a 'do not disturb' sign. She's wearing sunglasses, too, so she might as well be on a different continent. But then, even if she were listening, even if she weren't crushed into the farthest corner of the taxi possible, as if she's trying to put every millimetre of distance between us that she possibly can, it's not as if I would have anything to say.

My inability to express myself is another thing she always used to find charming. Or, at least tolerable. She said it was British and repressed in the sweetest possible way. When we were first seeing each other, we would lie in bed together, tangled and naked, and she would turn the lights out and ask me questions about my feelings. She knew I found it easier to talk to her in the dark. She didn't seem to mind. And then, one day, she suddenly stopped finding it endearing. She told me I was an adult, and I should be able to talk about complicated issues like one. But I couldn't. I still can't. All of the things I want to say sort of swarm around my head, but I can't catch any of them. I want to make her feel better. And I know that there is a combination of words which would do that. But I'm no closer to knowing which combination it is than I am to guessing the seventieth digit of Pi.

It was beyond shit of me to leave her to answer that caller's question. Unforgivable, actually. She's wanted to be a mother for as long as I've known her, and every month it doesn't happen is torture for her. I know that. Christ, what if she thinks that I don't know that? That I didn't answer the question because I wasn't sure? Obviously I tried. I opened my mouth. I wanted to think of something fast and flippant to say. But there weren't any words, because why the fuck were they asking us about that? Since when did being in our mid-thirties without kids make us some sort of poster couple for child-free life? I wanted to ask the woman on the phone why she was sitting at home watching breakfast telly, calling in to ask questions about the lives of strangers. But I couldn't even get those words out fast enough, and they would probably have stymied our career, which is the one thing that would have made Jessica even angrier than she is right now. So maybe it's not such a bad thing that I went silent. It's the same thing that happens all the time lately, when she says something that hurts my feelings and I want to explain it but I can't. This screaming silence, where words become so slippery that I can't force them out. Which meant that I left her there, on national television, to answer the worst question a person

48

can ask her. I'd like to say some of this to her. But I know
from previous experience that if I try to start a meaningful
conversation in front of the cab driver, it'll make her even
angrier. Obviously this guy neither knows nor cares who
we are, but sometime around hitting 100,000 followers,
she seemed to implement this policy that disagreements
needed to exclusively take place in private. And once we
hit a million, it became ironclad. We used to cheerfully
bicker on buses and call each other dicks at dinner parties.
But not anymore. She wants us to act like members of the
royal family, keeping everything on emotional lockdown
until we're away from the world, which means in a period
of time where we've been deliberately thrust into the
spotlight, there hasn't been a moment to let any of it out.
I want to say something right now, not wait hours until
we're home. But the only way to do that would be to break
her number-one rule and raise it in front of a stranger. So
instead I'm going to have to say nothing and compound
the fact that I sat there and left her to flounder on TV.

The car windows are blacked out, and I'm struggling to
work out whereabouts we are. The studio is over in West
London. For some inexplicable reason, they all are. The
car is dropping us in Central London and what should
have been a thirty-minute journey is taking forever. Or
the horrible purgatory between Jess and me is making
it feel like hours. Either way, we need to get a move on
because we're meeting with our management to discuss
plans for the year ahead. I never quite know how I feel
about being the kind of person who has a 'team'. When
we signed with CMA a few years ago, we'd both laughed
and laughed at them. The idea that we needed a team of

people to manage our social media account was hilarious. But, we agreed, we'd do it for a year. Make as much money as we could, and then cash out. We'd sworn blind that we would never say 'my agent' or 'my manager' out loud; it's a promise that only one of us ended up keeping. And three years later there is absolutely no sign of us tapping out any time soon. We haven't even finished the press for the first book and it's time to talk about the next one. Happily, Jess and I have agreed that whatever we do next, we're going to take a decent break first.

We arrive at the office, an open-plan one with lots of glass and a bike inexplicably hung on the reception wall. Clay, our manager, an oleaginous fuck who unquestionably has regular Botox, greets us. He's got a sort of frenetic energy, like he's perpetually on coke, but it's probably just untreated ADHD.

'My two favourite clients!' Clay exclaims as we get through the revolving door. He holds his arms out to Jessica first and she hugs him.

'I bet you say that to everyone.' She smiles.

'I absolutely do. But it's true in your case.'

It bloody should be. We've made him eye-watering sums of money. He steers us through the lobby and up to the second floor, where we get a sort of hero's welcome, if heroes were ever welcomed into meeting rooms. Jessica hugs and kisses everyone, remembering little details about people that make it seem like she actually cares. Or maybe she really does. I hang back, nodding and waving from a safe distance. Eventually, everyone makes a huge performance about sitting down.

Across the table from us, like an episode of *The Apprentice*, Clay is flanked by Maya, who is Clay's number two. She is terrifying, which Jessica and I agree is probably a good thing. Next to her is Alec, the Head of Vision for the company, whatever that means.

'So first things first, we want to say congratulations on your success. It's a genuinely astonishing debut. Official numbers aren't in yet, but from the preliminary figures the publisher sent over, it's looking very strong, and as we'd all hoped, we can confirm that you'll be on the *Sunday Times* bestseller list. Hopefully at number one. You should both be very proud.'

We both look at the desk because neither of us is sure what to say. Jessica is pink. I want to put my hand on her thigh and squeeze, because she's done what most people only dream of. But the memory of her pushing my hand away in the taxi back from Leeds stops me.

'The PR has been a huge success, and we know what a big ask it was to be constantly going from interview to event.'

We both make embarrassed noises to indicate that it's fine.

'How are you both feeling about the retreat?'

I've been trying not to think about it, but as part of the last push for PR for the book, we said that we'd take a group of readers – people who'd applied via a competition on our account – to some big house in the country and do a sort of marital bootcamp. The publishers are paying for it, and Jessica seemed into the idea, largely because (as she said, breathlessly excited), 'If it works, maybe we could do more of them?' I said yes because I always say yes to her, and then pretended that it wasn't happening because it's my personal idea of hell. But now the 'it's Sunday and I haven't done my homework' feeling erupts in my sternum.

'Jack?' Clay gets my attention.

'Sorry,' I say. 'I was just thinking about the retreat. Lots to prepare.'

'Really?' Maya sounds surprised. 'I thought the publisher had done most of the legwork? If you're spending a lot of hours, we should invoice them for additional services.'

'No, no.' Jessica quickly jumps in. 'They've done almost everything, we're just tinkering with things. We're very happy with how it's going. Right, Jack?'

'Right.' I nod.

'Lovely,' says Clay. 'And once you've done the retreat, publicity will be over and you'll have a little break.'

This is almost as exciting as the bestseller-list thing. Time off. A break. Some headspace from the brand our marriage has become and some time to focus on us and what makes us happy. I can write. Maybe if they get really desperate, they might let me pick up a few days of freelance at my old job. I long to come home after a day away from Jessica and pour her a glass of wine while I download all the gossip from the office, just like we used to.

'So it feels like the right time to start asking some questions. What's next for brand Jack and Jessica?'

There's a long pause. Alec looks at Maya and they seem to be taking a toss-up about who has to speak next.

Jessica is playing with her charm bracelet under the desk. From the chest upwards she looks serene, but I can tell she's nervous. She always seems to think that this lot are going to drop us, that they're going to tell us that we're washed up and there's no more road, despite the fact that she's now their highest earning client and a social media genius.

'Do you have any thoughts?' Alec asks.

'After the break?' I ask.

Clay laughs. 'Absolutely. But come on, we don't want you out of the game for long. Momentum is a powerful thing.'

Before I can reply, Jessica does. 'We've talked about it. We'd like to take a break and have a think. And then maybe a follow-up, more rules for marriage, based around us getting a bit older and having been together longer. A sort of "how to go the distance"?'

The fact that she's remembered about the break is a relief. It was one of the stipulations for doing this, that as soon as the book was done and dusted, we would take a proper period of time off to think about what we wanted to do with our careers. Hers, and mine. Not ours.

Everyone nods in a way that makes it clear they think this is solidly mediocre. 'That could work,' Maya says, which even I know is code for 'that's a fucking terrible idea'.

'And it's only six months until I finish my MSc,' Jessica says, 'so then I'll be able to dive a bit deeper into the psychological side of relationships. I'm excited to maybe move into a more science-based direction. The end goal is that I qualify as a therapist.'

Everyone nods with even less enthusiasm and now I'm starting to feel frustrated. I know they all think her MSc is a pointless vanity thing, and that she's only doing it because occasionally someone will point out that we have no actual expertise in relationships other than being married. And yes, they might technically be right. But my God does she work hard on it. She's never missed a lecture, nor been late for a deadline. She got on that course legitimately, not through the press office, despite what people suggest online, and she loves it. But apparently the idea of us doing something that might actually help people isn't appealing to this lot, who just want to keep making money off the same old formula for success.

'We talked about doing something a bit different,' I say. 'I liked the idea of essays on marriage, something a bit more reflective. Maybe an anthology with other writers. Maybe we could interview some experts and do something a bit more rounded? Or a series of profiles of long-term married couples for a newspaper?' I allow myself a moment to imagine Jessica and I sitting down with Zadie Smith and Nick Laird, asking them gently probing questions about the intersection of their marriage and their careers. Being invited to stay for a literati dinner party afterwards.

There's a very long silence and I realise that, by comparison, they were actually being really nice about Jessica's ideas because no one can think of anything to say about my thoughts. There's a long, very uncomfortable silence and then Maya clears her throat.

'We watched your slot on *Morning Chat* this morning, and that actually really dovetails with what we wanted to talk about today.' I think I know where this is going, and I very much hope that I'm wrong. 'We've done the numbers, looked at your comments online, done market research, produced analysis across all the socials. And basically, everyone is asking the same question.' She pauses, clearly hoping that we're going to jump in and finish the sentence for her. 'People are desperate to know: when is the J and J baby coming?'

'The J-bee!' Alec adds. He laughs at his own joke, but when the laughing stops, the room is painfully silent. There's a rubbish truck on the street outside. I listen to it beeping while the three of them work out what they're going to say. Jessica is doing an impression of impassive listening, switching her gaze from one person to another every few seconds.

'But,' Clay offers, 'having a baby is not the only option. We could also go in a different, equally exciting, direction.' He pushes an iPad across the table. It sits on the table between me and Jessica. It's a mock-up of a book cover. *Seven Rules for the Perfect Child-Free Marriage.*

'We're not committed to the title,' Alec throws in, 'we're still on the fence about childless versus child-free; it's such a difficult definition.'

They all nod and makes noises of agreement about how difficult the definition is. I try to read Jessica's expression in profile. I realise that I should say something. I left her to field the questions on the breakfast show and I can't do that again. I need to say something which will make them back off, and I'm not giving them any details about what's going on with us. I'm just not sure how—

'That's an interesting thought,' Jessica says. Slow. Almost robotic. 'So, to clarify, the strategy for our brand for the next twelve to eighteen months is that we should either have a baby, or announce that we're not going to have a baby.'

She's incredible at things like this. Her tone is so light, but there's something commanding about it too. Maya looks a little shamefaced. Alec, who I'm increasingly convinced is only half human, takes over.

'Pregnancy would be the next natural step for your brand, in terms of sponsored content and growing your following, and ...' Alec pauses. 'Your demographic.' He looks at me like I might not understand the word and my fists clench under the table.

Clay leans forward, silencing Alec with his body language. 'I realise this all sounds a bit heavy, but the publishers are pressing us for next steps. It doesn't matter whether you want to lean into the child-free life, or jump into parenthood. There's going to be speculation online about your plans, so it's cleaner and fairer to your following to just give a straight answer. I know you guys get it.'

How have these people created a world where it's normal to ask a couple to decide whether they're trying to have children or not, and then announce it publicly? This was supposed to be Jessica's side hustle, her lockdown hobby, a distraction from not liking her job. But somehow we have dehumanised ourselves so much that the idea of us having kids or not wanting to have kids has become part of the 'brand story' or, worse, the business plan.

'Okay,' I say. 'You've made your point. Jess and I will talk about it privately. Right, Jess?'

She nods. 'Sure.'

I can't wait for us to be alone so we can discuss what an insane fucking nightmare this whole meeting has been. It might even be awful enough to distract from the *Morning Chat* row.

'Great,' Clay says. 'Now, I know you both wanted a break, so we're going to propose you take two weeks.'

'Two weeks?' I say weakly. The last time Jessica and I discussed this, we talked about taking a year out, maybe going travelling, definitely me doing some freelance work if not going back to work full-time. That was the whole deal, that I put everything I was doing on hiatus while we did one book; there's no way in hell she's going to sign off on a two-week break. 'What? Jess?'

Jess pulls herself up in her seat. 'Let's talk about the break once we've decided about the next project. Shall we go over the potential new brand partnerships you emailed about last week?'

Eventually we step out into the street, blinking in the bright winter sunshine. She finds her sunglasses and looks around for a cab. I wrap my arms around her, and she doesn't resist. Is that because we're in public? Or because she wants to be held?

'Well, that was fucking awful,' I say.

She nods. 'The book idea ...'

'Yeah. And the fact that they won't let us take a proper break.'

She's looking at her phone, trying to summon an Uber. It would be quicker to get the Tube but this isn't the moment to point that out. 'I think they'll go to six weeks instead of two,' she says. 'So maybe we could still go away for a bit? Get some space?'

I played rugby at school and so I know what it's like to have someone smack their full body weight into you at speed. This feels like that. 'Six weeks? I thought we said we'd do a year?'

She looks confused. 'A year? Why would we take a year?'

'When we were writing the book. We said we'd take a year, I'd freelance, or go back to work, or write my own book. And you'd do your degree, and relax for the first time in your life. We were going to go on a big trip?'

'I mean, I don't remember that, but surely we were talking about it like if we won the lottery. It was a fantasy, it's not—You don't actually want to take a year out? When things are going this well? You heard what Clay said about momentum—' She stops because her phone buzzes. On the screen are the mock-ups of the book cover and an email: *See if you prefer child-free or childless! Xoxo Alec.*

She looks like she might be about to cry. The phone buzzes again, another interruption. 'He's arriving, the number plate ends in PCo,' she says, in a very small voice. I open the door for her, and close it gently behind her. Then as I cross behind the car to get in the other side, I take a steadying breath. She's not okay. I know she's not okay. Those people in there have done the most painful thing they could possibly have done and she's such a pro that she held it together the entire time. This is not the day to have the argument about what I really want.

Rule Two

You are your partner's greatest cheerleader, act like it

The Account

Jessica

It's summer, and we're in our early thirties, so obviously the only thing we do with our weekends is go to weddings. It's become our second job and our third most expensive activity after bills and rent.

In theory I love weddings. I cry when the bride comes down the aisle, even if it's someone marrying someone Jack works with and I've never met her before. I love the canapés and the small talk and the champagne (even when it's Prosecco). I love the getting ready, the gossiping with people I haven't seen for ages, the roast dinner they always serve even when it's thirty degrees outside. I even love the speeches. But sometime around the fifth wedding we went to last year, my appetite started to wane.

'Are you okay?' Jack asks, as he indicates at a roundabout and then cautiously changes lanes.

'Yes,' I reply. 'Why?'

'You're quiet.'

'I am quiet sometimes.'

'You've let me pick the music all the way from London and made literally no comments about how bad my taste is.'

I can't stop myself smiling at that. 'I can see how that might worry you.'

He glances across at me. 'What's up?'

'I'm just slightly dreading this.'

Even in profile I can see that Jack looks surprised. 'I thought you were looking forward to it? Gemma's dad is loaded, it'll be an open bar all night.'

He makes a fair point.

'Yeah,' I say, not sure how to carry on.

'But you're not excited?'

I shake my head, looking at the road ahead of us. Jack takes a slip road, sweeping us off the busy road and on to a lane surrounded by enormous fields. 'I just feel a bit … lumpy.'

He tries not to laugh. 'Lumpy?'

'Like I keep going to these weddings in a dress I've bought from Primark, and then I sit next to all these high-flying genius people earning mega salaries, and when they ask me about my job, I'm like, yes, I make spreadsheets in a Portakabin on an industrial estate, it's amazing, how about you? And we see all these people I haven't seen since last year's weddings and I've got no progress to brag about. We haven't bought a house, we're not trying for a baby, I haven't been promoted—'

'What about the online thing?' Jack interrupts me. 'That's amazing, you can brag about that.'

'It's not the same though, is it? Last time I sat next to Jaz and he told me that they're buying a ski chalet. As in, they have a house, and they're going to buy another one.'

Jack laughs. 'Yeah, well, I don't even like skiing. And I think having two houses is wasteful.'

'Yeah,' I say. 'And you'd always end up having things you needed for one house at the other one.'

He nods, accelerating. 'And it's bad for locals, and destroys communities.'

'And all that flying is bad for the environment,' I add, enjoying this now. 'And it's tacky.'

'Exactly,' Jack agrees enthusiastically. 'So even when we win the EuroMillions, we're only having one house.'

'Yes. We should actually start playing the EuroMillions.'

We arrive at the wedding and park by the church, and I enjoy being carried through the day, hugging people we only ever see on the wedding circuit. I'm still very aware of my £16.99 dress next to everyone else wearing real silk, but it's a nice do. Jack is absolutely right that Gemma's mega rich dad has thrown the chequebook at it and there's non-stop champagne for hours and hours. We get gently pissed while other people get yanked in for various different combinations of photos. It goes on so long that I'm kind of expecting him to ask for everyone with a winter birthday to join for a line-up, or everyone who did History GCSE.

Eventually we make it from the drinks reception to the dinner, filing into an enormous room filled with flowers and candles. Jack steers me to our table, where we've been placed with Tom and Grace and various other uni friends. We all fuss around pulling out the fake bamboo chairs and trying to find space for our clutch bags around the glasses, flowers, name cards and wedding favours we'll inevitably forget to take with us and then feel guilty about.

'Hello!' Patrick says, sitting next to me. He was on Jack's corridor in the first year, so I only got to know him after uni. He's a tall skinny guy with a wide smile and a slightly patchy beard. 'How've you been?'

I ask him about life and he explains that his wife isn't there because she's literally about to give birth and watching other people getting pissed while she's sober is her idea of a nightmare. I sympathise. He says they've just moved out of London to a village near Bedford and that they're doing up a house. He sold his first business so now he's 'taking a beat' to work out what he wants to do next, but it'll probably be consultancy.

'How about you?' he asks. 'I've been going on and on about us. What's new with you and Jack?'

'Nothing, really,' I say, my chest flushing. I don't know why I'm embarrassed about this. There's nothing new with us because we really like how things are. We're living together, married, he loves his job, mine mostly doesn't make me want to jump off a roof, and the evenings and weekends with each other are blissful. We haven't changed anything because right now we don't want to.

'Oh come on, it's been a year, you must have done something.'

Jack looks up from the other side of the table. He stops talking to Pippa, who I usually avoid because she insists on calling me Jessie and touching my hair.

'Tell him about the social media thing,' he says.

'Social media thing,' I laugh. 'You sound like such an old man.'

'Tell him!' Jack repeats, almost stern. He's not going to let this drop.

'I started posting about relationships,' I say, 'and it's picked up some traction.'

Everyone's listening now, and Jack takes full advantage of that. 'How much traction, Jess?'

I look down at my half-finished plate of pâté. 'A few hundred thousand followers.'

'What?!' Grace almost drops her wine glass. 'I'm sorry, how do I not know this?'

This isn't going to go down well. 'I was really embarrassed,' I admit. 'So I blocked everyone I know in real life.'

They all laugh, apart from Grace who is outraged. 'You've blocked me?'

'I thought you'd take the piss,' I counter. If I were being harsh, I'd point out that she didn't even notice me disappearing from her timeline because she's so busy posting hundreds of pictures of her toddler, Raffy, and her newborn, Ada.

'Yeah, obviously I would have taken the piss,' she laughs, refilling everyone's wine glasses with the fancy white wine Gemma's dad so generously provided. 'Okay, but how did this happen?' she asks.

I take a deep breath, and then a very large gulp of wine. 'Jack was working a late shift on our anniversary, so I made him dinner at like, one in the morning when he got back. And then someone tagged the restaurant I recreated the menu from, and people commented a lot saying it was sweet and they wanted more date night ideas. So then I posted more about dates, and then I started posting about dating, and long-term relationships, and I don't know. It just kept growing. And then some, like, semi-famous people reposted me and it got big really fast. But it's the internet, it's not like a real job or anything.'

Which is true. It's not a job. But – and obviously I can't tell them this because it would tip over into full-on bragging – it has started to earn me money. The first time a brand offered me cash to do a post for them I assumed it was a scam, but I went along with it just in case and to my absolute shock, a month later they paid me £500. As in, what I make in a week of work, for one post. And since then it's happened enough times that we've actually got a meeting lined up with a real-life manager. Obviously it's a side hustle (an expression that Jack truly hates) for now, but there are *people who are making real, proper money from this. And I guess it's not totally impossible that I might do the same one day.*

Everyone looks faintly impressed and I feel myself beaming.

The music starts and after Gemma and her new husband have taken a few steps around the dance floor, they gesture for us to join them. Jack winds his arms around my waist and we sway in a very safe version of dancing together. 'Thank you for that,' I say. 'It was very embarrassing and very sweet.'

'You're more than welcome,' he says. 'I told you that you had something to show off about.'

I rest my head on his shoulder.

'It'll probably dry up within six months,' I say. 'I'm going to run out of ideas eventually.'

'I wouldn't be so sure,' he replies. 'And if you get really desperate, I can always help you come up with something.'

'True,' I say. 'You're the writer, after all.'

He drops a kiss on my forehead. 'I heard a rumour that Patrick has cigarettes.'

I laugh. 'Let's go mug him for one.'

Jessica

It's the first Saturday morning since the book came out where we haven't had publicity for the book, or work to do on it, or something book-related to fill our time. We wake up and neither of us totally knows what to do with ourselves. I sort of assumed that once the book press was over, we'd fall back into the routine we'd been comfortable with before. But I can't quite work out what we'd have been doing right now, in before times. I find myself thinking how much easier it would be if we had children, if their dictatorial ways decided our weekend plans. I know my friends' routines intimately via social media. I watch their early morning cuddles in bed with sleepy toddlers and tiny prune-like babies. Their trips to ballet or football classes followed by coffee in the park, rushed lunches at Pizza Express. And I know it's much harder work than it looks because I used to go along for the ride sometimes, marvelling at how many things you have to do in a day when you're keeping a toddler entertained, at how quickly time seems to evaporate for them. But there's a different kind of hard in waking up in the morning and realising there's a vast stretch of unfilled time in front of you. Time and time again, my friends who are mothers tell me how lucky I am to have the luxury of empty time, that I can have a wee without an audience, but I wish I could make them understand what it's like to crave sleep deprivation and total dependency from a tiny person. How I hear them talk about their boring, stressful lives and simultaneously understand and envy them.

Obviously I can't say that. We have the luxury of time, of lie-ins and a clean, peaceful house. We're entitled to a cafetière of overpriced coffee and all of the newspapers spread out over our huge kitchen table. We can have the kind of morning our friends would trade a limb for. I should be grateful for it. But on weekends like this one, the silence of the house squeezes around my head and I find myself climbing the walls by lunchtime.

I could ask Jack if he wants to go to a gallery, or wander the shops, but he's lying on the sofa reading a book by someone with an unpronounceable French surname.

'How's the book?' I ask him.

It takes him a minute to realise I'm talking to him. 'Great,' he says. 'I'm enjoying it.'

I've known Jack for most of my life. I know without a doubt that this is his way of telling me to leave him alone so he can keep reading. So instead, I text Clay.

Busy?

Sleeping off a hangover.

It's practically midday.

Yes, thank you, Matron.

Fancy a walk?

God, no.

I feel a little wave of disappointment. Apparently no one I ask wants to do anything today. My phone buzzes again. It's Clay.

But I could be tempted to a bit of shopping.

'I'm thinking I might go out for a bit,' I say to Jack. He looks up from his book.

'Cool. Where?'

'There's an antiques market in West London.'

'Do we need any more antiques?'

'I don't think anyone *needs* antiques to start with.'

There's a little pause. I wait to see if he might suggest an alternative activity. But he doesn't. 'So, I'll be a couple of hours, and then I'll be home in good time for Tom and Grace's dinner thing.'

'Should be fun,' he says. To my surprise, because Tom and Grace are our university friends who live in a pristine house with their two pristine children and like to talk about all of the success that they, their children, and basically everyone they've ever met, are enjoying at all times. We usually agree that seeing Tom and Grace is objectively not fun anymore.

'Yeah. Totally,' I agree, not wanting to be the one with the bad attitude.

'Dreading it?' He gives me a smile and my shoulders sag in relief. He gets up to refill his coffee cup and gestures to me, offering me one, and I shake my head, without explaining that it's about my pregnancy-forum-induced caffeine anxiety.

'Yep.'

'How long do you think it'll take before they start nagging us to have kids?'

'An hour?'

'We could just tell them.'

'I'm really sorry,' I say, 'but I would rather let her patronise me all evening than admit to her that there's something she can do that I can't.'

Jack laughs, a proper, hearty laugh. I notice the fine lines around his eyes in the sun from the huge living room window. He's getting better and better looking as he gets older. I don't think I've told him that.

'I don't have to go out,' I venture. 'We could just go for a walk round here, or something.' I want him to say yes. To put down the book and shove his feet into his shoes like he used to when we were younger, when weekends were about having the most fun possible to fill my social battery before another shitty week at my shitty job.

He looks over to his book, to the sofa which is rumpled, all the cushions squashed to fit his body. 'Yeah,' he says. 'Yeah. Sure.'

'No, no, it's fine,' I interrupt, sensing his reluctance. He's spent the last two weeks doing dozens of radio spots and bookshop talks, and he clearly wants to be alone for a bit. That's fair. We have a whole rule about taking time to be selfish and doing your own thing. It makes sense that he would want some space. Though I'm not sure why I feel so hurt about it. 'We can walk over to Grace and Tom's together later.'

I pause at the front door, wondering whether I should tell him who I'm going out with. But he didn't ask. So maybe I don't need to announce it. While I doubt he'd say it in so many words, he would be annoyed that I'm seeing Clay as a friend rather than a manager. So it's easier and simpler for everyone if I just ... don't. In a perfect world, we'd have spent this weekend enjoying our post-press-tour freedom together. But things haven't quite snapped back like I'd expected them to, and the last thing I want is to exacerbate that.

Clay's already at the market when I arrive, standing outside a coffee shop wearing an impeccably tailored coat.

'Hello darling,' he says, beaming. He hands me a cup and kisses me on each cheek.

'Thank you,' I say, taking a long sip of coffee. 'Did they have sugar?' I ask, craning to see which café he bought it from.

'No.' He smiles.

'Liar.'

'It's coffee, it doesn't need sugar.'

'I like it!'

'Philistine.'

I roll my eyes. 'What are we looking for?'

This market is apparently one of London's best-kept secrets. Clay knows about it because an interior designer he had a fling with in the noughties brought him on a date. It lines a long Georgian street in West London, cars and tables overflowing. At first glance it looks like your bog-standard car boot sale. But the people selling here are dressed in moth-eaten cashmere, with scuffed Gucci shoes. 'It's where all the aristos come to flog something if they need to raise a bit of cash for school fees or a hole in the stable roof,' Clay tells me, taking my arm in his.

I can see why no one wants to let the secret about this place out. I pause by a scratched green Volvo, running my hand over a little wooden writing desk. It has turned legs, a leather top and a pretty little key in the lock. 'This is lovely,' I say to the man overseeing the stall. Overseeing is probably a strong word. He's sitting in the car with a door open, reading yesterday's *Telegraph*.

'Yes,' he says. 'It's 1850 or something like that.'

'You can't buy something now,' Clay says, batting my hand away. 'You'll inevitably find something you like better in half an hour and then I'll have to come back and beg for a refund. And anyway, it's got a chip in it – look.'

We wander further down, stopping to look at various framed family pictures of serious black and white people, a table covered in knives and forks, a huge box of buttons.

'You're too thin,' Clay says, as I reach up to take a hat off a hat stand comically placed in the middle of the pavement.

'Do you talk to all your clients like this?'

'You're more than just a client, you're a friend. And I'm worried about you.'

He puts the hat back on the hat stand and leads the way towards the far end of the market.

'Don't be stupid,' I say.

'I'm not. When I first met you, you had tits.'

I stop dead. 'Yes, and I also had back fat. Magic of spin.'

'Men don't want to fuck skeletons,' he comments, trying on a hat himself.

'You are so rude,' I reply primly.

'You know I'm right.'

'Maybe I don't care what men think about my body,' I say. I put the hat back and wander towards a stall selling cushions. Do I feel weird about buying second-hand cushions?

'Well, as long as you're not talking about dieting or weight loss online,' Clay adds. 'I had a client lose fifteen thousand followers last week.'

'Who?'

He drops the name of a reality TV star and I am suitably impressed. Clay chuckles. 'You're gloriously basic.'

'What did she post?'

'She did a story saying she "felt fat" and needed to cut the carbs. Eating disorder charities were crawling all over it. Jameela Jamil did her Shame-ila Shame-il act and the rest was history. No more *Celebrity Bake Off*, no more *Dancing on Ice*.'

'Shit,' I say, poring over another desk.

'See,' he says, 'far nicer than the other one.'

'I liked the other one.'

'To go in your study? You're mad. This is clearly the choice.' He flags down the woman the desk currently belongs to. 'How much?' he asks.

The woman is French and smoking a cigarette. She gives us a haughty look. 'Three hundred,' she says with a thick accent.

'Two,' Clay replies before I can answer.

The woman gives a Gallic shrug. 'Two fifty.'

'Done.' Clay smiles. He takes out his wallet and gives her a sheaf of fifties, then starts filling out a form for the delivery.

'Stop it!' I say. 'I'll pay for it.'

He shakes his head in refusal. 'Consider it a little rebate on my fifteen per cent.'

We wander back through the market and I spot someone selling jewellery. I find myself surprised by how sad it makes me. All of it probably owned by someone, once upon a time, who'd loved it. I'd like to have a look at it, but I'm worried Clay might try and pay again and the idea of him buying me jewellery feels oddly awful. The only pieces I own, apart from a handful of Claire's and Oliver Bonas bits, were bought by Jack, or inherited from Mum.

We reach the end of the road and it's not dark yet, but the streetlamps are prematurely bright.

'Shall I get you a cab?' Clay asks.

I say I'm perfectly happy to call myself an Uber and he insists on getting me a black cab anyway. He hands the driver a handful of £20 notes and waves goodbye. Sitting in the padded back seat, enjoying the warmth after the crispness of the weather outside, I look at my phone. *Thank you for today,* I type. *I had such a nice time.*

Is it bad, I wonder, that I've had such a nice time that I didn't think once about missing my husband?

Jack

I had good intentions this morning. I could sort of tell that Jessica wanted me to come out with her, and part of me felt like I should. But it's the first Saturday of freedom since the book circus started and I've been thinking about this bit of time like a kid thinks about the school holidays. A whole blissful uninterrupted day to write. Not Seven Rules stuff, which gets edited and double edited and changed by a sensitivity reader, and then edited again until it bears no resemblance to anything I put on the page. They don't need me for that. Proper writing. The kind I grew up dreaming of, the kind I studied at university.

Every writer will tell you, when interviewed, that he or she sits down at their desk every morning, like you would for any real job. They make it sound like the sitting down is what makes the books happen. So when I stopped working at the BBC and started working from home, I decided to do the same thing. I can assure you that if you sit at your desk every morning and then spend five hours fucking about on Reddit, you will not produce anything.

Thankfully, there's an email to help me procrastinate today. I see the name of the sender and my stomach does a little backflip. Edward Nestor. Edward is an agent. Not a manager like Clay, who represents people who have been on *Big Brother*. I don't think Edward would know how to negotiate a deal for me to get free veneers in exchange for two stories and a grid post, even if he wanted to. Edward is the kind of agent who represents the people I used to watch on telly as a kid. The funny, clever, tweedy Stephen Fry actor-writer types I idolised. The people I dreamed

I'd be friends with when I got into Cambridge and joined Footlights. Of course, then I fucked up my A-Levels so I didn't get into Cambridge, which made joining Footlights impossible (or at least moderately fraudulent).

I emailed Edward's office some months ago after a couple of glasses of red wine and another fight with Jessica. I'd sent some self-deprecating demi-essay about how I'd always admired the people he represented, that I had written something totally out of my usual 'brand' and that I wondered if he might consider reading it. I sent him something I'd agonised over, claiming I'd dashed it off out of interest, to see whether I might be half decent at writing. And to my immense shock, he replied.

Then, last week, I snuck out of the house while Jessica was meditating, claiming I was going to the pub with university friends. But instead, I went to Soho, wearing a jacket I'd had in the back of the wardrobe since my early twenties, one that Jessica hates. It felt important that I didn't look fashionable. I'd arrived at Edward's office with my heart in my mouth, turned down a cup of coffee for fear that I might have some kind of embolism if I added caffeine into the mix, then changed my mind and decided that I wanted to take the meeting while drinking black coffee because it might underpin the sort of image that I was trying to cultivate. Edward was going to think me gauche, I had decided. He was going to look down on everything I'd done so far. That was why I needed the black coffee and the tweed jacket.

Only it turned out that Edward, unlike me, isn't a pretentious wanker. He ushered me into his office, lined with all the books written by all the people he works with, and smiled at me across his desk. 'I have to ask,' he said. 'Why on earth do you want to stop doing all this? You've done so well?'

I tried to explain, without sounding like an intellectual snob, that I am a massive intellectual snob. That being paid to go to parties filled with people who add 'd'you know what I mean though?' after every sentence makes me tired. That my brilliant and intelligent wife finds it challenging and fulfilling, but I don't. That I want to write something that I'm proud of. That I know I'm not too good to write self-help books but that it feels completely wrong for me. Edward nodded along, either understanding or doing a very good job of pretending to.

'I liked your manuscript,' he told me with a smile. It took me a moment to realise that he means the fiction I submitted to him, not the book I've written with Jessica.

'Really?'

He laughed at my surprise. 'Yes,' he said. 'It needs work – it owes rather more to Evelyn Waugh than I think perhaps it should – but there is something there.'

We talked for a while about what I wanted to do, where I saw myself, what I wanted to write, and then he sent me on my way, telling me that he would be in touch in due course. I walked through Soho beaming at everyone I saw. Edward was the first person – the only person – I had shown the manuscript to. I have been writing it since I was in my early twenties, in stolen periods at work, in gaps between Seven Rules edits. It was a silly story about the least brilliant son in a brilliant family who acciden-tally ends up at a prestigious American university and gains entrée to the political classes. And while I knew there was a lot wrong with it, having it as my little secret, as something to work on while Clay told us how to write our captions and the publishers stripped out every vestige of my personality from my chapters of Seven Rules, had been like a little warm glow that no one else could steal.

I hover the mouse over Edward's message, torn between opening it or enjoying this blissful moment where I know that there is an answer but I'm unaware of what it is. In this moment, the news is good because I won't allow it to be bad. Schrödinger's email. Once I open it, I will almost certainly be disappointed. Of course, the stupid, optimistic voice in the back of my head is telling me that it isn't going to be bad news, that it's going to be the best news. There is no subject line. I find this endearing because my father also cannot use a computer, and I've already started casting Edward as a sort of paternal figure, something which I should unquestionably be working through in therapy.

Jack, it starts.

I wanted to echo what I said last week about your book. It's not perfect, but there really is something there. I believe with some editing it could be quite brilliant.

Unfortunately, when we met before I had misunderstood the nature of your arrangement with Clay McAvoy Associates, which is why I asked you to send over a copy of the contract. Sadly it transpires that you are an exclusive client of CMA and therefore I would be unable to represent you in any capacity.

If you were looking to leave CMA, I would be delighted to discuss offering you representation, but I understand, given the arrangement you and your wife have, that that may be complex.

I'm sorry to be the bearer of bad news – I really did enjoy your book.

All the best,
Edward.

I turn the computer screen off because I can't bear to look at the email again. When I left his office that day, strolling through Soho feeling smug, pretending I could feel the first stirrings of spring, I had felt so sure that something was going to come of this. I hadn't even thought about Clay. I hadn't really thought about Jessica. I suppose I thought they'd publish my book under just my name, and it would be a totally separate thing that I'd have been really proud of. Jesus, I really can be catastrophically thick sometimes.

It has always been made very, very clear to us that we are a package deal, that one of us can't work without the other. People are always saying that the brand is the two of us, that you can't be a relationship influencer on your own. And while I try to stay as naïve as possible about these things, I can't help thinking that the powers that be are probably right. But perhaps it's worth asking? Worth a try?

I slink into the kitchen, where Jessica is back from the market and about to start a workout on her Peloton. She's basically done an entire weekend of activities in the time it's taken me to read a book, have a shower and read my emails. She's wearing shiny Lycra clothes and her hair scraped back from her face. I find it's best not to make any comment about it, even one of approval, because we had an almighty row about her spending two grand on an exercise bike with an iPad stuck to it. She's on it a lot. She read something about endorphins being good for fertility, but I do occasionally consider that she might be asking quite a lot of her body.

'You're back,' I say, in a tone which accidentally makes it sound like I'm not pleased to see her.

'Sorry, I should have used the sign-in sheet at the door.'

I am pleased to see her, obviously, I'm just second-guessing everything I say in an attempt to find the right thing. Ironically, meaning that I say the wrong thing all the time, which means she's more annoyed with me, which means I'm even more inclined to say the wrong thing, and round and round it goes, like a really miserable roundabout.

I half laugh. 'Can I talk to you for a minute?'

She looks suspicious as she puts down her giant glass water bottle. 'Sure.'

I gesture to the kitchen stool, wanting her to sit down. 'I need to ask you something.'

'... Okay?'

'And I don't know how to put it in a way which won't seem offensive.'

'Are you hoping to revisit the topic of anal?' She smirks. It's sometimes annoying that I find Jessica so funny. On days like today, where I don't want to be jolly, she still makes me laugh. It would be very tempting not to say what I'm about to say, to enjoy the lightness in her, let it be contagious. But I've got to tell her eventually; I've already let my writing become a weird sort of half secret between us and I don't want it festering for any longer. Plus, she's in a good mood, which might help.

'Ha ha,' I say, taking a run up at it. 'No. I've actually been working on something.'

'Something?'

'A book. Well. Potentially a book. It's only a first draft, it needs a lot of work still.'

She looks horrified, which was what I was really hoping wouldn't happen. I'm aware that I'm butchering this.

'What book?'

'It's a novel.'

'You've written a novel? When?'

Mostly when I was supposed to be working on my chapters of Seven Rules and pretending to have writer's block. 'It's not very long. I don't know, between other stuff. That's not really the point. The point is, I've been writing it. And I was thinking ...' I decide that maybe it's best to soft peddle this, that I'll approach it in stages. 'That I want to look into getting an agent, so I can publish it.'

'We have an agent.'

'We don't have an agent, we have a manager. I want a proper agent.'

I've said the wrong thing. I look at the air, as if I can grab on to the words and shove them back in my body, undo the damage I've just done. She's back on her feet and she's angry. 'Clay is "proper".'

'You know what I mean. A literary agent, someone who handles books—'

'As opposed to what we wrote, which was what, a catalogue? A coaster?'

'You know what I'm staying. Stop being deliberatively obtuse.'

'That's a big word for your dumb–dumb wife with her low-brow book.'

'Why are you being like this? You know Clay isn't an agent. He's a manager. And you know Seven Rules wasn't the kind of book I wanted to write.'

'Yes, we're all aware that you'd have preferred to write the kind of clever book which sells about seven copies.'

I don't know what to say to that. I feel like she's hit me. Jessica is kind. She tips like a Rockefeller, holds doors open for everyone, lets strangers pour their heart out to her. So when she says something cruel it burns. And she knows me inside out, every cell. So on the rare occasions she wants to hurt me, she's really bloody good at it.

'Maybe I would,' I say, so pained that I'm actually enjoying the prospect of saying something nasty. 'Is it so wrong that I'd like to write a book aimed at people who can actually read? Rather than peddling incredibly obvious advice to anyone stupid enough to buy it because you take nice pictures and put them on Instagram? Just because you're happy to make money pretending that we're endlessly happy doesn't mean I am. Not everyone wants to sell snake oil.'

She looks horrified. 'Fucking hell, Jack,' she says, staring at me.

'Sorry,' I say quietly, looking at the floor.

We both stand there. I know I should say something conciliatory, but I don't know what. I think maybe I want her to lose her temper, to throw the kind of Mediterranean tantrum she was so fond of in her early twenties. I know what to do with that. But I don't know what to do with this miserable grey silence, and that's why we keep getting stuck like this, not liking each other. Not able to be properly nice to each other. How long has it been like this, I wonder.

'I should shower,' she says, interrupting my spiral.

'Right.'

'We've got Tom and Grace's dinner.'

'Can't let Tom and Grace down,' I say, sarcastic. I'm not even really attempting to be polite anymore. She rolls her eyes.

'I was thinking we'd leave at seven,' she responds, telling me without saying it that even if I had been attempting to clear the air with a blazing row, it's not happening. Sometimes I wonder if she does this on purpose, refuses to rise to it when I'm sort of asking for a fight.

'Look, I'm sorry,' she says eventually. 'I get that you want to do other things. And eventually I'm sure you can. But for now, can't we just enjoy what we've got? It's a pretty amazing job. No cramming on the Tube at rush hour, no last-minute bailing because you've got a breaking story – it's a sweet deal.'

'Yeah,' I say, looking at the floor.

The day I found out I'd got the job at the BBC was – after the day I kissed Jessica for the first time, and our wedding day – the best day of my life. I'd grown up idolising the place, probably because the only things my parents really valued were the Universities of Oxford and Cambridge, the NHS, and the BBC. Old, clever, brick sort of institutions which they trusted with their whole hearts. They weren't the only reason I enjoyed the job, obviously. I loved it, all of it. Finding stories, trying to cover them better and deeper than our competitors. Shrinking a huge, long-running news story down into a seven-minute piece which would leave the listener feeling equipped to debate it at dinner. It was brilliant. I worked there for the better part of a decade and I didn't ever think I'd leave. Seven Rules changed that. One afternoon I was at my desk and Helen, the terrifying and brilliant editor, asked me for a 'quick chat'. I cheerfully assumed it was about some long working programme she wanted me to produce. But instead she sat across from me and told me that I was distracted, tired and not myself, that my social media book project was clearly zapping my focus and that technically I wasn't allowed to moonlight anywhere else. She said it all nicely, obviously. She was a nice person. Then she put her very cold hand on mine and said, 'Why don't you take a sabbatical, and when the book stuff is finished, we can look at you coming back?' So I did. And then I went home and told Jessica, who didn't pause before she started jumping up and down about how great it was.

I didn't tell my parents. Still haven't. I don't mention work. My name isn't read out in the credits to programmes anymore, so they must know. I have absolutely no desire to discuss it with them, so I'm not going to.

'Jack?' Jessica says, in a tone which suggests she's been trying to get my attention for a while. I shake my head, dismissing the memory.

'Yep, sorry.'

'I was asking whether you minded going down to the wine shop and getting something to take to Tom and Grace's?'

'Of course,' I say, going to find my coat.

I close the front door behind me and breathe in the cold, pleasingly dirty London air. It's starting to get dark so the sky is orange-pink, the old-fashioned streetlights giving their best Mary Poppins impression. I stride down the road towards the wine shop, trying not to ask how it's possible that Jessica can have misunderstood my feelings about my career so completely.

Jessica

Ever since we took the Seven Rules money and bought the kind of house I used to salivate over on Rightmove, we've lived a ten-minute walk from Tom and Grace. If I'm letting myself be a cow, I'll also internally acknowledge that we now have a much fancier address than they do. Obviously thinking this, even privately, is not the hallmark of a good friend, but I'm still a bit bitter from the times Grace declined to come over to our house because she didn't think she could park their brand-new Volvo on our scuzzy street, her word.

As we stride down the pavement, Jack is half a pace ahead of me and I'm unfairly annoyed that his longer leg length means he's winning the race he probably doesn't know we're in. 'Slow down,' I whine.

'We're late!' he says, as if I need to be told.

'It's dinner with our friends, not a train.'

Jack slows. 'In fairness, I don't know why I'm in a rush. If we get there late, we might not have to hang out with their dreadful kids.'

I laugh. Jack isn't often bitchy about people, and I love it when he is. And I especially love it when he's snide about other people's parenting. Maybe it's that whole 'my enemy's enemy is my friend' thing, but there's something uniting about complaining about people together.

We turn a corner and see their house, big and white with a pale blue front door and somehow perpetually flowering window boxes.

Tom and Grace were the first of our friends to get married, in our mid-twenties. Jack and I were secretly a bit perturbed because we were engaged, expecting to be the first with our sweet little Central London church-and-then-pub affair. Then Tom and Grace swept in with their six-month engagement culminating in a huge country house wedding in the Cotswolds. Obviously we were both being wildly unreasonable, but we enjoyed driving down in our tiny little Peugeot, complaining about the expense of the whole thing, maligning huge weddings, and then obviously had a brilliant time pounding the free bar and hurling each other around the dance floor. When they got back from their honeymoon, they took their fat parentally gifted deposits and spent them on this huge great house. The rest of us still all lived in damp rented flats, so it became the default hang-out for us all. We cooked roasts in their kitchen, threw parties in their garden, treated it like a common room and a co-working space and a nightclub, all with Tom and Grace cheerfully loving each other at the centre of it.

Obviously, these days we're all older and more grown-up, and basically everyone we know is tied to a mile radius of their own houses because of nap schedules, so Tom and Grace's is not the social hub it used to be. When Grace first got pregnant, she had grim morning sickness most hours of the day, and understandably couldn't face hosting long boozy nights in their garden or roasts around their kitchen table, so they closed up shop, and to my massive embarrassment it left a sizeable hole in my social life. For years I didn't need to plan anything because Grace always did. And on balance it was probably good for me, having to think about what I actually wanted to do, who I really wanted to hang out with rather than just spending time with her friends and then complaining about the ones I didn't like. I wonder if tonight's dinner might signal a return to Grace wanting to be hostess again. And I wonder if I want that anymore.

Eventually we hear a small voice shouting, 'I want to do it, I want to do it, I want to do it.' After a long pause the door opens and a small child – Raffy – adorable in white linen pyjamas, smiles. 'I opened the door!' he exclaims.

'You did!' I reply brightly.

Tom stands behind the little boy, sleeves rolled up, smiling and slightly balder than last time I saw him. 'Hello, darling,' he says, kissing me on each cheek.

Raffy takes my hand. 'Come and see my Lego,' he instructs me. I swallow. I can do this. This isn't difficult. It's fine. It's fun. I'm a happy, child-free woman enjoying her friend's child.

'LEGO,' Raffy repeats.

'I don't know if Jessica wants to have a tour of all your Lego,' Tom laughs, doing absolutely nothing to intervene. He smiles as I'm dragged into the playroom. I know without a shadow of a doubt that later he'll either thank me for entertaining the kids, or even worse, act like he was doing me a favour by giving me some 'parenting practice'.

'If she's looking at your Lego, she has to look at my animal hospital,' Ada says, hurtling around the corner in the same White Company pyjamas and shoving her older brother out of the way.

'Can I see the animals?' Jack asks from behind us.

Ada studies him, considering his offer. 'Yes, okay,' she says gravely. 'But you mustn't break anything.'

'I promise I will do my best not to,' Jack replies with equal solemnity.

'Grace'll be down in a mo,' Tom says, retreating to the kitchen. 'I'll open a bottle.'

I follow Raffy to the playroom. They're so posh they have a playroom so the rest of the house looks like kids don't live here. When Grace comes downstairs, she looks perfect in a pair of oversized jeans and a paper-thin cashmere jumper. She's tanned and slim with delicate gold jewellery at her neck and her wrist, and lots of tiny hoops in her earlobes like a reminder that she's a Cool Mum. She looks at me, crouching over the Lego. 'So glad you made it in time for bedtime, would have been awful to miss the children.'

I nod, and don't say anything, but I pick up a little Lego man and put him in the car. 'He doesn't go there,' Raffy yells, smacking it out of my hand.

I wait for Grace to respond to her son's impressive right hook. Instead she smiles. 'You're so good with kids. How are you, anyway?' she exclaims. I get up to hug her and she puts her hands on my arms, looking at me searchingly. 'It's been ages. Have you even been here since Ada's birthday?'

I could point out that she hasn't been to my house since we moved in, but I don't. I know the rules. She's got kids. I don't. So we do things on her terms. Which is probably reasonable – at least, I tell myself that it's reasonable. But it's also half the reason I've stopped making plans with her; I just can't deal with hearing 'it's probably best we do things at my place, you've just got so much more flexibility' over and over again.

'All good,' I say. 'Before you came down, I was allowed to put five bricks into the new house he's building.'

'High honour indeed. Do you want a drink?'

It's probably not a test. But whenever one of my friends offers me a cocktail or a glass of wine, I feel fairly sure that they're really asking whether or not I'm pregnant. Not that many of them even know we're trying – just our age, our lifestyle, all of our demographics add up to wanting children.

'Yes, please,' I say.

Tom comes back into the playroom with glasses of wine for me and Jack, who has been released from Ada's Sylvanian hospital.

'You two would make great parents,' he says. Neither of us reply. I know we would, I want to scream. I fucking know we would. Sometimes I wonder if he might say these things to try to prompt a discussion, if he's asking without asking. But surely no one that smart could be so stupid? If I wanted to tell them, I'd tell them. And I don't. Grace would offer me advice, and supplements, and the names of doctors we could see – none of which she herself needed because she got pregnant with her perfect children the first months she tried, but she'd source them from her network of other barren women and then hand them over with a sympathetic grimace and I can't do it.

There's a long pre-bedtime routine starting with some French nursery rhymes, then Grace attempts to read them a lovely Victorian picture book while they both scream that they want the *Frozen* book, and eventually Grace takes both kids upstairs to bed. By Grace. Tom stays downstairs, holding court and laughing at his own jokes. I know I'm expected to follow Grace up and help her, but I just can't face it, and surely if anyone should be giving her a hand, it's her husband?

When Graces comes back there's toothpaste on her jeans and she looks suddenly exhausted.

'All okay?' I ask.

'Me? Oh yeah, of course. Brilliant. Great.'

She serves dinner in their dining room, a glass extension at the back of the huge Georgian house which absolutely could not be called a conservatory. They dub it a 'garden room' and while yes, it's pretentious, it's also so nice that it's made me jealous again. The table is laid beautifully, with cut roses and pristine glassware. We chat about work (Tom's is great, he's 'smashing' his target and thinking about starting a podcast, because he thinks the world needs to hear some of his thoughts), the kids (they're both in the top sets for every subject, but sadly their school just isn't stretching them enough) and holidays (Barbados has been ruined, so apparently 'everyone' is stumping up for Mustique). We've exhausted pretty much every subject possible by the time Grace brings out a Baccarat plate laden with brownies and a bowl of fresh berries.

'Very lazy pudding, I'm afraid,' she apologises as she serves the perfectly cooked brownies. 'Couldn't face anything more complicated.'

Everyone has a cup of coffee and then a strange hush falls over the room.

'So listen,' Tom says into the silence. 'Bit of an awkward one this, but we did actually ask you over here for a reason.'

'We're not sure we're up for experimenting with swinging, but we're very grateful to have been asked.' Jack smiles.

I laugh. Neither Tom nor Grace do. Instead they both adopt expressions of amusement despite clearly not thinking this was funny.

'We're getting divorced,' Grace announces.

'What?' I inhale, almost dropping my tiny hand-painted coffee cup.

'Tom and I. We've just filed for divorce.'

'I'm sorry?' Jack looks aghast. 'How is that possible?'

Tom shrugs. 'We've tried pretty hard, and we're not making each other happy, so we think it's best to call time. Before we make it worse and really hurt each other.'

'We just think it's easier this way,' Grace explains. She looks bone-tired, now I look properly. Really, really tired.

I'm not saying that I can read Jack's mind. Obviously that's not a real thing that people can do. But we've been together since we were twenty-one, and at this point I can certainly read every tiny micro expression on his face, and I'm sure that right now he's having the exact same thought process as me. We've known these people since university. We introduced them to each other, for God's sake. Grace was my best friend and club buddy, Tom was Jack's library bestie. We watched them flirt at our crass twenty-something attempts at dinner parties, pretended to be surprised when they admitted they were shagging. We saw Grace mop up after Tom when he got ill from a bad oyster on our group holiday to Cornwall. Tom queued with Grace for seven hours when she wanted to audition for *The X Factor*, and told Dermot that he thought she was the most talented woman in London (something we are absolutely forbidden from talking about now). We were there as he agonised over the ring he designed for her.

We were the first people to visit them when they were cocooned in their new baby bubble when Raffy was born. They have always been happy, and connected, and right for each other. They hit every single note of how you're supposed to build a life. If Tom and Grace, the two most perfect people in the world, who loved each other more than anyone else we know, who sometimes made us feel a bit shit about our own relationship because they were so happy, can end up getting divorced, then holy fuck. What hope is there for us?

It's hard to think of a conversational gambit at this point. We can't ask about anything they've got coming up, because presumably the answer is 'divorce admin'. Grace doesn't work, and Tom's job is so boring that I've managed to avoid learning anything about it, so beyond asking about the weather, I've got nothing. I can't even bring myself to gossip about our shared friends, because let's face it, Tom and Grace getting a divorce kind of tops the rumour that Holly from our corridor in first year is on Ozempic.

'Any big plans for you two?' Grace asks pleasantly.

'We're hosting an event for the book,' I say weakly. 'A sort of retreat.'

Oh God. Obviously we can't talk about this, it's a relationship bootcamp, I have completely fucked this.

'And we're going to finally tackle the garden,' Jack chimes in, his voice slightly higher than normal. This is an absolute lie, we've had no discussions at all about gardening.

'Oh very good,' Tom says. 'What's the plan?'

'We might redo the lawn,' I say, lying. The lawn is about three square meters of grass, I doubt you even could redo it.

'We loved the people who did ours.' Grace smiles. 'I'll give you their number.'

We finish pudding and make polite conversation until the clock hits 11.30 and I think it's socially acceptable to leave, and then we make our excuses. I want to ask whether we can still see them, whether Jack keeps Tom and I keep Grace, or whether we take it in turns, or all hang out normally. I want to ask whether they tried hard enough, what the kids think, whether it could be salvaged or whether they just don't want to try anymore. Obviously, I do none of these things, because I'm their friend not their child, and the fact that their news has sent shockwaves through me is not their responsibility.

Jack and I step out into the sharp cold of the street and I start walking, Grace's words ricocheting around my head. *We just think it's easier this way.* I thought we all agreed that this wasn't supposed to be easy. That marriage is hard work. And the more I think that, as I walk on assuming Jack is following me, the more I wonder why we're bothering. Everyone says it's hard – I say it's hard, I repeat it over and over again. But we never say when it stops being hard. We never explain what the end point is, what it is we're actually working for. I think about the war poem we read at uni, the one which goes 'the old Lie: *Dulce et decorum est pro patria mori*' – it is good and right to die for your country – and I wonder if in peacetime this is the old lie we tell. That it's normal to be unhappy. That marriage is working when it makes you sad. But is that really true? Is marriage actually supposed to be hard work? I've been unhappier than I have been happy for the last what? Few months, maybe even six months? I can see how Jack rolls his eyes or winces when I talk earnestly about my work. I can feel myself boring him when I talk about analytics and demographics, and I can feel myself getting angrier and angrier about it, holding him responsible for finding me boring. I increasingly like myself least when I'm with him. He used to look at me like I was every single one of his dreams come true, and for a long time his view of me was contagious. He thought I was brilliant, so occasionally, especially when we were together, I felt like I could be brilliant. But now he seems to think I'm some vapid social-media-obsessed bimbo. And I know that I'm not a nurse, or a teacher, or any of the other jobs which actually make the world a better place. But I am good at this, and there's more to it than just taking pictures. I love coming up with campaign ideas, and shooting content, and scripting videos. It's the kind of stuff I wanted to do, the stuff I might have been able to do if I hadn't missed the boat because I was looking after Mum while all my mates were doing internships.

'Are you okay?' Jack asks me, when he catches me up.

'Yeah, fine.'

'You look a bit freaked out. You're doing that thing with your jaw.'

I pull my scarf up around my chin, by reflex. He knows every single one of my tells. Just like I know his. 'I can't believe they're breaking up.'

'No. Me neither.'

'They were the happiest people we know.'

'Well. Apparently not.'

Without discussing it, we take the longer route home, walking in step, not talking until we arrive at our front door. I think maybe we both need the motion, to walk off the impact of this news, as if we can leave it outside in the night air rather than bring it back into our home with us. When we reach the house, we both go into the kitchen and I wordlessly pour us each a glass of wine. Then we sit at the kitchen island, staring at each other, trying to work out what to say.

'Sometimes I worry. That we could be … That that could be us,' I say.

There's a long pause, and then Jack looks up at me. 'Me too.'

I didn't want him to agree. I wanted him to tell me that there's no monster under the bed, no such thing as ghosts. I wanted the moment when you wake up and realise the terrible thing was in your dream and the real world is okay. And he hasn't given it to me. If I thought things were bad, his agreement makes them feel catastrophic.

'I think we might be in trouble,' I say slowly.

He's studying the kitchen counter and there's the faintest trace of a wobble to his bottom lip, which shouldn't surprise me because he cries at everything – adverts, books, TV shows – all of it.

'I think you might be right,' he half whispers.

My reaction to his agreement is totally unreasonable. There's an anger in me, coming from somewhere. I don't want him to agree with me, I want him to stop letting me say these things. I want him to tell me that I'm brilliant and he's brilliant, that we're brilliant together and we're going to be happy together for the rest of our lives. The alternative is too terrifying. And it's more than that. I don't just want us to stay together because we've got a book, or because I don't understand which way you swipe on an app. It's not that I don't want to be alone – it's that I want to be with him.

'I don't want that,' I say weakly. 'I don't want that for us.'

'Me neither.'

'We're supposed to be relationship experts. We should know how to fix this. We shouldn't have let it get this bad, but we should definitely know how to make it better.' I look up at him but his face is blank. 'I don't even really know what the problem is. Let alone how to fix it.'

I've been telling myself that once the book was published, everything would snap back into place, but I think by now I have to admit that it hasn't. Maybe it isn't going to. I swallow, determined not to cry. But how is this possible? Months ago we were the happiest couple I know, now we're talking about our marriage like it's terminal. I shake my head, as if I can flick away the reality that we're sitting with, that we're in trouble.

I stare at the kitchen counter. He stares at the floor. We sit in yet another long pause during which I will Jack to say something. But he doesn't. I want someone who knows what to do, to descend and tell us that we've made one simple mistake and if we just make a little course correction, we'll go back to laughing together and teasing each other and finding each other easy, blissful company. I want a monitor, a spirit guide, a specialist. I want to call someone, like I do when the dishwasher breaks or there is a leak in the roof; I want to hire the most expensive, best-reviewed professional to swoop in, diagnose the issue and solve it immediately. But of course I can't do that. Because if an expert like that – someone you can parachute in to fix a broken relationship – exists, it's us.

'What are we going to do?' I ask, as if he's going to have some solution.

He gets up and takes a packet of crisps out of the cupboard, pulling out a handful and chewing meditatively. 'Do you ever worry that the rules don't work?'

'What?'

'The Seven Rules. I mean, you said yourself, we're not doing so well, and we wrote the rules, so I guess I was just wondering—'

'Are you kidding?' This is surely not the time for Jack to get on his high horse about the account and the rules. We hold eye contact, neither of us willing to be the one to push this into an argument. We've never had a sensible discussion about the rules, because sometimes he laughs at them, sometimes he ignores them, and occasionally, when it suits him, he quotes them back at me.

I take a deep breath. 'Some of the time, I get the impression that you think they're a load of shit,' I say. 'And I think we're enormous hypocrites, because I don't think we take our own advice. Like, would you really say that you're my greatest cheerleader?'

I'm expecting a furious response to this, but in fairness I don't get one.

'No,' he admits. 'Not all the time, anyway. I try to be, but I guess ...' He pauses. 'I struggle. Especially since it all got so big, so ... I don't know. Public.'

I'm surprised by his frankness, and I rush to mirror it, wanting him to see that I'm trying too. 'And I don't think I'm exactly inviting you to make time for intimacy,' I add. He's not the kind of man to complain about a lack of sex, but we haven't slept together since

I was last ovulating a couple of weeks ago, and that was a perfunctory, half-hearted event. It couldn't have been less intimate. Every hotel room on the press tour seemed to expect sex. It felt a bit like the walls were disappointed by our attempts at conception, comparing us to other couples who'd stayed there and had delicious, chandelier-swinging shags.

'Look, I don't know what the answer is.' He reaches for my arm and I lean in to his touch. 'But I get it. Something is off. And if we don't fix it, we're going to be in real trouble, and obviously I don't like the idea of ending up divorced from you.'

'You don't?' It's not a great sign that hearing him say he doesn't want to divorce me feels like a triumph, but it's nice. Reassuring. Like when you take a bite of food and realise that you were starving hungry, I didn't know that I needed to hear it until he said it.

'No. Of course I don't.' He looks shocked at the question, which is unreasonable because – well – because he's made me feel recently like he'd love it if I weren't around. On my more dramatic days, I think that if I got hit by a bus he'd be sad and everything, but that then he'd really relish the mourning period where he didn't have to go anywhere or see anyone. No bitch wife nagging him to put on one of the outfits our stylist pulled or begging him to pose for pictures. But how the hell do you square the circle if doing the stuff which keeps a roof over your heads is making your partner like you less?

'I know I've been a bit ... distracted. With the book. And the baby stuff.' My voice is pathetically small. 'But I don't want to end up divorced from you either,' I tell him, when I realise he's looking at me and waiting for me to say something.

'Course not. It'd be bad for the brand.' He laughs.

If he thinks this is funny then he's the only person who does. I get to my feet. 'Maybe one of the things we need to work on while we're doing this "bootcamp" is occasionally having conversations which don't end with you being massively snide towards me?'

'I was making a joke,' he protests.

'It wasn't funny.'

'You very rarely think my jokes are.'

'Because they're always at my expense!'

There's a long silence. I get my Stanley cup, fill it with ice and screw the lid on. 'I'm going to bed.'

'Okay,' he says. 'We can work on things tomorrow.'

I know he means this nicely – genuinely I do. But his words hurt. I don't want to 'work' on our marriage. I don't want our marriage to need work, at least not in the sense that other people's seem to. It never did before. I only started writing about us because we were so naturally good. Maybe we tempted fate. I want the light, happy, casual joy that we had in each other for the first twelve years of our relationship. I just want it without the constant worries about money or the misery of working a job I loathed.

Rule Three

100% honesty, 100% of the time

Jack

For once we've been allowed to drive ourselves to a work event. Jessica pulls her duvet coat around her against the chilly morning air, wincing slightly at her hand on the frozen door handle, and then clambers into the passenger seat. I feel a prick of irritation because leaving at 6 a.m. was my idea, but it was supposed to appease her. I get ratty when I drive in London traffic, and at 6 a.m. there's very little. In my mind, that's a perfect problem-solving solution, but apparently not.

'It smells like damp in here,' Jessica says, as she takes a picture of her blindingly white trainers in the footwell and types *so, so, so excited, on our way to the first ever Seven Rules residential, cannot wait to meet the couples we're working with.* She does not look so, so, so excited. In fact, the first thing she said to me this morning was, 'It's so early I hate everything and everyone.'

'I'm sorry, the Ferrari is in the garage.'

'I'm not saying we need a Ferrari, I'm just saying we could probably get something a bit less battered now we're less broke.'

'It smells damp because we hardly use it.'

'Exactly, so time for a change.'

We inherited the car from her dad, years ago, when his second wife developed a burning desire for something smarter than the little Peugeot, and it was an absolute godsend. We were too hard-up to go on proper holidays, but we'd usually be able to stump for petrol, so when our mates were in Mexico or tagging along on a family villa holiday in Tuscany, we'd take a week off work, and then every day we'd drive out into the countryside until we saw something which looked pretty. My parents had given us a National Trust membership as a surprisingly un-shit Christmas present so we could sit in parks and gape at castles and then eat our Aldi picnics in the gardens. Jessica always liked the paintings and the interiors; she'd tell me that she was taking notes for when we had our own estate. I always liked the driving, the way she trusted me entirely with something so banal but so responsible, nipping across lanes and putting my foot down so London was behind us, the way she never let a song finish before she put another one on, and sometimes after a long day, she'd fall asleep with her cheek pressed against the glass.

I could tell her how much I miss that. Instead, I inexplicably say: 'The solution to having a car which smells of damp from underuse is not to buy a newer and more expensive car – which we will also barely use – which will then, eventually, also end up smelling of damp.'

She breathes a 'whatever' and sets about trying to connect her phone to the Bluetooth which plugs into the cigarette lighter. I had actually thought earlier that the guests at the bootcamp might be a bit surprised by our shit car, but if I say it now, it'll sound like I'm agreeing that we need a new one, and while we are making a decent whack, I do sometimes feel a stirring of anxiety about how cheerfully Jessica takes on new expenses. Times are good right now, but even so, the last thing I want is yet another direct debit winging its way out of our account on the first of the month.

'Seatbelt on,' I say, as I do mine up.

'I was just about to,' she snaps. She doesn't move to put the seatbelt on. I pull away from the kerb and turn in the direction of the North Circular. The dashboard makes a beeping noise.

'It's going to do that until you put your seatbelt on,' I say.

'Do what?'

'Make that beeping noise.'

'What beeping noise?'

I pause to make sure I'm not talking over it. 'That?' It's a very audible noise.

She's half smiling now. 'Don't know what you're talking about.'

'Has anyone ever told you that you can be quite annoying?'

'I'm actually quite worried that you're hearing imaginary noises.' She tries to suppress a giggle.

'I realise you're trying to be funny but that noise is actually making me want to drive into the central reservation,' I retort.

'I was just messing around,' she says, the smile gone. 'Sorry.' She puts her seatbelt on. The beeping stops and I briefly wish I'd been nicer about it. I change lanes and feel a sting of irritation when I notice her checking either side to make sure I've looked first. She doesn't even have a driving licence – since when did she have views about my driving?

'Are you listening to any podcasts at the moment?' she asks, after about half an hour of silence. I almost laugh at the formality of the question.

'No,' I reply. 'Not really.'

'Oh.'

There's another long pause. 'Are you?' I counter.

'No,' she says. 'I haven't been able to get into any lately.'

I put the radio on and for about an hour it's a welcome distraction, filling the silence. But then we get into an area without much signal and it starts crackling and whining. She turns it off. Neither of us says anything. More grass now, fewer roads. Still over two hours until we get there.

We pass Cambridge. 'Look.' I point. 'Cambridge.'

'Cambridge,' she repeats. 'We could stop and see your parents quickly?'

'Yeah. Maybe. Or maybe on the way home.'

'Yeah. Maybe on the way home.'

Somewhere past Northampton I hear her sigh. 'I know,' I say.

'I hate this,' she admits.

'Me too,' I agree.

'It's never been like this. Even when we've been fighting, we've never had to work to find things to say to each other. We've never been indifferent before.'

I know I've been thinking the same thing but hearing her say it really stings. She's indifferent to me. That's worse than her hating me. Indifference is pretty much the worst thing she could be feeling about me.

'I still love you,' I say eventually, looking straight ahead and grateful for an excuse to do this without sitting face to face.

. 'I still love you. It's just been harder lately, with the publicity and the book and all the pressure. And everyone goes through rough patches, we all know marriage is hard—'

Jessica and I used to laugh at people who said marriage was 'hard', on their socials, like they were accidentally telling tales on themselves. 'It shouldn't be hard,' we used to say to each other smugly as we lay in bed all weekend, shagging, reading, drinking red wine and talking nonsense. 'It's not hard for us.' Maybe we tempted fate. Or maybe it comes to all couples eventually. Either way, we're not smugly laughing anymore.

'We're fine,' Jessica repeats, more determinedly.

'Are we?' I look at her in profile and she looks back at me.

'Aren't we?' she asks.

'We thought Tom and Grace were fine,' I say, my hands tight on the steering wheel, in the ten and two position I was taught years ago and have always been too boring to deviate from. 'They thought they were fine. Actually, scrap that, everyone thought they were perfect. And now they're putting his stuff in boxes and she's probably downloading the apps.' It still doesn't seem possible.

'They really did seem so happy.'

'Yeah. But then I guess people would say that about us, right?'

'Are you saying you think we're going to split up?' she asks me.

Occasionally when I'm reading I wrinkle my nose at the lack of imagination in how people describe shock. It's always a twist of the gut or a punch to the chest. But maybe people describe it like that over and over again because it's the only really accurate way to put it. I do feel, as she says the words 'split up', like I've been hit in the middle of my body by something very, very heavy.

'No,' I say eventually, trying to keep my voice steady. 'I'm saying I'm worried about us. I think we're running on empty – we've spent too much time together but no actual quality time. We've been living in hotels, all we've talked about is work; it's honestly no wonder that we're snapping at each other constantly. But I don't think we can keep shoving it under the carpet and just go on saying that marriage is hard without asking each other why it's hard.'

She nods. 'I think you're right.'

At least we're on the same page, I suppose. The same horrible, miserable page, a page I literally never thought I would find us on. But in harmony here, if nowhere else.

'I mean, we are on our way to a marital bootcamp,' Jessica offers.

'Yeah, but for other people, not for us,' I reply.

'What if we change that?'

I'm genuinely shocked. 'You want to take part in a marriage bootcamp?'

'Why not? We've put together this incredible programme, we clearly need some help, surely we should take advantage?' She's sat up in the passenger seat now, looking at me expectantly.

The whole time Jessica was planning the retreat, she kept saying what an amazing project it was, that maybe we could run these things ourselves when she's qualified. But we were very clear from the outset that we were there in the background. We'd offer an hour session to each couple if they wanted to ask any questions about the book, but otherwise the experts would lead the workshops and we'd be a nice bit of colour at mealtimes. There had been absolutely no suggestion that we would take part in anything, aside from standing around the sides making encouraging noises. I'm not sure I can think of anything I'd like to do less than join in and bare my soul and our problems in front of everyone. But it's a shockingly agile suggestion from Jessica, the woman who won't bicker with me in the back of an Uber lest it ends up live-streamed on the internet.

'You'd really be willing to do that?'

'I would. Would you?'

'I'd give my right arm to make things right with you,' I tell her, entirely honestly.

'Great,' she says. 'I'll email Suze. Project Bootcamp is a go.'

When we pull up at the house, I have to take a moment to really look at it. It's a huge, beautiful former farmhouse. Natural stone with huge wood-framed windows, it's pure Countryside. Not really Jessica's taste, which skews more urban, but suitably escapist that it's the perfect setting for this kind of weekend. Jess unlocks the door with a key code rather than an actual key and pushes her way inside. It's incredibly warm and predictably luxurious, with pale-painted wood, thick carpets and wood burners. Not the kind of place I'd ever want to live – I'm a dull suburban boy at heart and the idea of not being able to pop out for a pint of milk terrifies me – but it's the kind of place I'm delighted to be staying, and hopefully the kind of place which will make these people feel it was worth giving up their time to come here.

'Suze? Are you here?' Jessica calls out as she walks down the long corridor.

Suze appears from nowhere, carrying a thousand files and looking a bit frazzled. She's followed by a very beautiful twenty-something man, and an equally terrifying twenty-something woman, both wearing trendy all-black outfits.

'Hi, hi,' she says, in a posh breathy tone. We all do hugs and then she realises that we're staring at the haunted twins next to her. 'Oh, this is Will and this is Cait, they're from our events team.'

'Will and Cait!' I point out, amused.

'...Yes?' replies Cait.

'It's like Prince William. And Kate Middleton,' Jessica points out. They both look very confused.

'We're not them,' says Cait eventually.

Jess and I exchange glances. 'No,' she agrees. 'You're not.'

'They're an absolute crack team,' Suze say, skating over my embarrassing joke. 'They'll keep the weekend running but you'll barely know they're here.'

Will and Cait carry on, clearly on a mission, but Suze hangs back conspiratorially. 'Listen. Saw your email. Are you absolutely sure you want to join in?' Suze asks, looking confused by our suggestion.

'Yes,' Jess tells her. 'We were talking about it in the car and we want to do it properly. Like we're one of the couples in the group.'

'Yep, sure, totally, and that's brilliant, but obviously the more private information you share with these guests, the less we can control what they post after the event ...'

'Sure, I hear that.' Jess smiles brightly. 'But we think it's for the best. Instead of us just hovering around, we can actually get involved. Way more authentic. Don't you think?'

Suze looks deeply sceptical.

'It'll be fine,' I say emphatically. 'We know what we're doing.'

Suze shrugs. 'Okay. If you're really sure.'

Jess catches my eye and gives me a nod so small it's almost invisible. 'We are,' we say in unison.

'I thought the Will and Kate thing was funny,' she says to me, as we tramp up the stairs to our room.

Jessica

Jack and I have very different attitudes to both packing and unpacking. He'll bring about three garments on holiday and then leave them in the suitcase for the entire time, even if we're away for a fortnight. I'll bring forty-five outfits and unpack every single item I've brought as if I'm moving house, even if we're just away for the weekend. Which is why I'm only halfway through folding pairs of tights while he's already found a shelf of books left by previous guests and ploughed into a biography of some dead American politician. He seems completely calm about what we're about to do, which is an enviable position because I feel like I'm about to throw up.

I spent a lot of time with Suze and our publishers planning this thing, finding the perfect balance of activities to really showcase how the rules can help a relationship. But I planned it for other people, I didn't think I would be joining in too. I didn't think my marriage needed help. But now I'm worried that I'm going to be exposed as a complete fraud for giving relationship advice when Jack and I are so far from perfect. I don't know how we'd survive if rumours found their way on to the forums.

I only found out about the websites a couple of years ago. Forums where people can post anonymously about any social media account as long as it has more than 10,000 followers. There was some article in the Sunday supplements. It talked about the women who have seemingly normal, happy lives, but who log on at night after the kids are in bed to discuss a stranger's weight gain, alleged surgery or any one of a variety of perceived failings. Obviously, the first thing I did was type our names in, my gut twisting as I waited to see what people had said.

So far we've got off shockingly lightly. Occasionally I've found the website useful. When they started talking about my Botox, claiming I was pretending I'd had nothing done, I waited a week or two and then threw in a mention of it, talking about how important it is to be candid about any 'help' you have, so that you don't perpetuate unrealistic standards. People seemed to like that. There are plenty of people who don't like us, obviously. A handful who say that I seem cold or that we don't deserve our big house, neither of which worry me especially. There were a couple of comments recently about me looking too thin, which I secretly quite liked. But most importantly, no one on there seems to have clocked that for the better part of a year, Jack and I can't go forty-eight hours without one of us winding the other one up.

Suze pushes the bedroom door open without knocking. 'You know you didn't need to take the smallest bedroom, right?' she says as I stand in front of the mirror debating between a white jumper and a striped one, agonising over which one will make the best first impression. 'We had you down as being in the main suite.'

'We thought Ken and Sue should have it. They're the eldest couple.'

'Sweet.' I cannot tell from the look on her face if she thinks I'm lovely or a moron. 'Can I steal you and Jack for pictures?'

Clay told us right at the start of all this that the people who do well are the people who behave well. 'Being an influencer is like being a royal,' he told us, over an expensive lunch. 'Put up and shut up if you want to survive.' So rather than saying that we're desperately trying to get on an even keel, I smile. 'Of course.'

'Where is he?'

I look around, unsure. The bed is rumpled from where I threw my very heavy suitcase on it. She follows my gaze and sees where I'm looking.

'You two!' she laughs. 'God, I wish Chris and I were still at it like rabbits.'

I could correct her. But I don't and we eventually find Jack in the kitchen, wrestling with a very complicated coffee machine. Suze manipulates our limbs while we stand in front of a huge window, Jack looking into the camera, my chin tilted upwards, looking adoringly at him. Suze has just got the shot when we hear the crunch of gravel on the drive and all three of us freeze for a moment.

'Show time!' says Suze brightly. She takes out a phone the size of a paperback and bolts for the door, presumably to capture everyone arriving.

'Ready?' Jack asks me.

'Yep.'

'I don't want to be a dick,' he says, which means he's going to say something dickish. 'But I don't think this is going to be easy. Airing our dirty laundry in public, admitting that we're not perfect. But if we're doing it, we've got to really do it.'

'I know that,' I say, indignant. 'I didn't agree to join in lightly. I knew what it meant, I get that it's a big deal.'

'Okay,' he says. 'Because I really do want to make things better.' He leans down and touches his forehead to mine.

'Me too,' I say earnestly. 'Me too.'

I asked for a bus to collect everyone from the station, so that they'd have a chance to chat and meet each other. I'm utterly vindicated when they pour off the bus and into the house already chatting and laughing. We need them to like each other at least a little bit because they're going to have to spend the next forty eight hours sharing their most personal, private secrets with each other. And, I remember with a twist in my solar plexus, so am I.

'I'm Verity and this is Noah,' the first woman introduces herself, shaking my hand then Jack's.

'Welcome.' I smile. 'Go straight through, and make yourself at home. They've been married for ten years,' I whisper to Jack.

'Ten years? But they look so young?'

'They *are* so young. They got married at eighteen.'

'Jesus. Why?'

'Jesus.'

'That's what I said.'

'No, as in, they got married because they were super Christian.'

'Oh. Well, that explains the marital problems. Three people in their marriage and all that.'

I laugh, and then try not to, because I don't want anyone to think that we're standing in the hallway being judgemental and superior. Which I suppose we are a little bit, not that we have any right to be.

'Well, there's actually five of them, because they've got three kids under three. We got the publishers to front up some money to get them childcare while they're here, so believe it or not, this is probably like a holiday for them.'

I smile at Sue and Ken, who are picking their way across the drive. They're the oldest couple of the weekend. Ken is bald and serious, Sue tanned and smiley. He's carrying her suitcase which is very sweet. I watch Jack, knowing he's wondering whether he should offer to take the suitcase from him or whether that'll seem ageist and patronising.

'What's their deal?' he asks after he's said hello and waved them through into the house.

'Ken retired a few months ago and they're struggling to know how to adjust to being at home together all the time. Sue had raised their three kids and stayed home while Ken worked on the trains so was away a lot. It sounds like it's been a big change.'

Chloe and Ben are next. Jack shakes both their hands and Chloe goes in for a hug. Chloe filled out their application. She explained that her family had issues with her marrying a black guy, so she and Ben cut the parents off. But then they had kids and she struggled and started taking them to see her mum and dad without telling Ben. Eventually one of the kids spilled the beans and it put a massive wedge in their marriage. It seems like Chloe applied to come here as a sort of *mea culpa* to Ben.

Last off the bus are Grant and Stuart. 'Grant is twenty years older than Stuart, and they apparently met when Stuart was his PA and Grant was still married to a woman. Grant's children are grown-up but won't meet Stuart, and it's all more complicated because Stuart wants to have kids and Grant thinks he's too old. Plus there's a bit of a mismatch about their sex drives.' I convey this to Jack under my breath as they approach the house.

'Are you going to be okay if they talk about wanting to start a family?' Jack asks me in a hushed tone as we turn to follow everyone into the house.

'What do you mean?' I play dumb.

'Their problems ... might be a bit close to home?'

'I've never shagged my PA.' I smile. It's a defensive smile that Jack can probably see through but I can't get upset and fall apart before the weekend has even begun.

Jack

At three minutes to seven, I'm standing in the kitchen, trying to work out what I should be doing while everyone else is unpacking and freshening up before the welcome drinks. There's a load of champagne in the fridge, designed to be carefully distributed so that no one is plastered but the awkwardness of what we're about to do is dulled slightly. I start very slowly unwrapping the top of a bottle for something to do with my hands. I freeze as I hear footsteps behind me, and look up. It's a very pretty dark-haired woman/girl with heavy eyeliner. She looks like a teenager who's been dragged to the country for a holiday with her parents. Which one was she? Chloe? Verity? I should remember her name, given how recently I was introduced to her.

'Thank fuck for that,' she says. 'I thought this might be the kind of place that doesn't provide alcohol. I'm Verity.'

'I'm Jack,' I say, returning the favour of repeating my name. 'Excited for the retreat?'

'Yeah,' she says. 'More so now I know it's not going to be dry.'

I pop the bottle, as quietly as I can. 'A no-alcohol policy was suggested by the people who organised this with us,' I say, pouring the champagne into a glass and handing it to her. 'But we insisted.'

She takes a sip. 'I can't think of anyone who needs a drink more than a group of unhappily married people trying to save their relationships.'

'The official party line is that no one is unhappy, and that we're all trying to "reinvigorate" our relationships,' I say, feeling Jessica would be proud of me.

She smiles, showing a little gap between her two front teeth. 'Sure.' Then, lifting the glass, 'Cheers.'

There's a silence so abject that I can hear the humming of the fridge. This is why I liked my old job. I'm good behind the scenes. I can set things up so other people can flourish, or more often, so that they can skewer a tricky politician. But standing in the middle of the room isn't for me. I think sometimes it might read like I'm not trying, like I think I'm too good for it all, but it's literally the opposite. It's been worse since things really started to take off with the account. More parties, more events, more dinners, but most of all, more pressure. If I embarrassed myself at the pub five years ago, then the only person who suffered was me. Now if I cock it up badly enough, apparently I could tank Jessica's livelihood too. Sometimes when we leave an event, Jessica will give me a review in the car on the way home. It started with her thanking me for going to bad parties with weak drinks so that we could 'network' and morphed into her explaining how I could make better small talk next time. I know she's trying to help, to make me more comfortable, and it comes from a good place. But sometimes it feels like we leave a party and I wait for her to start listing all the ways I've failed.

I'm quite relieved when Ken and Sue come down and fill the room with noise, chatting about how much they like their bedroom. Verity turns towards them and I step back just a little, smiling and nodding in a way I hope is acceptable.

Eventually everyone assembles, and it feels like an awkward school disco; the crowd has separated into two tribes, lining opposite walls. What I really want to do is walk over to Jess, put my arm around her and do the small talk together. I feel more confident at these things with her by my side, but I know we're supposed to be mingling. I can see that she's busy chatting to Sue, maybe because Sue's kids are all grown-up so Jess won't have to listen to what it's like having little ones. A couple of the blokes next to me have already formed a little cabal, predictably talking about football, and I feel on the outs, like the kid at school trying to pretend I'm interested in the same things to fit in better. There's a sort of frantic quality to the way that they keep repeating themselves, repeating sports clichés. They're nervous, and I get it. If you've spent your entire life keeping schtum about your feelings, it's quite the challenge to suddenly go away for a weekend and be expected to expose your innermost thoughts. A bit like being expected to take off all your clothes and bend over, really. Unlike the rest of them, I suppose I could probably bow out at this point. But even entertaining the idea feels wrong. I think, despite the nerves, it might actually be preferable to admit fallibility and join in, rather than just leading and acting like a pair of smug twats who know the answer to everything.

From across the room, I hear Jessica clinking a knife against her glass.

'Hi everyone,' she says. 'I'm Jessica, this is Jack,' as if they don't already know who she is. She's the whole reason they're here. 'Thank you so much for giving up your time to be here with us, for what we hope is going to be a really exciting, empowering weekend. We've got a jam-packed schedule of games, events and activities guiding you through each of our Seven Rules, which – as you all hopefully know – we believe can strengthen any relationship.'

She pauses to take a breath, obviously nervous. She's better in front of a bigger crowd, I've noticed. With a group this size, you can really feel everybody in the room. She sips her drink and then carries on, a bit slower now.

'Some of you will be here because you want to recommit to each other, some of you will be here because you're having some significant struggles in your marriage. Having struggles in your marriage is normal – we all know that. But being unhappy for an extended period of time is not. We want you to leave at the end of the weekend with tools you can use for the rest of your lives. We're going to ask for a lot of vulnerability and honesty from you all, and that's probably going to feel quite weird to start with.' People laugh lightly. 'But we promise you, it'll be worth it. Sometimes it's easy to fall into patterns in a marriage, to focus on the bad and forget the qualities that you love most about your partner and what attracted you to them in the first place.'

She pauses, fiddling with her bracelet and tucking her hair behind her ear. When she looks up she meets my eye, and I'm grateful that she's being honest although it hurts that I know she's speaking from experience. There are a few uncomfortable looks and murmurs of agreement, so it's clear that everyone can relate. 'Jack? Anything to add?'

I absolutely have to say something. I pick a spot at the back of the room and focus my eyes there, and then decide that it's probably best just to be honest. 'If any of you are feeling a bit apprehensive about this, join the club. I'm not into sharing my feelings by nature, especially not with a room full of strangers.' I pause, worried that was rude. 'Sorry. But you know. You are strangers at the moment.' They laugh, much to my relief. 'But yeah, Jessica and I agreed that if we were going to ask you to take part in this with your whole hearts, we should do the same. So we'll be doing all the activities with you. And if I can manage to nail this "talking about your feelings" stuff, then I promise literally anyone can.'

They laugh again, and the 'they' includes Jessica, which makes this a dramatic improvement on last time I did public speaking in front of her.

'So we thought we'd start things off nice and easy,' Jess says, taking back the reins, much to my relief. 'I know it's been a long day of travel so tonight we're just going to do a quick icebreaker where we go around and introduce ourselves and our other half, using rule two: always be your partner's greatest cheerleader. We'll give you a couple of minutes and then when you're ready, you just introduce yourself and tell us something amazing about your partner.'

The little gathered crowd eases back as each couple turns inward, talking in low voices.

'Can I borrow you both?' Suze motions to me and Jess.

We follow her out into the corridor and Suze hands Jess an iPad.

'Now you're joining in for the weekend, they need you to sign a waiver to say that you won't sue if you fall off anything high and that you're not pregnant, Jessica. I don't think they need you to say that part, Jack.' She smiles at her own joke.

For fuck's sake. Did she really need to ask? It's not even been a fortnight since Clay and the gang called us into the office to demand our fertility plans and now Suze has got us confirming our barrenness on a sodding form? I can see Jessica chewing at the side of her finger, like she always does when she wants to run away.

'Oh, yes. Of course. Great. Yep, I can do that, I can absolutely do that,' she burbles. 'Do you have a pen?'

My cheeks start burning for her.

Suze gives her a look. 'It's an iPad, Jessica.'

'So it is!' she agrees. She ticks the 'not pregnant' box and then scrawls her signature in the box. I take it and do my own form.

'Thanks. We should go rejoin everyone,' I say cheerfully, eager to have this exchange over with as quickly as possible.

'You know it took me and David three years to have the twins,' she tells Jessica, as we go back into the room. I stop. Please don't start telling her about how it worked out for you, I pray. I don't care that it worked out for you. I don't care about it working out for anyone else on the whole entire planet until it works out for us.

'That must have been really hard,' I interrupt with a tight smile. And then I go back into the room, where everyone is laughing at whatever Grant has just said about Stuart. Verity takes longer to think about her answer than she should need to, given that she's had the last five minutes to think of something. Eventually, without even looking at Noah, she says, 'The children adore Noah, and he's a very involved father.'

Not exactly being his greatest cheerleader, but it's only the first night. Noah smiles out at the group as if she's declared him the greatest man alive. In turn he says, 'Verity is a wonderful mother. She's sacrificed everything for the children. Her entire life is about them.'

I wince. The way Noah says it, I can really imagine just how much sacrifice she's made, and I'm not convinced we should be celebrating it.

'Your turn,' Verity says, smiling at Jessica. 'What does the world's most perfect couple like best about each other?'

'We're really not perfect.' Jess pauses for a moment. 'But I love the way that Jack is so genuinely curious about the world, about people – about everything, really. He constantly tells me things I don't know, it's like a real education.'

I look at the floor because I'm not sure where else to look. Pathetically, I can feel my neck getting red with pride. I can't remember the last time Jessica said something about me which wasn't a criticism. But then, when was the last time I said something kind about her? We're rustier at this than I had realised.

'This is going to sound a bit obvious,' I say, moving my gaze to the bottom of my champagne glass. I'd really like to brush this off with a joke. But that's not what we're doing here. 'But sometimes I forget that Jess needs a cheerleader, because she's got literally a million of them online. But that's me getting complacent about what a force of nature she is. We're all standing here because of her. She built this. She's a powerhouse like no one else I've ever known.'

My stomach twists as I force myself to look up, to see whether I've said the wrong thing again, if I wasn't supposed to suggest that the bulk of the Seven Rules work was done by her. But she's smiling her real smile, the one she trained herself not to do because her stepmother once said it made her look squinty.

'Well, what a great place to end the introductions,' says Suze. 'Shall we go through to dinner?'

The First Holiday

Jack

'Cabin crew, prepare for landing,' the pilot's voice crackles over the speaker.

'Ready to land?' I ask Jessica, who is gazing out of the window taking photos of the wing of the plane on her new pink phone.

'Can't wait.' She smiles. She's got heart-shaped sunglasses perched on her head and her skin is a deep terracotta from the tan I helped her apply last night. I find it a bit confusing that she can't go on holiday without already looking like she's been on holiday, but given that Jessica is miles out of my league and constantly looks incredible, I don't feel the need to share this thought.

'I know. An entire week of wine, sun, sleeping and shagging.'

'I thought you'd be looking forward to the museums and all that lame shit,' she laughs.

'Actually, the thing I'm most looking forward to is watching you speak Spanish.' I lean in for a kiss. 'Bonita.'

She told me once, when we were first emailing back and forth, that she's too self-conscious to use her Spanish in England, that she only speaks it when she's in Spain. This week, I'm finally going to get to see the woman I fancy so much I might explode do the sexiest thing that a woman can do and speak another language fluently.

She starts putting everything back into her handbag, haphazardly stuffing a paperback in, pages splayed open. 'In like, five hours, we're going to be sitting on our own terrace drinking wine and watching the sun go down,' she says.

We started planning this holiday, like a pair of total clichés, the day we got home from our families' for Christmas. We'd both *had miserable times, obviously, because that's the point of family at Christmas. The damp flat where she lived was freezing, she'd left a load of wet laundry in the machine by accident and it had grown a forest of mould. I'd dropped my phone between the train platform and the train on the way to her place. 'We need something to look forward to,' she'd announced, with complete certainty. 'Let's book a trip.'*

It turned out, in the process of organising our first grown-up holiday, that Jessica and I had different ideas of what a holiday looks like. For me it was always a long car journey, usually north of Cambridge, often to the Lake District. I'd be between my taller brothers, agonisingly bored, while we listened to a tape of Greek myths and legends. We'd arrive late and I'd get out with cramping legs, covered in crumbs from the car picnic. And then we'd spend the following days tramping through the rain to houses where famous politicians or poets had once lived. I'd watch my parents carefully reading little plaques next to paintings, and in the evenings they'd read their books on the floral sofas of whatever cottage they'd rented, while I wondered what it would be like to go to Center Parcs.

Jessica's parents were from a more glam school of travel. She describes flights to upmarket package holidays where smiling twenty-somethings who had trained as dancers would meet them at the airport and usher them on to an air-conditioned coach and drive them to a compound with a view of the sea where the food was reassuringly not foreign. She'd be packed off to kids' club every morning while her parents slow-roasted themselves on the beach. She mentioned once that she'd longed to be allowed to join them, that she had spent her childhood wondering how old she'd have to be before she was allowed to lie next to them in silence, feeling like a family.

So, given that we'd both had fairly depressing experiences of holidays growing up, we decided to do something different. Jessica found a little apartment on some new website where you can rent people's houses, and I rented us a car. And for the five months between booking the trip to Spain and getting on the flight, it became a sort of prayer, like a meditation. When we were cold or grumpy or had bad days, we'd talk about sitting outside the little villa drinking Fanta Lemon and eating crisps, swimming, rubbing sun cream into each other's skin. She talked about linen sundresses and buying really big tomatoes at the market; I talked about finally getting time to work on my novel, plotting away in a Moleskine notebook.

We arrive at Madrid-Barajas to discover that they're having a heatwave. We get off the plane, descend the metal steps and then wait for the better part of an hour, on the tarmac, in the bus which doesn't have air conditioning.

'Apparently this is the worst airport in Europe,' Jessica says cheerfully, looking up from her phone with a smile. 'One to tick off the bucket list.'

'A superlative is a superlative,' I say, kissing her. We're far too in love to be bothered. It was cold at home, it's hot here. 'Anyway,' I tell her, 'this way when we get through passport control, our bags will be waiting for us.'

Obviously this tempted fate, because we make our way through the longest, slowest queue imaginable and arrive at baggage reclaim to watch a handful of suitcases circling around like the last dishes at a YO! Sushi. We sit for another ten minutes before it becomes clear that our suitcases have not made it to Spain.

'Okay,' I say. 'Tell you what. I'll go and get the hire car, and you go fill out a lost luggage complaint.'

Jessica looks blank. 'Why me?'

'I don't think the car hire place will need much Spanish, but you're going to have to convince them to give you some money upfront to get new clothes, and give them the forwarding address for the house and stuff.' She looks blank again, which is starting to confuse me. 'You're the only one who speaks Spanish?'

A look of realisation crosses her face. 'Oh. Yes. Of course. Because I speak Spanish.'

I head off to the car queue, pick up the keys and locate the Fiat 500 we're driving for the week, which has been parked in direct sunlight and therefore has door handles so hot that I can barely open it. I sit inside, running the air con for a bit like some kind of billionaire, and thinking how great it's going to be when Jess gets here and I've made it all nice and cool for her.

Half an hour later, she's still not back. I call her, and there's no answer. So I lock the car, walk back to the terminal and arrive, sweating, to find Jessica standing in front of the lost luggage desk, her face streaked with tears, doing a complicated mime.

'Los baggos,' she says, very slowly. 'Mi baggage, est non ici.'

'Jess?' I say from behind her. She jumps, then whirls around to look at me.

'I thought you were getting the car?' she says, her voice high.

'I got it. I came to see if you needed some help.'

'I don't need help. I'm FINE,' she says, in a voice which sounds very not fine.

'Okay,' I say. 'You carry on.'

She's bright red under the tan.

'Have you told him our flight number? I've got it written down here if you want?'

'Can you just go and stand over there? On the other side of the baggage reclaim?' she asks.

'Why?'

'Because I'm asking you to,' she says, through gritted teeth.

The man comes back to the counter and says something in very fast Spanish.

'Mi baggos es dans Londres,' Jessica says slowly. 'Los siento, mi baggos esta en Londres porque?'

I'm trying very, very hard not to laugh.

'Me encanta los baggos, por favore,' she tries again.

I give in. Then the lost baggage man starts laughing too.

'That's just so many languages,' I manage to say eventually.

She storms away from the counter, and I scoop up her tote bag and water bottle and run after her.

'I shouldn't have laughed,' I say, still laughing. 'I'm sorry!' She's teetering between annoyed and amused, her bottom lip wobbling and her eyes creasing with giggles.

'Jack, I have to tell you something.'

'What?'

'I don't actually speak Spanish.'

'What?' I adopt a tone of shock. 'This is completely new information, I had no idea.'

She gives in to the laughter and then gently kicks me in the shin with her white Conversed foot. 'I don't even know why I lied. I barely even remember doing it. We were just like, newly sleeping together, and you said how sexy you found it when women could speak other languages, and I was like, fuck it, I'm never going abroad with this guy, I'll tell him I'm an eighth Spanish.'

'Hang on, you're not actually an eighth Spanish? You said you called your dad's mum your "abuela"?!'

'I didn't say that!'

'You bloody did!'

She shakes her head mournfully. 'She was from Hounslow.'

I lose it. I laugh so hard that I'm rasping for breath. Eventually, I pull myself together. 'Come on,' I say. 'Let's go and talk to him.'

The baggage man is coming to the end of his shift. He swaps with a colleague who speaks English and we're given an envelope of euros for compensation, and reassurance that our suitcases will arrive before we go back to London. We drive into the old town and park on a shaded avenue which smells like trees. Jessica takes her half of the money, which should have been enough for several outfits, and buys one coral-coloured bikini made of three scraps of fabric, which costs so much I wince at the label. Then she picks out a strappy linen sundress at a similarly mad cost, and beams all the way home clutching her bounty.

'What are you going to wear when they're in the wash?' I ask. I had bought a variety of sensibly priced garments.

'I'll be naked.' She beams.

'Fine by me.'

We drive on for a little while longer, the winding roads propelling us towards our destination. 'I think we should have an amnesty,' I say, after a little while. 'A truth amnesty.'

'Does this mean you've been keeping something from me?'

'I didn't pass my driving test the second time,' I tell her.

'Which time was it?'

'Fifth,' I say. 'And I failed my theory twice.'

She snorts with laughter. 'Okay.'

'How about you? Any other secretos?'

'Too soon!' she yells. Then she contemplates it for a minute. 'Actual truths?'

'Actual truths.'

'I faked it. The first time we slept together.'

I'm obviously horrified, but pretend not to be. I think back to our first time, in my single bed in Oxford, tangled in the duvet, her nipples pink and perfect against the white sheets, revelling at the idea that I was allowed to touch any part of her body that I wanted. No wonder I fumbled it. I consider telling her that that time was actually my first time. But it's still too embarrassing. I think I'd rather she thought I was selfish than that she knew I'd misled her to think that I'd slept with my childhood girlfriend before her.

'Thank you for telling me,' I say, trying to sound like a man rather than a teenage boy. 'Have you faked it since?'

She shakes her head. 'Are you annoyed?'

'Not at all. Just determined to make sure that every orgasm you have for the rest of our lives makes up for it.'

She pulls her legs up underneath her, already so golden. 'I like this,' she says. 'Let's keep it this way. Honest.'

'I agree. One hundred per cent honesty, one hundred per cent of the time.'

She offers up her hand, like the end of Thelma and Louise, and I grasp it.

'Deal?' I ask.

'Deal.'

Jessica

The next morning, as we all gather after breakfast, I'm feeling a little bit self-conscious in my Lycra leggings and top. I wish Jack had come down with me but I was so worried about being the last couple here I didn't wait for him. We stand around in the hall like we're waiting for a teacher to take us on a school trip. All the relaxed goodwill from last night, funded by champagne and food and candlelight, has evaporated and we're back to a friendly but slightly awkward chat. Stuart and Grant are talking about some football game they watched in their room last night, and Verity is FaceTiming her very violent-seeming sons while Noah stands behind her saying nothing. Ken is helping Sue with her sturdy walking shoes. Just as I'm starting to get annoyed at Jack for leaving me alone this long, Chloe and Ben run down the stairs, tanned and toned in their matching Lycra, with Jack trailing behind them.

He pauses at the bottom of the stairs and puts a pair of leather brogues on his feet. I feel the irritation stir. The packing list for the trip was unbelievably clear. I realise that he's much more comfortable with concrete than countryside, but I'm 100 per cent sure he must have something which would be at least a little bit weatherproof. I knew I should have packed for him.

'Is that what you're wearing?'

He looks down at his clothes. He's wearing a blazer, for God's sake.

'What's wrong? I didn't know we were going to be doing the activity!'

'But you knew we'd be going … outside?'

'Yes, Jessica. I knew we'd be going outside.'

'Fine. Well. You're going to get very wet feet.'

'Yes, well, that'll be my problem, won't it?' he says cheerfully.

Once we're all ready, we're guided on to the bus by Scary Will and Cait, at which point we sit in silence listening to the radio until we pull up in the leaf-strewn car park of

SEVEN RULES FOR A PERFECT MARRIAGE

a national park. Waiting for us as we step off the bus is a
meaty man dressed in camouflage.

'Everyone fall in!' he shouts. We booked him from a
website of army types for hire. He might have done something in a war zone once upon a time a long time ago,
but for the last two decades he's been running corporate
retreats for financiers.

'Welcome to North York Moors,' he booms. 'I'm Darren
but you can call me Daz. Is everyone ready to have some
fun?'

Everyone answers quietly in the affirmative. Daz isn't
exactly who I picture when I consider the concept of 'fun'.

'I said, is everyone ready to have some fun?'

We make slightly more noise, but not much. It's not
really a fair question because we are technically not here to
have fun, we're here to remember that honesty is the key
to good communication in any relationship.

'We've got a really fun challenge for you today,' Suze says,
full of pep. She's dressed like a PE teacher; she's even got a
clipboard. 'We're going to walk over to the river. When we
get there, there are going to be lots of lovely supplies for
you all to build rafts. You'll have fifteen minutes of building
time, and then we'll have a competition for who can get
across the river on their raft the fastest. We'll time each of
your attempts to get from one point to another, quickest
wins. And, just to keep it fun and competitive, there's a
cash prize for the couple who wins – and the couple who
comes last doesn't get a place on the bus home.'

'The only snag,' Suze adds, 'is that you won't be given
quite enough materials for your raft. So, to get more kit,
you're going to need to go to Daz as a couple and tell

him – and each other – some home truths. For every truth you share, you can pick something from his pile of goodies. Got it?'

I was about to start worrying what would happen if Jack and I won (we could hardly take a cash prize from our own event) but I don't think there's any risk at all of that happening. Everyone starts talking and we're on the move. When we get to the river, there are little stations with our names on them, so we all take up position.

'We should probably go easy,' I tell Jack. 'We don't want to win at our own event.'

'True. But we also really don't want to walk home.'

He's right about that. Especially as his silly leather shoes are already soaked and there's a tide mark around the bottom of his jeans.

'Ready? Get set. Go!' booms Daz, blowing his whistle. Everyone jumps into action. Chloe and Ben leg it straight to Darren and start machine-gun-firing home truths. I hear snatches of 'not as up for it anymore' and 'dented the Tesla', but I'm trying to focus and sort through what we've been given. There are empty plastic barrels and some bits of wood, but nothing to join them together with. I can see Darren guarding a load of rope, duct tape, floaties, pool noodles and all sorts. No chance of doing this without the truth-telling bit, then. God, I wish I'd designed these activities with a loophole.

Across the field I'm surprised to see Verity working enthusiastically, given that her attitude so far has seemed a bit like she doesn't want to be here. She stops for a moment, looks around, and then drags a reluctant-looking Noah towards Darren. I wonder, way too late, whether the cash prize thing might have been quite a bad idea, or at the very least a bit insensitive. Financial strain was a big part of Verity and Noah's application. It's not a fun game for them. If they go home knowing they could have had five hundred quid then the entire weekend will be soured for them. I should have thought about this. It's the exact kind of thing I'd have hated back when I was working at the marketing company, spending my lunch break putting clothes in my basket on Net-a-Porter and then deleting the whole thing miserably because I could barely afford the Tube.

'Jess?' Jack shouts, holding up an armful of plastic floats. 'I don't know what to do.'

I crouch down and start arranging them into a sort of underside for our raft. 'Aren't you supposed to be doing this? You're the man.' Ten meters away I can see Ken and Sue laying out their materials and methodically building their raft, like the couple in the instructions that come with IKEA flat-pack.

'We both know I'm not that sort of man. Can I interest you in a sonnet about the raft? A witty comment about the raft? Maybe a wry observation?'

I laugh and then try to stick a couple of the bits together, but it's just impossible with the bog-standard Sellotape they've provided clearly out of a desire to torment us. 'I can't do it,' I say, practically stamping my foot in frustration.

'Let's just go and see Darren,' Jack says, standing up.

Stuart and Grant seem to have finished their raft. They're carrying it carefully towards the water and everyone pauses to cheer for them. Chloe and Ben have been working quickly and aren't far behind, either, so that only leaves us three other couples. For fuck's sake! If we end up being the ones to walk home, everyone's going to think it's really funny and I'm going to have to pretend to have a sense of humour about it.

'We can't go and see Darren,' I hiss, 'we're supposed to be one hundred per cent honest all of the time already. How are we going to have any home truths to spill?'

Jack gives me a 'Babe, please' look.

'I'm serious! Isn't it going to look bad if we run over there and start talking about all the secrets we've been keeping? And wait, hang on, have you actually been keeping secrets?'

'I'm sure I can come up with something,' Jack says weakly as he sees Sue and Ken, almost twice our age, carrying their rafts with surprising speed.

'Fine,' I say. 'We can just make something up.'

'We said we were going to do this properly!'

'Okay, okay,' I say, taking him by the hand and dragging him over to Darren who seems to be having way too much fun playing God.

'Hi,' I say. 'We're Jack and Jessica, we wrote the book that this weekend is based on.'

Darren looks out at the couples throwing themselves around the floor trying to make junk into boats. 'This is based on a ... book?'

'Yes,' I say, determined. 'It is. And we need to just grab some duct tape and whatever else you'd recommend so that we can join in.'

'Great,' says Darren. 'Spill.'

Jack laughs.

'You couldn't just slip us some rope?' I say, higher pitched than intended.

'Afraid not.' Darren smirks.

I take a deep breath. Jack wants me to be honest? Really? He wants me to tell him that I message Clay when I'm worried about work because I know he'll take me seriously? Or that I've been spending hundreds of pounds on pregnancy supplements with no proven medical benefit on a secret credit card? Probably not.

'I moved your bookmark,' I bark.

'What?'

'In the hotel, after our launch party. You were in the bathroom. I deliberately moved your bookmark so you'd lose your place.'

He laughs. 'You psycho.'

Darren hands us some rolls of duct tape while giving me a concerned look. There's a huge shout from the water where Stuart and Grant's boat has capsized.

'Thank fuck!' I shout.

Jack shakes his head. 'How am I always surprised by how competitive you are?'

'Honesty, please? Jack? Time is of the essence right now because I don't want to walk back to the house later.'

'I can't think of anything.'

'Yes, you can, come ON.'

'I'm trying.'

'Try harder!' I shout. 'Try faster!'

'I WAS A VIRGIN WHEN WE SLEPT TOGETHER THE FIRST TIME,' he shouts. There's a silence across the field. Everyone turns to look at us. Darren bites his lip, then finally hands over the rope we wanted.

'Good luck,' he says. 'And listen, mate, I think it's nice to wait.'

I start frantically binding the plastic bottles together with the duct tape. 'You were a VIRGIN?' I hiss at him.

'Yes,' he replies, delicately screwing the lids on to them so they don't fill with water the moment we're on the river.

'And you LIED about having slept with "some girl at school"?'

'Do we really need to talk about this right now?' he pleads. 'And I had done basically everything with her apart from that.'

'Still!' I stand up, hands suddenly still. 'I'm the only person you've ever slept with!'

He looks up at me, bright red. 'Oh, piss off,' he says, also sort of laughing. I put my hand over his. Look at him. His handsome, beautiful profile.

'I wish you'd told me,' I tell him.

'It's embarrassing.'

'It's not embarrassing. It's romantic.' I look at him again. 'Jack. It's lovely.' I reach up, running my hand over the stubble which shadows his jawline. I brush my lips against his. 'I just wish I'd known.'

'Yeah,' he says. 'Well, everyone now knows that I was a virgin until I was twenty-two, so if we could crack on and make this thing float so we don't also lose this game, then that would be a little bit of a help.'

We work together, me directing and Jack listening, offering suggestions intermittently, and eventually we've got a sort of raft-looking thing. We drag our attempt down to the water and Suze gets ready to time us. We get into the water and paddle frantically, splashing each other, the boat (boat in the very loosest sense) rocking madly from side to side. The water looks cold and brown underneath us, my trainers are soaked, but we're doing it. We cross the finish line made of life buoys and float gently back to the shore. I jump down in relief. Jack attempts to avoid standing in the deep water and whimpers slightly as he looks down at his brogues, soaking and caked in mud.

'How did we do?' I ask Suze, panting.

'You made a really good attempt!' she says.

'Are we one of the fastest?'

'Uh. You had one of the smoothest turns ...'

Jack laughs and puts his arms around me. 'I'm sorry, darling.' I lean into his body, warm despite the wet day. He's always so warm. Before we lived in a house with reliable central heating and double glazing, I used to use him as a radiator in bed at night.

The rest of the group are standing around by the water and Suze waves to get everyone's attention. 'Right,' she shouts, 'we have a tie for the win!'

Everyone makes an 'ooo' noise.

'Verity and Noah, you had the same time as Chloe and Ben. So it's time for a tie-breaker race.' Ken and Sue applaud good-naturedly while Verity and Noah look a bit bashful. Chloe and Ben do quite an aggressive high five, clearly in perfect unison with their competitive spirit.

There's a surprising amount of excitement as the two teams get ready, standing by their rafts, primed to push them in. Daz is standing with his lace-ups almost ankle deep in water, like an Antony Gormley made of meat. He puts the whistle to his lips.

'When I say three, you can get in the water, and the first to reach the red life buoy is the winner. One, two, three, GO.'

Both couples give their rafts a shove into the water and start paddling madly. We're all cheering. Verity's face is twisted in effort; she's paddling harder than any of the rest of them.

'Faster,' she screams at Noah.

'God, she's really going for it.' Sue turns to me. 'Good on her.'

Chloe and Ben reach the buoy slightly ahead and an enormous cheer goes up. They all make their way back to the shore and Chloe and Ben high-five each other, delighted.

'Congratulations!' Suze says, holding their hands up to celebrate their victory. 'This is for you.' She hands them a cheque which they rip open.

'Five hundred quid!' Ben says, delighted. 'Woah!'

'That's a weekend in Paris,' Chloe says, beaming. 'A mini-break.'

They hug. I look over at Verity who is staring at the ground. It looks like there might be tears in her eyes but that could just be the cold air. I can feel her burning, and I get it. That's not money that should have gone on a mini-break. It would have made her life better. Not so long ago I'd have felt the exact same.

'And now we come to the losers of the task.' Suze smiles. 'Any guesses?'

There's a silence and it seems like everyone is looking at us. 'Surely not us?' I ask, aghast.

Suze laughs. 'By almost two minutes slower than everyone else, Jack and Jessica came last.'

Everyone thinks this is very funny. I try to swallow my pride. There's quite a big part of me which wants to go and ask Suze if I can see her numbers, but luckily my desire not to seem like a total psycho stops me.

Jack nudges me in the ribs. 'Let's not have a Twister moment.' I half pout, half laugh at the memory of the time I tried to play sexy Twister with him in our first flat and ended up shouting at him for not bringing his best game.

I push his hair, damp with sweat and water, away from his forehead. 'Fine.' I smile.

'The good news,' Suze continues, 'is that while this task was about getting you to embrace honesty, we weren't totally honest with you. We never intended to make the losers walk home.'

Everyone claps, and we make our soggy way back to the coach, ready for long baths and dry clothes. Sitting next to each other on the coach, I smile at Jack. He smiles back, one hand on my thigh.

'I can't believe we lost,' I say.

'I'd rather lose with you than win with anyone else.' He grins.

'What a line.' I roll my eyes and then rest my head on his tweed shoulder. Ironically, given how spectacularly we lost, this morning has ended up feeling like a win.

Rule Four

Sex and intimacy have to be a priority,
even when life gets in the way

Jack

Dinner is prepared by a chef they've brought in, who presents us with some incredible beef thing (delicious, tiny,
I could still manage an entire pizza) paired with some
massively expensive wine (delicious and by contrast, very
generous) and then leaves the kitchen completely spot-
less. Everyone seems to be getting on well with their
other halves, considering we're on a My Marriage is in
Trouble holiday. I do wonder if perhaps the simple fact
of not having any domestic duties might be making us all
happier. Usually at this point in a weekend Jessica and I
have already had a row because she's changed where 'we'
keep a utensil without telling me about this unilateral
decision, or because I've insisted on keeping last week's
newspapers to catch up on. There's the ongoing war about
whether it's okay to leave pans to soak (obviously I say yes,
she says no) and the perennial dishwasher-stacking debate.
None of them are moral failings, we're not going to break
up over them or anything, but they're the kind of micro

fights which make the whole thing feel heavy and hard, like thousands of tiny paper cuts. It's only now we're here, and there's nothing small to fight about, that I realise quite how much they all add up.

After we've eaten, we move into one of the snugs, a room with massive great sofas and a log burner, which I read recently is terrible for lung health but makes it all feel quite cosy. The walls are mostly glass but it's so eco and high-tech that they're warm to the touch. I'm worried that everyone is having too nice a time and is too relaxed to be up for this evening's task, which involves starting a massive row with your other half.

Suze rolls in, having declined dinner with everyone else in favour of a protein shake and replying to emails in the kitchen. Her work ethic is staggering.

'I'm sure everyone is looking forward to some down-time this evening after our antics out on the water today,' she says, with the air of a primary school teacher. 'But we're not just here to relax. So, on to the next rule!'

No one seems enthused, but Suze ploughs on, reading off a cue card. 'The old saying tells us to never go to bed angry, but it's actually much worse to stay up late, going over the same ground, getting too tired to make sense of the argument and then waking up in a bad mood because you didn't get enough sleep. So tonight you're going to tackle this practically.'

Ken murmurs that he's much more of a morning person and doesn't feel his best late at night anyway and Chloe says she's the same. The rest of them nod in agreement.

'Jess?' says Suze. 'Did you want to introduce the activity?'

'Yes,' she says, almost convincingly. 'Yes, absolutely. So, Jack and I believe that one of the keys to positive arguments is to approach them prepped and ready. That means you've had something to eat, and you've had a good night's sleep. Never fight hungry or tired.'

It's actually incredibly good advice, when I hear her say it like this.

'Now I should say,' Jess tries again to garner some enthusiasm, 'this doesn't mean that you just bury the problem. You need to wake up in good time the next morning so that you can have a proper, calm, sensible discussion about what started the fight, once you've had a decent sleep and a change of scene. This isn't about avoiding the fight, it's about rescheduling it until you're ready for it.'

'I'm already almost asleep,' says Sue cheerfully from her armchair. 'I don't think I've got another activity in me.'

'Maybe we could leave it for tonight?' Stuart ventures.

I drag myself to my feet with superhuman effort. 'Come on, guys. We've got the rest of our lives to chill on the sofa. We're here to do some work. Let's crack on.'

Jess looks surprised, which is a fairly damning indication of how helpful I've been recently.

'Jess?' I gesture. 'Shall we?'

'Sure,' she says. 'So, we're going to ask that you go and find space in the house, somewhere you feel you're private and comfortable, and then we need you to start a fight.'

Everyone laughs.

'I know.' Jessica laughs too. 'I get it. But you need to start a fight. And then, once you're full flow, I want you to stop it and go to bed. Then you can wake up refreshed and settle it before breakfast.'

'It just sounds so mad,' Chloe says from her sofa, where she's positioned slightly closer to Ben than she was when I last noticed them sitting together.

'I get it,' I say, before Jessica can jump in. 'But just give it a go. That's why we're here, right?'

Everyone stands up, stretching, still very much not in the mood. But they file out, their voices moving across the house. And then it's just me and Jessica, standing in the snug, alone.

'So,' I say, standing closer to her, so I can smell the dry citrus scent she wears, the one she'd just started wearing when we first met because she'd read that some French actress wore it.

'So,' she replies.

'We have to go and have a row.'

'We're usually quite good at that,' she says, smiling up at me.

'Yes.' I smile too. 'We are.' I grab her hand and lead her through the corridor, up the stairs to a nook on the landing next to our bedroom. 'Go on,' I encourage her. 'Let's fight.'

She just stands there.

'I mean it,' I say, taking her hands.

'You can't wash up for shit,' she blurts out. 'Sometimes after you wash up, I wait until you've left the room and then I redo all the wine glasses.' She takes a deep breath like she feels better to have got that one out.

'Is that really the best you've got?' I smirk.

'You want more?'

'I want more.'

'You complain about going to events that people would kill to attend, you're ungrateful for all the amazing things about our lifestyle, you refuse to learn which kitchen spray is for what purpose, you're snooty about my influencer friends, and you're obsessed with pleasing your parents, which is literally impossible.' She inhales before launching into her next slew. 'You snore, you eat like a teenage boy, you forget plans which are in the diary, you don't hide how much you dislike Clay and you refuse to learn how to make our bed properly.' She grins. 'Okay. Your turn.'

Nothing I didn't know. Maybe we can do this. I squeeze her hands.

'Everything in our house is organic and natural, you act like I've brought a bag of heroin in if I order a Chinese, there are fifteen hundred cushions in our house and you continue to buy more, you complain about all your friends but insist on seeing them anyway, there are a dozen half-empty bottles of beauty products in every room of our house but I'm not allowed to throw them away, you used to eat McDonald's in bed when you were hungover and now you won't let me take a packet of biscuits upstairs.'

'We're supposed to be fighting,' she tells me as I push her against the bedroom door.

'We are fighting,' I reply.

'No, we're not.'

'Kind of proving my point here.' I laugh.

I wrap her arms around my neck and then brush her thigh and slide my hand down her jeans. 'Problem is,' I tell her, 'I want you, and I'm getting the sense that you might want me.' I kiss her neck and she does her familiar purr-shudder. 'And if we start a fight, we might spoil that.'

'Oh, I don't know,' she responds, pressing her body against mine. 'Maybe it'll be a turn-on to get to complain a bit.'

I laugh. 'Go on, then. Try it.'

She speaks quietly, into my ear, like she used to when she stayed at my place in Oxford and we couldn't wake my housemates. 'The way you stack a dishwasher is a war crime, and you wear too much corduroy.'

'Low blow,' I say. 'There's no such thing as too much corduroy.'

She smirks up at me, her lips full and her cheeks flushed from the teenage snogging. 'Your turn,' she says.

'You insist on taking taxis when it would be quicker to get the Tube or to walk. You ask me what you should wear even though you know I've got no taste. You're on your phone when we're watching films, even films with bloody subtitles, and you also snore.'

And weirdly – very weirdly – it's proving to be something of an aphrodisiac. It feels so good not to try to be good all the time, not to obsess over being kind and getting it right. Admittedly these aren't the big, heavy truths that we should probably have used this time to unpack, but I'm only human and anyone who prioritised doing an assignment over getting into bed with Jessica would have to be absolutely mad.

'Also, all the kitchen cleaning sprays do fundamentally the same thing,' I whisper in Jess's ear.

'They fucking don't.'

She's laughing as I kiss her and lead her into our bedroom.

'And I do not snore,' she says breathily, as my hand moves between her legs and I increase the pressure, just the way she likes it.

'Yes, you do.'

She kisses me urgently, pressing her hand against my crotch, teasing through my jeans, then she pulls away from me just when I don't want her to stop.

'Aren't we supposed to go to sleep? If we're doing this properly?' she asks.

I shake my head. 'You need to reread your own book, darling. It doesn't say we have to go to sleep. It says we have to go to bed.' And with that, I pick her up and drop her down on the mattress.

'Excellent point,' she says as she rolls over and climbs on top of me.

Jessica

I wake up early on Sunday morning and go for a run, lacing my trainers in the half-dark bedroom, enjoying the silence of the house as I slip down the stairs and revel in the feeling of putting space between me and everyone else. It's a cold, grey, misty morning, which I think might turn into a bright blue sunny one. I used to think that people who ran for fun were mad. I'd go to the gym if I wanted to look thinner than the other girls on a hen do, or if my jeans felt tight, but that was it. It was only ever about wanting to look thinner (even if I told that lie we all share, that it's just about 'feeling fit' and 'wanting to be strong'). But then, when the fertility problems started, I needed something to do with myself, and I found that this helped. I liked pounding the pavements, and I liked getting better and better at it. My body was getting it wrong in so many other ways; at least this was something it could do right.

When I come back to the room, my face flushed and my T-shirt soaked with sweat, Jack is sat up in bed reading on his phone.

'Tell me you haven't been for a run.'

'Lie to you? My lawfully wedded husband?'

'After all that wine last night. And those fucking rafts.' Jack groans and rolls over and pulls a pillow over his head. 'Everything hurts. All of my limbs are going to fall off.'

'It's the best thing for a hangover,' I say smugly. Then I peel off my leggings and top and I realise I'm standing in my underwear in front of Jack, and I feel very, very naked. I don't know why this feels so weird. We had sex not ten hours ago. And I used to do this all the time, wandering around our flat in my underwear, fake-tanning in my knickers in the living room, sleeping naked when it was hot. But, like so many things, it changed since we've been trying to get pregnant. I feel more protective of my body. Guilty, I suppose, that it's failing us. And even when I've got clothes on, I still find myself trying to hide from him, from everyone. Increasingly I'm drawn towards oversized cashmere jumpers and massive linen shirts, tentlike dresses, anything which puts up a barrier between my empty body and the rest of the world.

I notice that Jack is staring at me. 'What's wrong?'

'Nothing.'

'But you're staring at me?'

'I just can't remember the last time I saw your belly button.'

I half laugh. 'Is that a thing for you? Belly buttons?'

'Yes. I've been harbouring a secret belly button fetish for years now. I thought this was the time to tell you.'

I take my sports bra off, and I stand there in front of him for a moment so he can see me. Jack sits up with a big grin on his face.

'Honestly,' I say, taking my knickers off. 'You'd think you'd never seen a naked woman before.'

'It's not my fault I've fancied you for the better part of twenty years!'

I'm standing under the water, my wet hair pushed back from my face, when Jack walks in. He stands for a moment, watching me shower.

'Do you really still fancy me?' I ask him, meeting his eye in the mirror.

'Have you seen you? How could I not?' Jack joins me under the water, kissing me, and I'm enjoying the sensation of our wet bodies against each other. 'You've got sexier every year I've known you, and you were already stunning.'

He slides his hand down my body, between my legs. We've been doing this for a lot of years. We know every trick, every motion, every movement. Friends of mine have lamented the predictability of having sex with the same person over and over again, the lack of variety, but I love that Jack knows how to make me come. I lean against the shower tiles, my arms braced, eyes tightly shut. I wonder for a moment what he's thinking about, whether he's managed to divorce this from the kind of mechanical conception sex we've fallen into, but dismiss the thought. One hand is on my hips and he's moving against me, grinding the palm of his other hand against me in the way I taught him when we first started sleeping together, just enough contact but not too intense. As we have so many times before, I come slightly before he does, my orgasm the trigger for his. We stay in position for a moment, both slightly shaking, both – I think – slightly surprised.

It's probably not quite the impression we wanted to send, arriving to breakfast late, both of us still pink in the face from the exertion and the shower.

'Good morning?' I overhear Ben ask Jack in front of me at the breakfast buffet. 'I'm not exactly a reader,' he tells him, loading his plate. 'But if your book gets my wife looking like that,' he points back at me, flushed and happy, 'I might give it a go.'

Jack certainly isn't the only person around the table with a hangover – in fact, everyone seems a bit worse for wear. Plus, we did ask them to deliberately start fights with each other last night. In short, it's no surprise that the atmosphere in here is absolutely dreadful. There's no conversation, which means that the sound of people chewing is unbearably loud. Eventually Suze shows that whatever she's being paid isn't enough, and puts the radio on. But it's the show Jack used to work on, doing a very depressing report about a drought related to climate change. It's the kind of topic that he used to spend days grappling with, trying to distil down into a report that anyone could understand. I used to worry, occasionally, that it must be a bit bad for a person to constantly be immersed in terrible news, all day and all night. I get up and switch it to Radio One, and the music hums a much less depressing soundtrack to breakfast.

'Shall we?' I turn to ask Jack, when everyone seems finished.

'Okay.' Jack gets up. 'I know no one wants this, but let's go to the snug, where the chairs are really comfortable, and if everyone makes it there without crying, I'll make sure someone hands out a round of very cold Diet Cokes.'

Everyone sort of laughs and murmurs their approval, and people start making their way to the snug. Suze looks pained as she stage-whispers to us, 'The official beverage partner for this weekend is Rafe's Alkalised Water. We really shouldn't be providing any other soft drink, in case they mention it in their end-of-weekend interviews.'

'Suze,' Jack says beseechingly. 'Have you ever had a hangover?'

'Yes,' she says. 'I have.'

'Did you want a Rafe's Alkalised Water, when you had that hangover?'

She smiles. 'No, Jack, I did not.'

'So do you think maybe just this once we could sack off Rafe and give the people what they want? Maybe talk really nicely to the chef about doing some bacon rolls for lunch later?'

Suze rolls her eyes. 'I'll tell Cait and Will to sort something out.'

Once everyone's had a restorative Diet Coke, we're ready to start this morning's activity. I've played Mr and Mrs on more hen weekends than I can count, and while I'm now officially over watching a scared-looking man answer sex questions at the behest of his fiancée's bridesmaids, it's a good format for today. Light and silly, which is what we need, because we're going to spend today talking about all the problems we've got with each other's families.

Suze is playing master of ceremonies for this one and brings each couple up in turn to sit on bar stools like they're on a game show. Chloe and Ben are first up, with Ben taking his turn at wearing the noise-cancelling headphones.

'Has Ben's family ever hurt your feelings?' Suze asks.

'Yeah,' she says. 'A bit. But mine have been way worse.'

'How?' Suze asks.

Chloe looks tired. She glances across at Ben, who is in his own world for a moment, tapping his toes to the *Dolly Parton Greatest Hits* Suze inexplicably chose. 'To start with, they kept talking about how okay they were with us being together, like there was something to object to. They said the wrong thing a lot – like I remember one time my dad randomly told Ben that he really liked Tiger Woods. We thought they were just being awkward. But then we started talking about a family and they had all these questions about how they'd look, what their hair would be like, and then one day out of the blue, my mum just told us, unprompted, that she didn't approve of us being together. Just straight out. Over lunch. She said she thought Ben was great, but that it had gone too far, and she couldn't support it. And my dad just sat there. Said nothing.'

I knew the overview of this story from their application for the workshop, which was written by Chloe. We picked it because it was clearly hastily written, full of spelling mistakes and unfinished sentences. It had all the signs of someone who needed help. She talked about how sorry she was, how she needed some way to make it up to Ben.

Suze gestures at Ben to take his headphones off.

'What did I miss?' he jokes, grinning into the painful atmosphere in the room.

'Chloe shared with us about her family, and how they've behaved towards you.'

Ben's face clouds. 'Oh. Right.'

'What do you think she said?'

Ben laughs, clearly trying to keep his tone light. 'I mean, they told her they didn't want her to have kids with a black guy, so I'm not excited to buy them Christmas presents. But look, I was the only black kid in my village, it's not exactly the first time I've experienced racism.'

Everyone in the room looks painfully uncomfortable, like they don't know what to say, or how to explain that they think Chloe's parents are being horrific.

'And then I started seeing my mum again,' Chloe blurts out. 'We'd cut them off. But she's my mum, and I—' She's welling up. 'I know it was shit. But then you just wouldn't talk to me about it.' Chloe looks at me, as if I can help. 'He literally never wanted to acknowledge it.'

'It's a hard conversation,' Ben says, after a long pause. He looks at the floor. 'And I didn't want to talk badly about your family.'

'I wouldn't have cared,' Chloe insisted. 'I don't care what they think.'

'But you do care,' he counters. 'Because you still want to see them, and be around them. Even if it means hurting me.'

She swallows, and thinks about it for a moment. 'I'm sorry,' she says.

Ben puts his hand on her thigh. 'She's your mum, Chlo. I get it.'

I'm not sure I would have been so forgiving. Chloe leans into him, looks him straight in the eye, and it's like no one else is in the room.

'No, really. I'm sorry,' she says, from somewhere right inside her chest. I feel it. I think we all feel it.

'I know,' he says quietly. 'I know you are.'

There's a pause while Suze, who is more brilliant at this than I'd anticipated, gives them a moment to breath, to feel the connection that they've found. I wonder if everyone else in the room is thinking the same thing I am, that we want that moment Chloe and Ben have just had, where something clicks and there's real, meaningful progress.

'Jack and Jessica,' Suze says. 'You two next.'

We settle on to the stools and Suze passes Jack the headphones to put on.

'Jessica. Do Jack's family think that you're a help, or a hindrance, to him?' Suze reads off the card.

Jack puts the headphones on and I try to think of a diplomatic answer. Do they think that I've been a help or a hindrance? I mean, in any normal person's logic, I've been the biggest help imaginable. I founded the thing which bought our house. But would his parents see it like that?

'Oh, such a good question,' I say. 'I think they'd think I'm a hindrance because Jack's so smart. They probably think he could be winning the Booker Prize if he wasn't with me.'

'Jack?' Suze asks, after prompting him to remove the headphones.

'Sorry. Um. I think my parents have a different idea of success to Jessica. They only really like old books and professors and stuff. So I guess they'd say hindrance.'

There's a noise of approval from the group.

'Did I get it right?' He laughs. 'Oh, amazing!'

Arguably it's not amazing that his parents regard my career as detrimental to their son, but okay.

'Next question!' says Suze. 'What do you think your family would change about Jessica to make your relationship better?' Then I put the headphones on and listen to a blast of Dolly before Suze motions at me to take them off. Everyone's looking at me all misty-eyed, like they just watched the last five minutes of *The Notebook*.

'What d'you think he said?'

'I don't know,' I say. 'Hopefully not that many things.'

'It was lovely,' pipes up Ken. 'He said he'd not change anything about you, and if anyone suggested it, he'd be telling them to get stuffed.'

'He said it nicer than that,' Sue adds.

I look across at Jack, who is blushing because he always blushes.

'Thanks.' I smile.

'Welcome,' he says, looking at the ground.

It's not quite the seismic breakthrough that Ben and Chloe had; it doesn't change the energy in the room the same way theirs did. But it's something. I can feel that it's something. And I think maybe he can too.

The Abortion

Jessica

In films, when someone takes a pregnancy test, they turn it over and wait for three minutes until they can see a result. I assume this is a narrative device designed either to build tension or to let the characters talk about what might be, because when you take a pregnancy test in real life, it shows both lines almost instantly. I know this because I'm currently sitting on the loo with my jeans around my ankles, watching my pee soak down the stick, bringing up two vividly pink lines, crossed over each other in the middle.

I am pregnant.

This is not good news.

We could not be less ready to have a baby. I'm twenty-five. If I break a glass I still wait for an adult to come and tell me that I need to put some shoes on while they clear it up. I don't want to do this. I don't want to be a mother. I don't want to get through it and learn to love it. I want more of my life. I want more time to be selfish, to believe that my career is going to take off. I want more time to be me.

We have absolutely no money and we live in a one-bedroom flat, the entirety of which would fit comfortably inside my child-hood bedroom. I am working in a job that I hate, that I'm not very good at, for almost no money. Jack and I drink too much. We smoke too much. And clearly we weren't responsible enough to use contraception properly. God, isn't it ironic that being irresponsible results in the biggest responsibility a person could have?

I look at my phone. Jack's at his work Christmas party. He caught my eye in the mirror this morning, while he was getting dressed, and beamed. 'I can't believe I'm going to the BBC Christmas party,' he'd said. I'd laughed at him, pointing out that he does work there so it would be a bit weird not to be invited. He just laughed, and despite the disparity in our career satisfaction, I can't help being delighted for him. They're paying him about six pounds a week, he works the worst hours imaginable, and he's the happiest person I know. Tonight he's at some pub near Great Portland Street, mixing with all the people he wants to be when he grows up. It's the best things have ever been for him. My finger hovers over his name. I could call him. I know I could. I would have every right to tell him that I need him, that I'm not okay and that he needs to come home. But I don't want to. Ruining his evening isn't going to change this.

Instead, I search for the Marie Stopes phone number. I think I knew when I saw the lines that I was going to do this. I just wanted to pretend that it was a hard choice – that I searched inside myself and really tried before I gave up. It's not like I'm a teenager anymore. You don't tell people that you had an abortion at twenty-five, in a long-term relationship, and expect them to feel bad for you.

Jack comes home a little after midnight. He's pissed but full of joy. 'Merry Christmas,' he says, tumbling in the front door. Our flat is so tiny that I can feel the cold air from our bed. 'I missed you.'

'I'm pregnant,' I say, abandoning all my good intentions about breaking it to him gently.

I've heard people say before that they sobered up instantly thanks to a shock, and I've always assumed that it's bollocks. But the warm boozy glow around Jack is instantly gone.

'Are you sure?' he asks.

'Yes.'

'Wow.'

'Yes.'

'Are you … okay?'

He is desperate to say the right thing. He's wearing the expression that he always gets when he is frightened that he's about to fuck up and say something which will haunt us for the rest of our lives. He wants to ask what I want to do. Whether I want to keep it. But he's worried that the way he asks the question will bely a preference about the answer.

'I've been better,' I say. 'I don't want to do it.'

He nods, and says the only sensible thing a man can say in this situation. 'It's your choice. Whatever you want to do, I've got you.'

Five days later I have an appointment at a clinic in Warren Street. We ignore a busker playing a Christmas song outside the Tube, and push our way past a couple of religious nutters on the way in. I am relieved that the waiting room isn't full of weeping teenagers. It's mostly couples, some a little younger than us, some a little older. I'm given pills. We get a taxi home, which we absolutely cannot afford, and then we wait. Jack makes me chicken nuggets and spaghetti hoops, which makes me cry. We watch The Secret Garden.

There is more blood than I was expecting. It's so early that I thought it would just be like a period, but it isn't. Not at all. For a while I lie on the floor of the bathroom, curled up because it's not big enough to extend my legs. The cold of the tiled floor feels good underneath me, easing the nausea. Jack stands in the doorway watching me and saying nothing, which is preferable because I don't want to talk about it. I read online that I'd know when it was over, and it turns out that's true. Eventually it is, so we go to bed. He holds me and I wake up awash with relief, knowing I have made the right choice.

The weeks pass, the bleeding stops, and we go back to our normal lives. I fill Tupperware with leftovers and we take the Tube to work. He stacks the dishwasher, I empty it. We finally start watching Game of Thrones, which everyone has raved about; we go to the pub and hang out at Tom and Grace's house and just sort of get on with it. With one pretty major difference. We can barely bring ourselves to touch each other. I get into bed each night wearing pyjamas which cover me from ankle to wrist. I put a pillow between us. When, half asleep, I roll over and run my hand along his torso, under his T-shirt, he flinches. We are terrified of what our bodies did. Terrified it will happen again, despite the fact that I had an implant put in my arm to remove any risk of forgetting to take the pill ever again.

Eventually Valentine's Day rolls around. We try to ignore it. The date pisses me off every time I see it because it reminds me how much time has passed. I want to shout, 'Yes, I know, it's the middle of February and I haven't had sex since before Christmas, I fucking GET IT.' I buy Jack a card because I always have done, but it takes me ages to choose one which feels even close to right. Our messages to each other are half-hearted. On the morning of the fourteenth, I get a surge of determination and I put a bottle of champagne on my credit card, then when Jack gets home we drink it and watch more Game of Thrones. During a particularly violent beheading, I feel briefly better, but it's all too brief and before I know it it's a sex scene. A really long, really naked sex scene. And the atmosphere is like I'm watching it with my dad. I want to go and make a cup of tea.

'Right,' I say, as the woman on the screen orgasms, and the atmosphere between us becomes unbearable. 'This is mad.'

Jack turns his body to face mine. 'I know. I know! I was just sitting there thinking that I'd actually rather be watching this with my parents.'

'Me too!' I say. 'Thank fuck for that.'

I refill both our glasses with the champagne, which isn't properly cold anymore.

'What's going on?' I ask.

'I don't know,' he replies, dropping his eyes. 'Well. I mean. I do sort of know.'

'Is it the abortion thing?' I ask.

Jack looks guilty. 'I'm just so scared of it happening again. I know it's not going to. But I am. And, I don't know. It's pathetic, but it was so horrible for you. And it was my fault.'

'It wasn't anyone's fault.'

He looks unconvinced.

'Okay,' I say. 'Then it was both of our faults.'

Mollified, he puts his hand on my thigh. 'The more we didn't have sex, the more I felt like we shouldn't have sex, and then I sort of thought that we should, but the last thing I wanted was to pressure you.'

'I get it,' I say. 'I felt the same.'

We both look across the tiny flat, to the door of our bedroom which opens directly into the living room. It's like it's goading us.

'This isn't going to be very sexy,' I say, 'but I'm going to make a suggestion.'

'Hit me.'

'I think we go to our room, and we make out like teenagers for five minutes. And if we don't feel like shagging once we've done that, we call it a night, and try again another time.'

He smiles, stands up and offers me his hand. I feel consumed with disappointment that he's agreed to my suggestion because I don't want to take my clothes off. I don't want to be touched. I don't want to repeat the stupid act which got me into this shitty miserable place. But I've said it now. So I follow him to the bedroom, and we lie down. He runs his hand under my top, along my spine, kisses my neck and twists his hand in my hair, just firmly enough that it's sharp but not enough to hurt me. I gently bite into his lip. He smells right, he feels right, he knows exactly what to do, how to trace the skin at the side of my breasts to make me whimper. We're good at this. We like this. This is not a bad idea.

Five minutes later the timer goes off on his phone, sharp and loud. I reach over and silence it, one thigh either side of his torso, our clothes twisted on the floor. We don't call it a night.

Jack

My smugness from winning at Mr and Mrs (Suze had to tell us four times that there were no winners) is short-lived, because it's almost time for the 'intimacy workshop'. If there was one part of this weekend which I have been actively dreading, it's this. The intimacy rule, where we moot that you have to make space for sex and intimacy even when it doesn't feel wholly natural.

I didn't really want to talk about sex in the book at all. Maybe I read too much John le Carré as a teenager, but I've always taken the view that sex rarely comes over well in writing, so it's best avoided. Obviously the publishers didn't like that view, and once Clay got into Jessica's head and convinced her that the book needed a chapter on sex, I left it to her to write. Jessica begins the chapter by talking about going to the gym – you often think you're not in the mood, but once you've got your trainers on and you're pounding the treadmill, you're glad to be there. Sex, she tells our readers, is much the same. Give it five minutes of foreplay and if you're not in the mood, park it for today and try again tomorrow, or next time you both feel like it. In fairness to her, it's very good advice that we've benefitted from in the past. But we were still worried it might come across like we were telling people to force it. Aside from a very small handful of blue-haired teenagers online, no one took it this way, and it's the piece of advice which we are most often complimented on by couples who have kids, as it's helped them make time for each other. But it was always going to be a difficult rule to bring into the retreat. I suggested we just give people the night off and put a 'do not disturb' sign on their rooms, and a nice bed and time away from their real lives would probably be enough.

Eventually, after a lot of agonising over what an appropriate activity might be, Jessica and the team settled on a massage workshop. The idea was to focus on the physical-intimacy side of things, rather than sex, reminding people that if their sex life isn't panning out, then it's better to get some skin-to-skin contact in place and then worry about the actual shagging later. I know it's a good concept, but I was then, and remain now, very unconvinced that all of us taking off our clothes and rubbing each other in the same room is a good idea. The itinerary for this evening reads: 'A light vegan or vegetarian meal, with a variety of alcohol-free cocktails, followed by a massage workshop led by a local healer.'

I'm, broadly speaking, pretty liberal. I go on marches against things like war and poverty. I like quinoa and avocados. I live in North London and I worked for the BBC. But even I have my limits, and it turns out that limit is pretending to be excited about a Sunday evening where I eat a vegan grain bowl served with a cup of kombucha and then have a local hippy tell me how to rub Jessica's body so that her chakras open. But I want to fix my marriage and I want to stay married to my amazing wife.

Obviously all my internalised objections are pointless, and I find myself wrapped in a towelling robe and swimming trunks, standing in the 'spa' area of the house. It's not actually a spa, it's a sort of conservatory where they hold the drinks reception if they're having a wedding, but they've put a load of massage tables in the room and cranked the heating up to an unbearable level. There are branded towels on every bed, candles burning, spa music playing and pots of oil all over the place.

'Welcome, everyone, very happy to be with you today,' says the woman leading the workshop, in a thick Yorkshire accent. 'I'm Hibiscus, and I'm going to teach you how to explore each other's bodies.'

There is no way that woman was named Hibiscus.

'First of all, I'd like you and your partners to each find a massage bench,' she says. We all do as instructed. 'Then I would like one person from each couple to take off their robe and lie on the bed.'

There's lots of faffing about which makes me feel more awkward. 'Do you want to go first, or shall I?' I turn to Jessica.

'I don't mind.'

'Not super helpful,' I mumble.

She gives me a look, like I've just said I want to kick a puppy in the face. 'Sorry,' I say. 'I just, you know me. This really isn't my thing.'

'Yeah, I get that,' she says. 'And it's probably not Ken's thing, or Ben's thing, or any of the blokes' thing, but they're doing it with good grace.'

Her criticism cuts me to my core. She's probably right, but I don't honestly care at the moment – I'm in a room full of strangers, expected to take my clothes off and then lie around in swimwear being oiled; I'm allowed to feel a bit stressed. I look around the room and immediately feel worse when I'm confronted with Grant's madly toned torso, befitting of a man half his age. Noah's bizarrely well built for a man of God, presumably from doing wood-work or whatever Jesus-esque activity he's been cracking on with in lieu of spending time with Verity, and obvi-ously Ben, who used to play rugby professionally until he got injured in his twenties, has the kind of muscles they use to sell steroids on the internet. Ken, the only man whose body might make me feel better about myself, has opted to go second and therefore is still wrapped in towelling.

I shrug my robe off and lie down as quickly as possible, hoping no one's looking at me, noticing that I somehow manage to be both skinny and a bit fat at the same time. Obviously I've always felt a bit ashamed of my body – I'm a moderately uncool man who sunburns easily and is one quarter of an inch below six foot. I can't dance, I wear the clothes Jessica picks, which I think are probably designed to hide the less appealing parts of my physique, and in conclusion, yes, I am pathetic about anything which involves getting my kit off, especially in public and in front of people I don't know. I lie down on the table and then do an undignified sort of wiggle as I try to cover myself with the towels. I hear Jessica snigger and consider getting up and walking out, but the more reasonable side of my brain says that since we've been throwing ourselves into the activities, sniggering aside, we have been getting on better, so I resolve to entertain the idea that, like Jessica said, everyone else is doing it with good grace. Hibiscus dims the lights and turns up the spa music.

She gives directions on how to massage, starting with legs and arms, then shoulders and back. And I admit, it's nice. The oils smell sweet and comforting, and it's nice to have a lie-down. I close my eyes, take a few deep breaths.

'We have to swap,' Jessica whispers.

'What?' I rub the heels of my hands into my eyes. 'Huh?'

'You fell asleep, it's been twenty minutes. We have to swap.'

Blearily I get up and pull my robe back on. Jessica takes hers off, lying down in her bikini, which is bright pink and made of almost no fabric at all. Her body is utterly beautiful, just as it always was, when we were in our twenties and she'd go out to clubs in black jeans and a cropped black T-shirt with a tiny band of puppy fat above the waistband, cold to the touch when we'd queued for a bar she wanted to go to and I wanted to skip completely. Through those years – when our McDonald's and box-set habit saw us both put on weight, and her face was a little rounder, then later into our twenties when she fell in love with cooking; when she grew her hair out, when she chopped it off; when she developed little lines around her eyes; when she shrank, grew, dressed provocatively, covered up; in her gym leggings, her linen pyjamas, her bridesmaid dress at dozens of weddings, the Primark bikini on our honeymoon – at every single juncture, she has just been a different kind of perfect. I've never, not once, taken for granted that I'm allowed to touch her.

Hibiscus comes around and refills the pots of oil, telling us how to start with the feet and ankles. She keeps up a running commentary. 'This pressure point is good for releasing any stress in the lower spine; this pressure point helps support immunity.' Obviously everything she's saying is total bollocks, there is not some mystery point in your wrist which is connected to your liver function any more than there's a muscle in your arse which can make you better at playing the guitar.

'Now,' instructs Hibiscus, 'the same as last time, we're going to use a pressure point for emotional release, under the scapula. This can be done lying down or sitting up, depending on the intensity you would like to experience.'

'Lying down or sitting up?' I ask Jessica. 'I went for lying down, obviously.'

'You went for being completely unconscious. Actually.' Her tone is a bit strained. Surely she's not cross that I had a sleep during a massage? It was supposed to be relaxing?

She turns and sits up, making her decision clear. Hibiscus comes and guides my hand into the right position. 'When you're ready, take three deep breaths, and then, Jack, apply firm and direct pressure. Okay?'

'Okay,' I say, trying not to roll my eyes. 'Three deep breaths.'

Jessica takes the three deep breaths, really takes them, slowly and deliberately, holding the breath in at the middle point. And then I press. And to my absolute horror, she starts to cry. Jesus. Did I do something? Did I hurt her?

'Are you okay?' I ask, panicking. She doesn't reply, because she's crying. It's not one little tear on her cheek, either – it's crying, the kind of crying you spend your entire life as a man trying to avoid making a woman do, especially in public. Huge, deep, shuddering sobs. I look around to see if anyone else is having this reaction, but of course they're not and now everyone is looking at us, which is my worst fear when I'm stood half-naked, covered only by a robe which makes my legs look like matchsticks. Jessica is so good at everything that she's overachieved at having an emotionally manipulative massage. This is fucking awful and I can't find a way to make it stop.

'Jess?' I say, gently trying to put my arm around her. She pulls away, and I'm surprised, and hurt, and honestly pretty confused. But then, fuck me, she must be really hurting to let it all out publicly. 'Jess, are you okay?' What the hell has happened and how have I got this so wrong?

She's still really, really crying and she's got snot running down her face which she definitely wouldn't do on purpose.

'It's very normal.' Hibiscus comes over. 'It's all part of the process. Jessica, would you like some privacy?'

She manages to nod.

'I think that's a good idea. Well done for today, duck, you did so well,' Hibiscus adds, patting her on the shoulder.

Jess pulls her robe around her and hurriedly makes her way out of the room. I stand, dithering, not sure whether to go make sure she's okay or just give her some space. Everyone else is standing around like they're at the site of a road traffic accident, wrapped in their robes with ashen expressions on their faces. I look to Hibiscus, as if she's going to tell me what to do. Then I notice Suze in the corner of the room giving me a hard stare and looking at me like I'm a complete fucking idiot, which is probably a fair assessment.

'I'm going to, uh, just go and check that Jess is okay,' I say.

I knock, gently, on the bedroom door. 'Jess? Are you there?'

There's no response. I wait a couple of minutes, agonising about whether to go straight in, or leave her alone. Eventually I knock again and then gently push the door open.

'Jessica? Can I come in?'

'Sure,' she answers. When I get inside, she's sitting on the bed wrapped in a towel, clearly having just got out the shower. She looks both much older than usual, and somehow like a teenage girl. Her face is still swollen from crying, her eyes red, beads of tears on her eyelashes.

'What happened?' I ask.

She looks confused. 'It was the pressure point?'

'Okay. Sure. But what really happened?'

'What do you mean? Hibiscus said that it might prompt an emotional release, and it did.'

'Okay. But you don't really believe that, right?'

'Why would I not believe that? It happened.'

I've got to believe that she's being deliberately obtuse at this point. 'Because pressure points are bollocks?'

She gets up, picks up a hairbrush and starts pulling her hair into a severe bun with the parting in the middle. 'They're not bollocks, there's plenty of research around alternative medicine, including massage and acupressure; it's even offered on the NHS for some illnesses.'

'I don't think this is the moment to debate the efficiency of alternative medicine.'

'You're only saying that because you're in the wrong.'

'I'm not in the wrong, I just don't want to have you crying for another half an hour.'

That was unkind. I don't like that I said it. I'm frustrated and I feel like a complete idiot for not knowing how to fix this, which is a really illogical reason to start making things worse.

'The idea was to cry,' she reminds me. 'That was the point of the exercise.'

'Right, so you were crying because you'd been told you were supposed to.'

'Or maybe I was crying because I've got a lot of shit going on in my life which I don't have time to deal with on a day-to-day basis, and my body is holding a lot of stress chemicals and hormones, and the massage just happened to release them. I suppose once I started crying, it was an outlet and I cried about everything else which is hurting me and making me miserable.'

'Why does it have to be the massage? Why can't it just be all that stuff about your feelings?'

'Do you realise how insane it is that you just heard me saying that I'm miserable and that I've got all these unre-leased feelings, and the only part that you picked up on was the bit about the fucking *massage*?'

Jesus. She's right.

She starts getting changed, pulling on a white T-shirt and jeans.

'You just want to go and pretend everything is fine right now?' I ask, surprised.

'Yes,' she says.

'Why?'

'Could you perhaps hazard a guess as to why I want to go downstairs and finish the evening properly?'

I want to explain that whatever the reason, pretending that everything is great all the time, to our friends and the internet and our management and every single stranger on the street, is exhausting. But I don't have the words. So instead, I shrug. 'For "the brand".'

She stops in the doorway, framed by the bright light of the hall against the darkness of our room.

'Do you seriously think that's why?' she asks.

'Sometimes. Yes.'

'Right. So it couldn't possibly be that I want to keep our private life private?'

'Why are you the arbiter of what gets to be private?' I ask, genuinely stumped by her inconsistency. 'I don't understand where the line is. You share our marriage so easily, and then suddenly there's all this stuff you want to hide. We agree to participate in this retreat, but that's supposed to mean being open. I don't get what the rules are. I'm trying to get it right but I'm not clairvoyant.'

She sighs. 'We've got a load of people waiting for us downstairs, and I feel like I've been hollowed out. So I'm going to go down, talk to everyone about how they felt that went, drink one glass of wine, and then I'm going to bed so that we can finish this bootcamp, because those people have given up time to come here and try to learn something from us.'

I quickly pull on some jeans and a jumper before following her downstairs. I realise as I put my clothes on that I'm still sodden with the massage oil, which is presumably why Jessica rinsed herself off in the shower. But it's too late now, so I resign myself to being massively uncomfortable for the rest of the evening.

When I get downstairs, everyone's decamped to the snug, mostly in some form of loungewear, though Ken is back in trousers and a shirt, the uniform he's been wearing for the entire weekend so far. Jessica is sitting, legs underneath her, in an armchair. Her face is back to the perfect alabaster, with the tiny smattering of freckles across her nose and her temples. She's holding a glass of wine between two hands and looks serene.

'Jack,' she says, smiling. 'Come and sit down.'

I have been a Jessica Richards superfan since the day she asked me if I had a pen outside the exam hall. I think she is the cleverest, most beautiful, most charismatic woman on earth. But there's something about this, the performance she's putting on, which makes me feel very, very uneasy.

'Did you enjoy the workshop?' Stuart asks cheerfully. 'I was just telling Jessica, I cried too.'

'I almost did,' Ben adds. 'Mad shit, that.'

Great, we've instigated mass hallucination. We might as well call it a cult. 'How about you, Grant?' I ask, searching for an ally, and feeling a bit depressed that my best chance at an ally is a man who I overheard in the kitchen yesterday saying that 'this country is too tough on landlords'.

'No tears here,' he says, which is a relief to me.

'Me neither,' I agree. 'I had a nice kip.'

'Shame, that,' says Ken. 'Missed out on something quite special.'

Everyone whips around to look at him. He and Sue are sitting close together on the sofa, hand in hand. 'Sue and I are talking about taking a proper course when we're back at home. We'd like to get in touch with our spiritual sides.'

'Where are Noah and Verity?' I ask, realising that the group is two people short.

'They went upstairs.' Chloe giggles.

'Well, that was the idea of the task.' Jessica smiles. 'Right?'

'On that note,' Grant says, smugly offering his hand to Stuart and pulling him up to standing. 'We're for the wooden hill to Bedfordshire.'

He pats him on the arse and Stuart chuckles, then they head upstairs, at which point I realise that the expression he just used was posh old guy language for 'going upstairs to bed'. Obviously it's nice that they're reconnecting, especially given that a disparity in sex drive was part of their problem, but I can't help asking myself: what the fuck is going on in here? Was there Viagra in the massage oil? There's no way that a massage workshop has genuinely reinvigorated all these people's sex lives. And Verity and Noah haven't touched each other the entire time they've been here – surely she isn't actually upstairs, with Noah? Some cold, *On Chesil Beach*-style scene where they solemnly undress and make sedate, controlled love? I can see Noah's serious face set in an expression of restrained enjoyment, and it makes me feel a bit queasy. Why am I thinking about this? What's wrong with me?

Jessica gets up too. 'Thank you all so much for being so open-minded and open-hearted about the workshop. Hibiscus has provided a QR code so if you want to access the tutorial at home, you can, and there are worksheets on there too. Otherwise, tomorrow morning is the last session and we'll tackle rule five, then, to bring the whole thing to an end, we'll do rule seven and you'll each "leave the party together", so to speak.'

She picks up her glass, because she insists on putting everything in the dishwasher despite Suze having told us multiple times that William and Cait will handle it and there's an army of cleaners coming in after we leave. Everyone choruses their goodnights and I trot after her, wondering how it's possible that she could go from sobbing to hostess in such a short period of time. I used to reassure myself that the Jessica who belongs to the internet wasn't my wife but just her work personality. We've all got one. I allegedly supported Brighton and Hove Albion at work, so I could make cheerful chat about the game last night. I also pretended to want a cup of tea if anyone was making a round so I could be friendly and join in. But even if that was true once, even if there used to be a pretend Jessica who existed on a server somewhere, I'm worried now that the fake version has started to subsume the real one. Surely this can't be good for her? The constant pressure to paint on a happy face and pretend that everything is great? It's Stepford-wife stuff and I don't want it for her. I don't really want it for me, either.

She does her complicated skincare regime, then lies down with her eye mask and her earplugs, every barrier up. Has she noticed that before all of this Seven Rules stuff, she used to fall asleep quickly and easily? I take a long, steadying breath. The retreat is almost over. I've seen so many blissful reminders of the real her, the real us, over the weekend, and this is the last stretch of the Seven Rules tour. We're so, so close to getting our normal life back, and thanks to this weekend, I think we're even ready to enjoy it.

Rule Five

*Self-care isn't selfish; make time to make
yourself the best possible person*

The Big Move

Jack

*I've lived with other people plenty in my life. My parents spent
all the money they had on sending me and my brothers to a
cheap boarding school, which is still an insane amount of money
to spend on anything. So from thirteen to eighteen, I shared a
dormitory with other boys. At university I lived in halls; after
university I lived in a houseshare with a load of guys from school
who still called me Jacko and talked about the Old Days all the
time. I've shared space with a lot of people and, generally speaking, I've enjoyed it. But I've never lived with a romantic partner
until now.*

*The decision that we should move in was made, like all great
romantic gestures, on the basis of our finances. Initially when we
all got to London, Jessica lived with her friends Grace, Sophie,
and Katie (known collectively as 'the girls') in a very damp house
in Clapham. Only, they all had deposits to put down on their
own flats, and therefore found themselves buying various Victorian*

ground-floor conversions, to fill with fairy lights, ornamental gold pineapples and neon signs.

Jess, on the other hand, wasn't in line to get a nice big 15 per cent deposit like the rest of the girls, who had rich parents or dead grandparents. So she went to look at various squats with available rooms to rent before coming to stay at my shared house with mascara under her eyes. 'It's fine,' she says, as we make carbonara in the kitchen. She grates Parmesan with a grater so blunt it's barely making shavings. I wash up the pans which are sitting in the sink, filled with grey water and marbled with soapy fat. 'I'll find something. There's got to be a houseshare of non-psychos in an okay area for less than half my salary.'

She opens the fridge to get something and does a strange sort of whimper noise.

'What?' I ask, across the kitchen in a second.

She points into the fridge. There's a half-smoked cigarette stubbed out into the packet of bacon we'd bought at the nice supermarket over the weekend.

'Maybe we should move in together?' I ask.

And so we do. Initially Jessica was talking about us finding a mews house on a cobbled street, somewhere more central so that we could save money by walking to work. 'I'm going to grow sweet peas and tomatoes on the balcony,' she'd announced. This idea was very short-lived when we realised that our budget wasn't going to stretch to the garage of a mews house. In the end we found a bedsit on the top floor of a big family house in North London. It has a bedroom, a little kitchen with a sofa and space for a telly, and a tiny bathroom. There are skylights in every room, and while it's a long walk from the Tube and the family who own the house made us swear never to have more than two people over, it's ours. For the first few weeks, we lie in bed watching the

sunset through the hole punctured in the roof and hold hands.
We sleep in jumpers to save putting the heating on and all our
saucepans are from Poundland, but we're happy. So happy that
we stop doing anything other than going to work, coming home
and being together. Being together becomes an activity. We no
longer put things in our diary or ask each other what the plan
is for the weekend. The plan is Jack and Jessica. Living together is
the activity. I talk to Jessica as I wake up, as I brush my teeth,
as she makes us breakfast, as I get dressed, as she gets dressed,
swapping over because there isn't space to both be in the bedroom
at the same time. We walk to the Tube together, text each other
throughout the day and sit down together in front of the TV at
night before we fall asleep next to each other.

It was nice, until it wasn't. Now it feels like the sloping ceil-
ings are getting lower and lower. Every noise she makes feels
loud. She puts Gilmore Girls and Friends on her laptop in the
background while she's pottering around, and the chatty, cheerful
dialogue drives me insane. There's no silence and nowhere I can
stretch out. Her clothes are strewn across the bed and on the floor
like a sort of fabric salad. She has dozens of bottles in the bath-
room, splayed paperbacks on the kitchen table and leaves as
many glasses and bottles of water on her bedside table as it can
accommodate. Within three weeks, the woman who I once said
'wasn't capable of being annoying' is irritating me like I had
never dreamed possible.

I get home from the office, throw my keys on to the table and
within seconds, Jess has bounded from the bedroom. She leaves on
the dot of five because she hates her job. She's wearing pyjamas
and she's got some kind of goo on her face.

'Hello,' she says, throwing her arms around me. 'I love you.
How was your day?'

'Fine.' I start putting my things away, hanging my jacket up behind the door, placing my shoes in the shoe rack.

'Any gossip?'

'Not really.'

'Oh, boring. I think Amy is pregnant again, and she literally just got back from mat leave so Sharon is going to be fucking fuming ...' She pauses. 'Are you okay?'

'Still fine. Just like I was two minutes ago.'

'Someone's grumpy. Do you want—'

'I'm not grumpy,' I hear myself snap. Shout, if I'm honest.

She looks taken aback. 'Yeah, doesn't sound like you're grumpy at all.'

'I'm sorry,' I say, slumping a bit.

'What's going on with you?'

'I just—' I swallow, knowing that what I'm about to say is going to ruin the happy, lovely bubble that she's inside, that she's so happy and I'm going to take that away from her. 'I'm struggling a little bit. With living together.'

'Okay,' she says, going to the fridge. 'What do you want to do about that?'

I don't really know how to process this because I was expecting her to shout at me, or cry, or do something befitting of the news that I'm not finding our blissful life totally blissful.

'Did you – you realise – I just said that I'm struggling. With us. Living together.'

'Yeah, obviously,' she says.

'Sorry?'

She pours herself a glass of wine and offers me one. I shake my head and she gives me a pitying look. 'Jack, this is a massive adjustment; we've totally changed the whole nature of our relationship. I swear, men really need to read more magazines.'

'Wait, are you finding it hard too?'

'Of course I am. I love you. I love living with you, but like, more in theory than in practice right now, you know? Like you're great, love you, but having someone else around the entire time is a lot. And you're really easily irritated by my very normal living habits. And there's all this stuff I can't do when you're here.'

'Me too!' I say, equal parts shocked and delighted by where this is going. 'I just want to sit and write for a while, and there's nowhere to do that. I can't sit in front of you and just not talk.'

'Okay, so why don't you take your laptop to the pub for a couple of hours?'

'Am I ... allowed?' I ask.

She laughs. 'Are you allowed to take a couple of hours for yourself? Yes, Jack. Yes, you are.'

This is the most obvious suggestion imaginable. 'I was worried you'd be hurt that I didn't want to hang out,' I say sheepishly.

'I love you, but the idea of an evening here alone to do all my gross beauty shit without you around and then watch an episode of something you'd judge me for? That sounds like the most perfect Friday night.'

'Are you sure that's okay? That it's not a bad sign?'

She rolls her eyes at me and points at the door. 'Out.'

I wander down the road to a sweet ivy-covered pub I've never been to before. I write half a chapter of the book I've been working on since I was twenty-two. Drink a pint of the Hobbitty ale I can't usually order because I share a bottle of wine with Jess. And then I walk home and crawl into bed with her, smelling the sweet citrus of her neck and her hair.

'Did you have fun?' she asks.

'I did. It was a decent place. Burgers the size of your head, served on actual plates, none of that slate nonsense. I want to take you there at the weekend.'

'Sounds lovely,' she says, stretching and pulling another of my pillows into her arms. 'Sleep well.'

When I'm lying next to her, I always do.

Jessica

'This morning you're going to spend some time being self-ish,' Suze tells us, as we all sit around in the armchairs and on the sofas. 'Jessica, could you explain a little about the rationale?'

'Sure,' I say, getting to my feet. 'So, selfishness gets a bad rep. But we've found that by taking some time to be selfish, we're way better partners to each other. You need time where you're not thinking about other people's needs, where you can focus on yourself and recharge your batteries. You can't pour from an empty cup. When you live together and spend a lot of your time together, there's a bit of a risk that you sort of lose yourself. There's a lot of compromise in a good marriage, and we love that. But in order to maintain that original version of you − the one your partner fell in love with − you need to do things which recharge you.'

I recount a story of when we first moved in and Jack went out for the night and how it turned out to be the best thing for us.

'See, love?' Ben says to Chloe. 'She's saying that I need to be able to go golfing all weekend!'

'That's not really what I'm saying,' I say, trying to be patient. I know Ben is joking, and he's actually a very decent guy, but it's a criticism I've heard levelled at our method a lot, and it's one which annoys me. This isn't about men going off on a four-hour cycle while their wife looks after the kids at home. It's about improving yourself so that you're a better person, and by extension, a better partner. 'There's a place for the golfing,' I say, trying not to sound like a primary school teacher. 'What you absolutely don't want to do is have a situation where one of you – and let's face it, in a heterosexual relationship, it's usually the bloke – spends their weekend seeing mates, and the other partner picks up all the domestic labour. You also want to try to avoid a situation where the "fun" stuff that you do to be selfish is actually like, having a shower or going to the supermarket. That's essential maintenance, not self-care.'

'How does that work when you've got kids?' Verity asks. 'Or you work full-time?'

'That's a really good question,' I acknowledge. 'I used to try to take a bit of my commute each morning and listen to an audiobook I was really looking forward to, to make that dead time into a bit of a treat. And of course if you're in a two-parent relationship, then you can tag in and tag out to make sure the other person gets a little window to read a book, go for a walk, or see friends.'

It's a pretty textbook answer – I'm basically quoting the book – but it's not a bad one, and I do mean it. I get that it's easy for us with our flexible job and zero caring responsibilities to sit here and preach at people like Verity who've got three young kids and probably mounting bills to go with that. But I've been there, at least with the money and the job. I didn't come from a life like this one, and I don't like the idea that if you've got kids and a busy life then you can't be selfish occasionally.

'You'll have a couple of hours,' Suze says, 'and you're going to go off individually and do whatever you would like. We have the pool open, there's an entertainment centre in the lounge, you can go for a walk, take part in a crafting session in the library – or do whatever else you most enjoy. Cait, Will and I will be around if you have any additional requests.'

Everyone stands around a bit awkwardly trying to work out what to do next. Ken makes noises about watching some sport on the telly, Noah wants to pray, Stuart wants to work out, and I'm not sure where everyone else is going, but within moments they've all dispersed, including Jack, and I'm left standing alone in the snug wondering what to do.

An old version of me would put on an old season of *Real Housewives* and exfoliate, pluck all my ingrown hairs and paint my nails. But now I have a dermatologist-pre-scribed shower gel which exfoliates chemically. My hair is lasered and I've got shellac on my nails. All my grooming is outsourced. There's an essay I need to start work on for my course, but that's hardly the point of the exercise. I could go for a run, I guess. It would be nice to move my limbs, and the rhythm of my feet on the ground always helps calm the gnawing in my stomach. But we've got this photoshoot later which I have to look decent for, and if I go for a run, I'll have to wash my hair, and I'll still be pink in the face by the time the photographer arrives – and again, I don't know if it would really fit the bill. My actual current activity of choice when I have the house to myself is to sit on a pregnancy forum for several hours and read about treatments I haven't tried, and comment on posts from strangers about their potential pregnancy symptoms. Again, obviously not something I'm going to want to share when we all catch up later. What I'd like to do is plan and schedule some content about the weekend, but then I'll have to try and explain that working is genuinely my favourite way to spend my time, and usually when I try to explain that, people look at me like I'm a loser.

Maybe I could go and have a nap? That would kill a couple of hours. But that's not going to sound great when everyone asks what we did. I'll read. Reading is a perfectly safe, sensible activity that no one can take issue with. And maybe I'll spend a couple of minutes thinking about how I've got no idea what to do for fun. Which really can't be a good sign.

I wander the corridor and eventually I see Ken watching snooker on the TV. I linger in the doorway, not sure whether to go in or not.

'Have you ever played?' he asks, without turning around.

'No,' I say. 'I mean, I've tried it a couple of times in the pub.'

Ken laughs. 'I can't see you in the kind of place that's got a snooker table.'

'You'd be surprised,' I say defensively. 'I used to be fun when I was younger.'

He laughs again, and I take this as an invitation to sit on the far end of his sofa. 'Have you always played?'

'Sue and I used to go to the working men's club every Saturday night when the kids were young. Left 'em with the grandparents, or on their own once they were a bit bigger and happy with a video. She was a demon at poker.'

'Sounds like a very happy time.'

'It was.' He pauses. 'That's why you stick with it, when it's hard. She's the only one who remembers all of it, like I do. When I'm with her, I'm right back there again, with all our friends and our kids. Best years of my life.'

'That's lovely,' I say, really meaning it. 'You're very lucky.'

'Aye,' he says. 'D'you know how to use the remote? There's darts on the other channel.'

Between us we make the monstrously complicated television work and we put the darts on. He gives a satisfied sigh as it starts.

'You and that husband of yours have been a marvel this weekend. Shouldn't you be doing something you actually enjoy?' he says, after a few minutes.

I look up at the ceiling. 'I can't think of anything to do,' I admit.

'You sound like me, when I retired.' He smiles.

'Really?'

'Absolutely. I've been driving Sue bananas, walking around the house. I'd been to work every day for nearly fifty years, I'd not thought of a thing to do when I stopped.'

'I don't know what I'd do,' I admit, drawing my knees up to my chest. 'I used to say that we'd take a break when the book published. But I never thought about what we'd do. To be honest –' I don't know why I'm saying this – 'I assumed by then we'd be having a baby.'

Ken looks at me, straight on, for the first time since I came into the telly room. 'You two having trouble?'

I nod, and swallow at the same time, because if I try and form any words I'll start sobbing and I've already embarrassed myself enough doing that last night.

'I'm sorry to hear that,' Ken says. 'I really am.'

There's a long pause, and I get enough control of myself to say, 'Thank you.'

'It'll come right,' he says, looking at the television again. 'One way or another. It always does.'

I have a horrible feeling that when he says 'one way or another' he means that there's a world in which Jack and I aren't together anymore.

I'd be lying if I said I'd never thought about it. If in our worst moments, I hadn't wondered what it would be like to share a home with someone who actively loved my work, or to spend the night with someone I haven't known since I was twenty-one. On the handful of occasions I've allowed myself to think about it, I've imagined one of those grown-up, sensible splits where everyone is mature, but you just go from sharing a bed to never seeing each other again. It's not like we've got children. Nothing binding us together if we decided we didn't want to be married anymore. And within seconds of giving it any proper consideration, I know that I absolutely cannot let that happen. It would break my heart.

Jack

My laptop is upstairs in our bedroom and I can hear it calling to me. It feels like ages since I've had a proper stretch of time to write. I've been hearing people talking about the sacrifices that they make for their partners this weekend, a lot of which make me look like a spoiled brat by comparison. And I think I could do with reframing this. Yes, I've been unhappy with some of the changes to our lives since the account snowballed. But we've built it to such a level, we've written a book together (ish) and we're done now. When we get home, I can reasonably tell Jessica, properly – not by sulking and seeming sad and hoping she'll work it out – that I want the break that we agreed to. Something substantial. And if she's not upset, and I don't handle it horribly like I did last time, we could talk about me doing my book, signing with Edward Nestor and finally working on the thing I've been trying to write since I was twenty-two. Or go back to the BBC, cap in hand. But either way, I want to do something I'm proud of, something that is mine.

I make my way towards the stairs and I'm almost halfway up when I hear the doorbell go. Who the hell is that going to be? I pause, hoping someone else will go. But the house is eerily silent, everyone absorbed in their own personal time.

I open the door and to my complete horror, standing there, looking like he teleported from Soho, is Clay.

'Hello,' I say, trying to summon enthusiasm. 'What are you doing here?'

He walks into the house without waiting to be invited, and while I know I don't own the place, I still find it rather objectionable.

'Where's your lovely wife?'

'I'm not sure.'

'You might want to go and find her. I've got news.'

Jessica

Jack appears in the library, just as I'm trying to find a book to read. Like a proper grandfather, Ken gave me some very sage advice then implied quite clearly that he'd like me to bugger off and leave him on his own.

'What are you doing?' Jack asks, apparently irritated about something.

'Oh, just sort of working out what to do with myself.' I shrug, hoping he's not going to point out how weird it is that I don't know what to do with free time.

'Right. Clay's here.'

'Clay?' I reply, something fizzing in my upper abdomen.

'Yes. About yay high? Dresses like a Danish architect despite being from Surrey? Takes fifteen per cent of our money.'

'What on earth is he doing here?' This has got to be big, but is it good big or bad big?

'No idea. He said he had something to tell us.' Jack turns to walk back into the hallway as my stomach drops to the floor.

We find Clay sitting on a sofa with his feet up. He stands and kisses me on each cheek.

'In the nicest possible way,' I ask, 'why are you here?'

'I have news,' Clay says, beaming. 'And I thought it would be nice to deliver it in person.'

I feel light-headed. Relief and nerves, surely this means it's good big? Back when Jack and I first got into this stuff, we learned that there's a sort of hierarchy with managers. They email with bad news, phone with good news. And now we're about to find out what it means if they come halfway across the country to see you in person.

'I heard from the Americans,' he tells us.

I grip my hands together. The Americans have been umming and ahhing about publishing our book for months. I've been hoping and praying and embarrassingly even manifesting that they would, because it's the first step to cracking America and opening us up to a massive new audience. It's the one I've wanted since we first signed the book deal. 'And?'

'Well, as you know, they wanted to see how the sales figures here were, and how your demographic was developing internationally. And they were impressed. Very impressed. So impressed that we had a call yesterday and they've officially made an offer.' I try desperately to drink this in, so that I can remember what this feels like. 'And that's not all.' He pauses dramatically. 'They've got a first-look deal with a production company. So they want the film rights, as well as the book.'

I scream and throw my arms around Jack and then Clay. 'I can't believe it!' I gasp. 'Oh my GOD.'

'I haven't even told you the number yet,' Clay says, almost purring.

'Oh my God, how much?' I ask, almost scared to hear the answer.

I feel like I'm going to simultaneously throw up and burst into tears. I look at Jack next to me who's stood there in total shock, probably struggling to process the enormity of what Clay's just told us.

'What does this mean in terms of next steps?' Jack asks after a minute.

'Good question. It'll be another edit; they'll want a version of the book that works for the US market. And then it'll be a publicity tour over there, at least a month. They're talking about doing ten cities – and I don't want you to get your hopes up, but apparently they're shooting for the talk shows.' I make another very uncool squeal at this. Clay looks at me, indulgently amused. 'In terms of the film,' he goes on, 'I know less at the moment, and I imagine it'll be more of a ceremonial position than a writing one, but they'll want you to be producers on it. And then assuming the film comes out, there'll be a whole second wave of publicity around that, though who's to say when that would be,' Clay explains.

'So what about our break?'

Clay and I both turn to look at Jack. Neither of us saying anything.

'We'd said we were going to take a break?' he repeats.

'I mean, I don't think anyone knew just how much demand you two were going to be in.' Clay chuckles. 'When things like this come knocking, you don't say no. But listen, I can get you a couple of days to recover from this thing. Maybe head out to the US early? Actually, with all the edits and the next PR tour, you might find it's easier just to be based out there for a few months.'

'We could stay in New York for a couple of months?' I whisper and look over at Jack. Surely the *Sex and the City* dream has got to be better than a break? I get that he wanted to catch his breath, but we could stay in a brownstone in Brooklyn, wander across the cobblestones for brunch, spend the weekends at the Met. He'd be living where people like Herman Melville and Edith Wharton lived – his literary heroes.

'Can't you see us walking along the Hudson? Long lunches at Balthazar? Martinis at the Carlyle?' I ask, desperate for him to see the vision. It's surely the best place we could be without children. 'We could do weekends upstate, you can look at every picture in the Met while I'm at Bergdorf?'

'Yes,' he says, still a little shell-shocked. 'Yeah, that's definitely a plan.'

'Right?' I smile, wrapping my arms around him.

'Wow. So does this make a second book more likely?' Jack asks Clay.

Clay gives Jack a look. He never really understands Jack's self-deprecation. 'Jack, there was always going to be a book two. The pre-orders and early sales surpassed the publisher's wildest dreams; you're a debut that landed at the top of the *Sunday Times* bestseller list. Of course they'll want to take up their option for the second book. They've already made that clear.' He laughs and I almost jump up and down. The entire time we were doing the book, it always felt so flimsy, like one wrong step and it could all disappear. When we bought the house, it felt so dangerous, like we were letting ourselves slip into a world we couldn't afford to stay in. But this is different. This is the rubber stamp I've been waiting for. And with the kind of money Clay's talking about, that terror that it's all going to disappear, that I'll be back hoping my card doesn't decline when I get on the bus, that's gone. They say money can't buy happiness, but what I'm feeling right now, this kind of bullet-proof optimism about our future, that's a feeling that only money can give you and I'm so unbelievably grateful for it.

'Jesus, Jack,' I say, hugging him again. 'We did it. We really, properly did it.'

He smiles down at me. 'You did it,' he says.

I shake my head. 'I couldn't do any of it without you. And I know it's a lot, to have to keep going, not take a break. But it's not like we'd be doing anything important with that time.' I glance down at my stomach, empty and hollow. I can't bring myself to say it, that I couldn't get my head around the break if we weren't having a baby. But I think he knows.

'Right, lovebirds,' Clay says, picking up his bag. 'Shall we go over some quotes for press about the retreat?'

'Absolutely,' I say, getting to my feet. 'Let's go and find a bigger table so we can stretch out.'

'It's supposed to be selfish time?' says Jack.

I stop halfway to the door. 'Sorry. You're quite right. Clay, can you wait for a bit? Jack and I are halfway through one of the sessions for the weekend.'

Clay looks perturbed. 'I said I'd have this back with the team in a couple of hours.'

I look at Jack, and then at Clay, and wonder for a moment why I seem to get stuck between them so often. 'Would you mind? If I did a couple of hours with Clay on this?' There's a loud silence.

'Sure,' Jack says eventually. 'I guess this is what makes you happy, so it's kind of appropriate.'

'Exactly.' I smile as he leaves the room.

'How's it been?' Clay asks as he unpacks his laptop, an iPad and a sheaf of papers on to the dining table.

'Really good, actually,' I reply. 'I was nervous about it, joining in and being part of the activities. But it's been great. I think it's helped us a lot.'

'I wouldn't have thought Jack would be able to get off his high horse long enough to join in,' Clay laughs.

I bristle at this. Occasionally I've let myself confide in him, because it was easier than talking to Grace, who seemingly had things perfect, or any of my other friends who I worried might think I sort of deserved it as karma for bragging about my amazing marriage. But I realise, as Clay cheerfully makes a snide comment about my husband, the person I'm allegedly the world's biggest cheerleader for, that I've got something wrong. If he feels like he can languidly snipe at Jack, that's because I've made it seem like that's okay.

'He's been brilliant, actually,' I say.

Clay seems to understand that I'm telling him to shut up, without telling him to shut up. He acknowledges me with a little nod, and then opens the laptop so we can pick between ten almost identical quotes and ten almost identical headshots of us.

Jack

I head towards the kitchen because I want to drown my sorrows in biscuits, and because obviously there's now no point in using 'selfish time' to write. I woke up this morning with a purpose. Get through the last part of the retreat, get back to London and get back to the BBC, to some version of myself that I recognise. Finish the book. Convince Edward Nestor that I'm worth representing and put some distance between me and the Seven Rules era, without hurting Jessica or seeming ungrateful for all that nice money they threw at us. Easy. Perfect.

Too perfect, it turns out. In retrospect, it was painfully naïve of me to think that we'd be allowed to stop making money for Clay and the publishers. We're golden geese, so obviously we're not going to be allowed to run around free range. And now the next year of my life is going to be spent doing this whole thing over again, but in America this time. Months and months more of Seven Rules. Then, inevitably now, the whole circus will start again with another book.

I know I should be happy. I want to be happy. This is the seal of approval Jess has dreamed of since she started making money this way. She spent years sitting at a desk being patronised and ignored, she applied for job after job and got rejected for all of them because she didn't have the right experience or know the right people, and then finally, when she'd made her peace with never having a career she was in love with, this all happened. I want it for her. I just really, really don't want it for me. And I don't want it for our relationship either. The unavoidable truth is that we were better together before all this started.

For a while I latched on to the idea that all this was worth it to buy a house instead of moving every time a landlord sold up. I even bought into the logic that it was a way to put something into savings, catch up with our friends who have wealthy parents. But I can see now that if it went well, it was never going to be an in-and-out thing. I'm done with pretending that I can extricate myself from this. Of course it's not going to work like that. It's going to be like we're at a casino, chasing a win by throwing the dice over and over again, not caring about the cost. Jessica's never going to want to stop doing this because it's making her feel alive, and I'm never going to be allowed to bow out because despite having fuck all to do with the content, I'm part of the package. I am stuck. Not important or necessary, not central to the work, not creatively fulfilled – not even really creatively consulted. But locked in.

I let the kitchen door bang as I walk in, and then head straight to the cupboard.

'What's wrong?' Surprised to hear a voice behind me, I turn around to see Verity standing in front of a stand mixer, weighing out ingredients.

'Sorry,' I say, stopping on my quest. 'Sorry, I was just being clumsy. What are you doing?'

'Baking.'

'Stupid question,' I say, looking at the very obvious evidence around her.

'Want to help?' she offers.

Not really. But I can't write now, and at least if it looks like I'm in conversation with one of the guests I can't be dragged back to Clay and Jessica's production line. 'Sure. What can I do?'

'Preheat the oven. To 180, please.'

I put the oven on, and she looks impressed. 'Well done.'

'It's really not complicated.'

'Wouldn't have stopped most men from asking how to do it.'

I laugh. 'Who does the cooking in your house?'

She gives me a look.

'Another stupid question.' I hold my hands up.

She passes me a bowl, some icing sugar, cream cheese and a wooden spoon. 'You can start on the icing. Beat half of that into that.'

I do as I'm told, surprised to find myself really thinking about it, trying to get the measurement right, not make a mess. There's something rather meditative about it, watching the icing thicken. Ironically, given my feelings towards the book right now, I find myself remembering why so-called 'selfish time' is a very good rule. I feel my rage dulling to a simmer.

'So what's actually going on?'

'What makes you think there's something going on?'

'Oh please. That whole thing at the massage session?' She's looking at her work, not at me, but somehow it still feels like she's gauging my reaction.

'Oh. That. Nothing really, just that whole pressure point thing, Jessica felt like she'd had a big emotional release. Processed a lot of hard stuff.'

'What does *she* have to process?' Verity says. She stares me down, her eyes straight into mine. I expect her to backtrack when she realises what she's said, to apologise, even. But she doesn't. She keeps looking me straight in the eye. 'Aren't you two supposed to be the perfect couple?' I laugh, and she reads this as a response. 'No?'

'I don't think she'd appreciate me talking about it.'

'Course not,' Verity says, sifting flour into the bowl. She's madly neat, not getting a speck on the counter. 'Though, I would say—' She stops.

'Would say what?' I want to know.

She looks like she's searching for the words. 'For ages I wasn't saying anything about my life or my stuff. Because I wanted to protect Noah, I didn't want to say anything that made him sound bad. But that meant I wasn't talking about my stuff either.'

I nod. 'Yeah. I get that. I think it's pretty normal to want the world to think well of the person you love.'

'I know it's different for you two,' she says. She puts her finger in the icing I've made and licks it. 'Sorry!' she laughs. 'Just cost you your five-star food hygiene rating. That's good!'

'I promise I won't tell anyone.' I smile, pathetically buoyed by the feedback.

'Thanks.' She grins back.

'Is this really what you wanted to do? With your free time? Baking?'

'Sure. Why not?'

'Just seems a lot like the kind of thing you'd be doing at home. Something which benefits other people.'

'True.' She stirs for a moment. 'I think it would have taken more time than we were given to work out what I actually want to do. For myself.'

'That makes sense. I can understand wishing you could put yourself first a bit more.'

'Really?' She seems surprised.

'I shouldn't really go into it,' I say, knocking the toe of my trainers against the kickboards of the kitchen island like a moody teenager.

'You do talk to someone, though, right?' She opens drawers, whispering the word 'scissors' as she looks for them.

'Uh,' I reply. 'No. No, not really. I've tried therapy a few times but it's not really for me.'

'I don't mean a therapist, I mean like a friend or something.'

'Still no, honestly. Most of my mates have kids so they're nigh on impossible to get hold of, and then when we do go out, they're always talking about how great my life must be because I'm child-free and assuming I don't have any problems, even though the child-free thing is actually kind of part of the problem, so I don't want to bring them down, and Jessica doesn't want them to know that we're trying to get pregnant. It's always supposed to be a secret, so she's privately obsessed and publicly we have to just act like the question of kids has never occurred to us. I used to have some work mates I talked to, but then of course I got canned from my job because I was doing this book and it was bringing "the wrong kind of attention", and Jessica thought that was some brilliant triumph, like she wanted everyone to know our book was doing well enough that we didn't need to have other jobs, but fuck me, I miss it. I miss it so much. I wake up in the morning and I'm just totally lost, I don't know what to do with myself. Every time I tried to help with writing the book, it was like anything I suggested was stupid, and then the publishers had all these plans and they just spoke to Jessica like I wasn't there. It all sounds so stupidly futile, complaining about not being allowed to work, having all this free time and free-dom – you must hear this and think I'm such a prick, and I probably am; God knows I am to Jessica most of the time, you know? I'm really shit to her, I'm pretty much always in a bad mood and she doesn't understand why. I just miss us when we were younger. I know she hated us being broke, but we were happier, we really were.'

I once tried to drink the top shelf of the bar at a pub in Oxford, after I'd eaten some sushi from the discount bit of the petrol station. It's never been clear which of them caused the great hurling incident of 2009, but whatever the cause, that was very much like this, only then it was actual vomit and right now it's word vomit. Streams and streams of it, everything I haven't said to anyone for the last couple of months, just spewed over the pristine walls and floor of this designer kitchen.

Verity has stopped doing anything to do with baking. The cake mix, yellow and wet, sits in the bottom of the pan, half full, and drips on the marble counter. She looks at me like she's genuinely very sad for what she's just heard. 'Have you said any of this to Jessica?' she asks.

'No,' I reply. 'Not really. Bits of it, sometimes, maybe. But not properly. I think I keep waiting for her to realise, like it'll mean more if she decides to rescue me when she notices it herself. But she never does. Sometimes I worry that maybe she has, and she thinks that it isn't important.'

I feel like a teacher who's invited a student into their office and then started crying about their divorce. I'm supposed to be helping Verity, not putting all my misery on her plate. But saying all of this to her, despite being wildly inappropriate, has helped clarify that I need to pull myself together and talk to Jessica. I want her to be happy, but she's not going to be happy if our marriage falls apart, and if we keep on like we've been for the last few months, it's going to. Her happiness is important, but – and this is very hard to admit as a British man who wants to repress every feeling before he's even felt it – mine is too.

'She should have noticed,' Verity says, putting her hand on mine. 'That's her job. She's your wife.'

'I think maybe that's part of the problem,' I say sadly. Probably self-pityingly. 'It's literally her job, being my wife.' I feel tears pricking behind my eyes, and I try to blink quickly enough that they're gone before they escape, but I'm not fast enough and they run down my face. I brush them away with the sleeve of my jumper. Why am I doing this? Why am I talking to a semi-stranger about this intensely private stuff? But then, Verity's the first person who's asked me. I think maybe I would have told anyone who asked. And there's something reassuring about the fact that this will leave with Verity. I'll never see her again. It's like the Catholic kind of confession, speaking into a void and taking the catharsis from saying it all. 'Jesus. What are we going to do with ourselves?'

'Well, I'm going to get divorced,' Verity says calmly.

'What?'

'Yes. I did some sums, and I know how much money I need. It'll take me a while because basically none of my work pays. But once I've got it, I'm going to take the boys and we're going to leave Noah.'

'Are you sure? That's a big decision to come to.' Jesus. Is this our fault? Have we accidentally inspired her to make some huge life-changing decision? And is there anything in place to make sure we can help her if we have? I briefly think about quiet, stoic Noah finding out that he's not going to live in the same house as her anymore, and about their kids being shuttled between them, and the thought comes with a surprisingly sharp pain.

'Yes.'

'He doesn't seem ...'

'Horrible?'

'I, uh. Well. No.' I cringe.

'He isn't. He's not much of anything, really.'

There's a long, heavy pause and yet again I feel completely unequipped to deal with the situation I find myself in. The person who would know what to do with all of this is Jessica. Because it's always Jessica. Which must, I realise, be a bit draining for her. When something in the house breaks, she knows where the manual and the warranty are, or finds the right number to call and get it fixed. When we're double-booked, she massages the diary. She organises our holidays, arranges our social life, makes sure that the fridge is full and the house is clean. Even if she doesn't really go in for cooking anymore, she makes sure that there are snacks and meals and plans and routines and everything around us is safe and functional. I used to do things for her, for us. Back in the day I'd go to the supermarket on the way home on Tuesday, when fresh flowers went on yellow-sticker discount. I'd come home with a battered bunch of tulips and she'd perk them up in some water, do something clever with taking off the leaves, and they'd look great. And then, after the account took off, some flower company offered her a free weekly subscription. She was elated that the flat was suddenly filled with all these expensive, beautiful flowers all the time. It seemed a bit stupid to buy her the supermarket flowers after that. So one of the little things that I did to make her happy got retired, and

I didn't replace it with anything else because pathetically, I felt hurt. And I didn't say anything because I didn't want a row. All the same lazy excuses I've been making, and that I need to stop making.

I glance up at the clock on the kitchen wall and realise, with relief, that selfish time is almost over. It's almost time to go home. 'I should get going,' I say to Verity. 'Thanks for this. It really helped.'

Jessica

After selfish time we have a last lunch of fancy salads and talk about the last rule, 'always leave the party together'. There's no official activity for this one, because they're all kind of leaving a party together, but we've got cars to drive them all home to their front doors, so that they can properly leave together. The idea being that they'll chat about their time here, have a bit of a gossip about the other guests – whatever they want, really – and focus on being a unit rather than running for a train or having a row over the satnav. But before we can go home, it's just the final photoshoot.

The stylist has outdone herself in terms of wardrobe. I've always been nervous about asking to borrow things or letting brands send me freebies, so when Clay said they'd send someone to style the shoot, I was massively relieved. Plus, if I'm really honest, I don't hate playing dress-up in expensive clothes. There's a hanging rail in our bedroom, filled with the most beautiful dresses, tops and trousers I've ever seen. I pull a silk blouse off a hanger and hold it up against me.

'What do you think?' I ask Jack. 'I love it. But if I wear this, I'll have to wear the trousers.' I gesture to a pair of cream cashmere trousers with a wide leg. Then I think better of it. Cream trousers probably aren't a great idea, because about an hour ago I went to the bathroom and, with the same familiar, disappointing, miserable feeling it always brings, I saw a faint trace of pale pink blood. Sometimes I like to allow myself a fantasy, to pretend that it's just an implantation bleed, that I am actually pregnant, because sometimes bleeding can actually indicate a pregnancy; you're not out until it's a full-flow period. But today I didn't have enough energy for the pretence. I just shoved in a tampon. I didn't even have it in me to cry this time. Maybe this is how it goes. You just stop letting yourself feel all those huge feelings, resign yourself to the fact that it's not happening, you're not having it, it's not for you, and get over it. Sometimes I read articles from women who never had the family they wanted and I wonder if maybe they used up all their allotted pain for that specific issue, and that's how they found their peace.

'Are you going to get dressed?' I ask Jack, who is sprawled out on the bed, reading. There's an entire row of beautiful men's clothes. Merino wool jumpers, buttery soft jeans, suits if he wants to look formal. I asked them to include some tweedy, corduroy options so he didn't feel like he was being made over, and maybe something 1950s vintage, in case he wants to channel any of his literary heroes. But he still doesn't look interested at all. 'Please?' I say, trying to get his attention. He's miles away.

'Sure,' he says, getting up. He pulls the closest garments off the rack and puts them on without looking at them.

He looks great, he always looks great, and these are thousands of pounds of designer clothes so they make him look even more handsome. But I wish he could find the fun in it like I do.

'Okay,' I say, 'I'm going down to hair and make-up.'

'Okay,' he replies.

'Are you okay?' I ask, waiting in the doorway.

'Yeah. Just a bit sad.'

Instinctively I go to hug him. 'I know. I am too. It's been a really intense weekend, it's bound to bring some stuff up for you. But I think we've made real progress. I feel like we're doing so much better.' I look at him, praying he's going to agree, that he thinks we're doing better too.

He smiles. 'I'll see you down there,' he says.

'Sure? I can stay up here if you want to talk about anything?'

'No, no, it's fine. I think I'm just tired, it's been a long few days.'

I kiss him gently, pressing my lips to his. 'Okay. Home straight now. And then we can go home, I'll roast a chicken and if you're really nice to me, we can watch *University Challenge*.'

I love photoshoots. I know that sounds spoiled and vain and shallow, but I do. We have a team of hair and make-up artists at the house to make everyone look beautiful. It's optional – they set up downstairs and anyone who wants to be made over can, anyone who'd prefer not to is welcome to sit it out. Predictably all of the women opt in, and I like watching them enjoy it just as much as I do; the space has been transformed with rolls of brushes and pots and jars, styling tools, big mirrors, and lights. At the far end they've put up a sort of set, a pink backdrop for people to pose in front of. The room smells like hairspray and hot hair, the lighting is bright and warm, and we're all chatting gently as they put our rollers in.

'I feel so famous,' Chloe says, as someone hands her a cup of coffee to drink while her hair is being straightened.

'Me too,' I say. 'I know it's bad, but this is one of my favourite parts of the job.'

'Why is that bad?' Stuart asks. 'It's fun.'

It's a very good question, actually. I always tell myself off for liking this part. But maybe that's the mean voice in my head talking, the one which is always disparaging about anything light and feminine and sweet. The one which often takes on Jack's mum's voice, even though she's actually mostly very nice to me.

Verity is the only one who doesn't seem to be having a good time. She's sitting on the chair next to mine while foundation is dabbed on to her perfect skin. All morning she's been quiet, much quieter than she was all weekend, and withdrawn.

'Are you okay?' I ask.

'Me? Oh. Yeah, fine.'

'You seem a bit ... down.'

'Yeah. I guess I just don't really want to go home,' she says, surprising me.

I put my hand on her forearm and then wonder whether that might be a bit overfamiliar. 'I get that. We'll stay in touch, though, and the weekend doesn't end here.'

'Jessica, they're ready for you and Jack for interview questions,' Suze says, standing in the doorway. 'Are you done?'

The make-up artist gives me a nod, I check myself in the mirror and then follow Suze down the corridor.

'I don't think Verity is very happy,' I say to Suze's back.

'Has she made a complaint?'

'No, no, she just seems off.'

Suze looks at me like she has no idea why I'm telling her any of this.

'I'm sure she's fine,' I say. 'But will you make sure they've all got our direct details for afterwards? So we can stay in touch?' I ask.

'Is that a good idea? You don't really want to set a precedent for that.'

'I think we need to – we've had a really intense weekend together, we owe them all some aftercare.'

The journalist who has come to interview us – Kayla – looks like she's in her late twenties. She's wearing a black top, black trousers, and black glasses, and she's not very smiley. Usually we're interviewed by good-natured showbiz journalists, but when I googled Kayla, it turned out that she's spent more time in war zones than interviewing ITV actors. I sense that coming to Yorkshire to do a puff piece about our brand and our book probably wasn't what she dreamed of when she decided to get into journalism. This isn't going to get her nominated for a Pulitzer. But obviously as soon as I sense that she doesn't really like me, I become absolutely obsessed with trying to change her mind.

'So,' she says. 'Is there really such thing as a "perfect" marriage?'

Jack laughs, and I try to too, even though I think she's signalling that this isn't going to be the easy interview Suze thought she'd lined up.

'Sort of,' I say. 'There's no objectively perfect marriage, and if you're taking perfect to mean faultless and blissfully happy at all times, then maybe not. But there are lots of perfect marriages in the sense that they suit the people in them perfectly.'

'Ours isn't perfect by anyone else's metrics,' Jack adds, slipping his arm around my shoulders. 'But it's perfect for us.'

'So is it a bit misleading to suggest that if a couple just follows Seven Rules, they'll be happy?' she goes on. Suze straightens in her seat. We're not famous enough that she can provide a list of questions that we are and are not willing to answer, but she's not above giving a journalist a dirty look or, if she's feeling really pissed off, asking, 'Is that relevant?'

'People seem to find that our method really helps,' Jack answers before I get a chance to. He's doing an incredible job handling this. I shouldn't be surprised. He spent years asking people difficult questions for work, and he's learned from politicians, celebrities and world leaders how to answer cleverly. Weirdly, I wish his parents could see him like this, how sharp and brilliant their least praised youngest son is. 'We hear from hundreds of couples a month who've been struggling long-term, and who've found that buying the book and working through the rules has been a lifeline for them. I don't think anyone buys it thinking it can fix every problem they've got, but the fact that they're trying at all is half the battle, right?'

'The book's only been out for a week and you've heard from hundreds of couples?'

Jack smiles. I think he might actually be enjoying this. 'We've been developing our method on social media, and have offered free online activities and worksheets for almost two years now.'

Kayla looks mollified by this and moves on to questions about how we grew our social media account, whether we worry about influencers being a short-term trend, and how we see ourselves progressing going forward. Her eyes glaze over a bit when I'm talking about my degree, and I can hardly blame her, I'd find it boring if I wasn't me.

'Have we got everything?' Suze jumps in, which is the universal PR language for 'your time is up'.

'I think so.' Kayla nods. 'So I'm going to have a quick chat with the couples who've been on the retreat, get some background, and then that's it.'

'Perfect.' Suze gives her approval.

'Oh, last question,' Kayla adds, once Jack and I are on our feet. 'Some of the forums online have a lot of speculation about your not having kids, some people saying there's trouble in paradise. Any truth to those rumours?'

I freeze.

Jack looks appalled. 'Sorry? Are you asking if our marriage is on the rocks?'

Kayla holds his gaze. 'You used to be a journalist, right? You know I'd be mad not to ask.'

Jack gives her a wide, sweet smile. 'Of course. But no, there's no truth to the anonymous comments made in an online forum which deliberately facilitates conspiracy theories and fantasies. And I think it's a bit problematic to conflate not having children with being unhappily married, don't you? I think you'd risk alienating a lot of readers there.'

And with that, we leave the room. I take his hand and squeeze it tightly. 'That was incredible,' I say. 'You were brilliant.'

'I was not.'

'You were!'

In the hallway, I step closer to him and wind my arms around him. 'Thank you,' I whisper.

'You don't need to thank me,' he replies.

Back in the makeshift photography studio, we find Sue and Ken posing for the camera, laughing their heads off as they do James Bond poses. Grant and Stuart are holding hands. Chloe is sitting, leaning into Ben. Verity and Noah are on the same sofa. We've done well, I realise. We really have done well.

Like the circus coming to town and then leaving, the make-up artists and photographer and assistants tidy their things away, and they and Kayla disappear into their cars as quickly as they arrived. The house is eerily silent in their wake. And then it's finally time for goodbyes.

Will and Cait, who seem to appear from nowhere and who, I've just realised, seem to move in complete silence, bring us all into the library. Everyone settles down for the last time, and we ask everyone to tell us what leaving the party together means to us. I find myself, yet again this weekend, with a tear running down my cheek when Ken and Sue kiss after telling us that they can't wait to start having adventures together again.

'I'll tell you a secret,' I say, when it comes to my turn. 'Jack and I weren't supposed to join in this weekend. The idea originally was that we'd just be around, helping out. But I'm so glad that we did. I feel like we really needed to recommit to each other and refocus on what really matters. So, for me, leaving the party together means that we're going home more together than we were when we got here. More unified. More connected.' I look over to catch Jack's eye, expecting us to share a conspiratorial smile. But he's looking out of the window.

'Right,' says Suze. 'We've only got the house until five so we'd better start moving.'

I thank Will and Cait for their incredible work behind the scenes all weekend. 'It's been amazing,' says Cait, her face still completely impassive. 'I found the parts I observed really moving.'

'So did I,' adds Will, again totally monotone. I have no idea what I'm supposed to say to this because it seems staggeringly unlikely that they were even listening, so I give them a weird bow/curtsey.

Then there's lots of hugging and swapping of phone numbers and more hugs. Suitcases dragged downstairs, people remembering that they've left their phone chargers plugged in, and finally, they get into their cars. Jack and I stand in the doorway of the beautiful glass house, waving as each of the cars slips away into the afternoon. It's a little warmer out here than I'd expected it to be. Like spring is coming.

'Well done, both,' Suze says. 'Brilliant work. Honestly. You should be very proud of yourselves. And joining in with the activities was a master stroke,' she continues. 'I'd have said no if you'd pitched it – risk management and all that. But clearly, it's gone down a storm. Well done.'

'How did the interviews go, with the couples?' I ask, because that's the stamp of approval we really need. 'Did they seem like they'd had a good time?'

'Perfect. Lots of nice colour, they said some great things about you and the method, and it all felt pretty genuine.'

'Good,' says Jack. 'I mean, I assume it was genuine?'

'Yes, yes, of course,' Suze reassures us. 'You know what I mean. Right, we need to be out of here by five, and you'll be home at midnight unless you get going.'

We arrive home at 10.30 p.m., and mercifully there's a parking space right outside our house. We drag the bags in.

'Weird, there's no post,' I say, pushing the door open.

'We've only been gone since Friday morning.'

I suppose he's right. That's actually really not very long. It feels like much longer. So much longer that I'm sort of surprised when everything is where I left it, my book on the kitchen table, the spare phone charger I'd meant to pack curled into a snake on the stairs. It's strange to think that the version of me who left it there didn't know about the US deal, or Jack being a virgin the first time we slept together. She'd never met Chloe and Ben, never laughed at one of Ken's dad jokes. It feels impossible that I could have changed very much over the course of a few days. And yet, somehow very possible. True, even.

'Thank you again for today,' I say. 'For the whole weekend, really.'

'That's all right,' Jack replies, kissing me.

'No, really, you were great. With Kayla, with everyone. You did an amazing job.'

'I'm glad you think so.' He drops another kiss on the top of my head.

'I'm tired. I might go and have a bath,' I say. 'Get all the make-up off from the photoshoot. Then get an early night. God, I can't wait to be back in our own bed.'

'Okay,' Jack says, sounding like it's not okay.

'What?' I ask. 'What's wrong?'

'Nothing, nothing. I just wanted to talk to you about something.'

I assume he's noticed the Tampax packet in the bathroom back at the house, and doesn't know how to talk about it. We've been so bad at this bit lately but I'm determined to keep moving in the right direction.

'I got my period this morning,' I tell him, looking at the floor. Obviously I'm not squeamish about periods around Jack; he's bought me tampons dozens of times. Occasionally when we were younger and shagging all the time, I'd pull my tampon out before we got down to it. No big deal. It's not the bleeding. It's the shame of not being pregnant, yet again.

'Oh,' he says. 'Did you think . .?'

'No, no, not really. I just. You know. As soon as it's half an hour late, I'm picking out nursery paint colours.' I laugh as I say it but that only makes me sound sadder. I am sad. Properly, grippingly, miserably sad. I knew I wasn't pregnant – we'd made one perfunctory, obligatory attempt during the middle of my fertile window. I think I knew even then that it wasn't going to happen. So this isn't a logical kind of sadness, it's the kind of confused and obsessive sadness which not being pregnant drives you into and which is so difficult to comprehend for someone whose body doesn't crave pregnancy.

'I'm sorry,' Jack says lamely.

'Yeah.'

He wraps his arms around me, and I hate that after this many years he doesn't know what to say, but I'm not sure I actually know what I need to hear in this moment either. I think perhaps I just want some reassurance that he is as sad as I am. Or that he's not disappointed in me for failing us once again. That's the problem with infertility, it makes you irrational. I want him to pull me back, sit me down on the sofa and pour me the glass of wine I couldn't have had if I were pregnant. Even though I think there's every chance that if he offered it, I'd be angry with him for thinking that a glass of wine was any kind of compensation. I want him to tell me that we can actually do something about this, something proper and medical, with tests and chats, but if he suggests it, I'll think he's telling me that I've failed, and I'll be terrified to find out if there's something wrong with me. This entire thing – all the supplements and sex positions and online forums – they've turned me a little bit mad.

'What are you thinking?' Jack asks, interrupting my train of thought.

'Nothing,' I say. 'Just that I need to put the recycling out.'

'Leave the bins,' he says. 'Just go and enjoy your bath. I'll do it before I come to bed.'

That's love. Doing the bins. Trying to cheer me up, even when he knows that anything he says will be wrong. Giving me space to process alone, then coming to hold me when I'm ready.

'Jess?' Jack turns back.

'Mm?'

'I'm sad too. It's just—' He pauses. 'Sometimes I don't want to say that. In case it sounds like I'm making it about me. Or worse, in case you think I'm somehow blaming you.'

'Are you actually sad?'

He nods. 'Desperately. For both of us.'

I step down the three stairs I've taken, still standing on the bottom stair, and wrap my arms around his neck. 'Thank you for telling me that,' I say. 'It really helps.'

'I wish I knew how to do more,' he replies.

'That was what you wanted to talk about? Right? You'd clocked that I'd got my period.'

He nods and buries his face into my neck.

Jack

When we first met, I was the early riser and Jessica loved a lie-in. I grew up in a puritan household where cold rooms and plain food were regarded as good, and things that teenagers enjoy, like lie-ins and PlayStation, were regarded as akin to smoking crack. Not that my parents would know what crack was. I would wake up at 9 a.m. and be drenched with guilt about having wasted half the day, despite the fact that obviously half the day hadn't actually elapsed.

Back when we were young and stupid and fun and would stay up until three in the morning, I would always envy Jessica's ability to fester in bed until long past noon and then wake up perky and refreshed, while I'd have forced myself into clothes, gone for a walk, bought a newspaper and spent the entire day pretending that I felt absolutely fine. At some point in our thirties, things shifted. She started getting up early and then, to everyone's horror, became an I Got Up Early person. She started telling me in great detail how much she loved getting up early, how much she was getting done, how peaceful the world is at 6.30 a.m. and how empty her spin class was. I realised that I used to preach much the same thing to her eye-rolls, I just didn't know how annoying it was. All of which is to say that when I got out of the shower on Wednesday morning, two days after we got home from the retreat, I wasn't worried that there was no sign of Jessica. In fact, I wasn't even worried when I went downstairs and there was no trace of her. I noted that there wasn't her usual bowl of berries and granola half eaten on the side, because she likes to have half her breakfast when she wakes up for some complicated reason pertaining to insulin. But, it's Jessica. She'll probably have read an article about going out for a walk before breakfast improving your nail strength or something. I pottered around, made coffee, and then took my phone off airplane mode.

Usually there's a little row of notifications – various social media platforms, an email or two, a couple of messages from friends if I'm lucky and they've finally replied to me because they've had five minutes not chasing their toddler. But today when I pick up my phone, they don't stop coming. I stand, confused, watching as notification after notification flashes up on my screen.

Are you okay? says a message from my friend Chris, who I worked with at the BBC.

What's going on? reads the one in our WhatsApp group with Tom and Grace.

I have seven missed calls, one of which is from Clay, and one of which is from my parents' landline. Four voicemails. I can't even remember the last time someone left me a voicemail. Social media notifications keep coming and coming and coming, so quickly that I can't work out which one to press. Something is very wrong.

By reflex, I go to call Jessica. Her phone goes straight to voicemail. I try it again and the same thing happens. I'm not sure what I think is going to happen when I try it a third time, but the panic is really rising now. Why would she have disappeared? And then I start thinking horrible things, about how low she seemed about getting her period, and more dejected than I've ever seen her before. I never know what to say when it happens, how to tell her that I'm sorry for once again letting her down and that I really truly believe that we will get there, but that maybe all the workouts and supplements and tracking might be making it harder, that the line we hate about 'just relaxing' and 'enjoying the trying' might be right. But she was in a state. What if she went out for a walk and something awful happened to her? Is this what would happen if something had happened? Would my parents and Clay know first? I look at the clock on the wall, it's just after nine. She could have gone out at what, six? Three and a bit hours. A lot of things could have happened to her in three and a bit hours. I call her again, my heart thumping cartoon-like in my chest, my breathing fast. Everything feels tight and terrifying, but as I dial her one more time, the front door opens.

Jessica storms in, carrying a pile of newspapers. She's on the phone, via her headphones, and she's still wearing her pyjamas with a coat over them, and sheepskin slippers on her feet. She pulls the sunglasses away from her face and throws a paper down on the kitchen table.

'I've got to go,' she says. 'Jack's up. I'll call you when we know exactly how bad it's going to get.'

I go to hug her. 'Jesus Christ, Jess, the one time you don't pick up your phone – I was terrified, I thought something really bad had happened to you.'

'What?' she snaps, gives me a bemused, angry, icy look, a look I've never seen before. It's pretty jarring for someone you've spent your entire adult life with to suddenly have a new facial expression. 'What are you talking about?' she asks, as if I'm the one who's acting strangely.

'I was calling and calling. I've got all these messages, I thought something was wrong.'

'You haven't seen it?'

'What? I haven't seen what?' And the panic that I thought had subsided hits me in another wave again.

Grimly, she sits down at the kitchen table and opens the newspaper. Not our usual newspaper, but a lurid tabloid that neither of us would ever buy. I'm a *Guardian* person, and Jess doesn't really read anything, but would pick the *Times* for the aesthetic if she was buying one at the week-end. She opens it, leafing page after page until she stops. And there, on a double-page spread, in big black block letters, is the headline.

SEVEN RULES FOR A PERFECT SHAM-IDGE

'I've already read the online version,' she says, horribly calm. 'But it's longer in print.'

'What is this?' I'm staring at the pages but I can't make them make sense.

'It's an article,' she tells me. There's still an unnerving tone to her voice. 'About how our entire marriage – and, by extension, our entire brand – is a sham.'

I have a horrible, terrible, fucking terrifying feeling that I know what's coming.

'How? Why?'

Jessica gets up and starts very precisely making a coffee with the several-thousand-pound coffee machine I was sure we didn't need. 'Read it.'

'Hot stuff social media duo Jack and Jessica Rhodes present the impression of having a marriage so perfect that they can tell you how to improve yours,' I read. *'But the truth below the surface is a bit different. Over the weekend, they hosted a retreat at 1.5-million-pound Winchlowe Hall in North Yorkshire, where four couples came to learn about their secrets for a harmonious marriage. But in a shocking turn of events, one workshop attendee told us that behind closed doors, Jack and Jessica's own marriage is far from ideal.'*

'Oh Jess,' I say, pausing. 'Are you okay?' I go to hug her but she steps backwards.

'Keep reading,' she demands, her gaze fixed in the middle distance.

'I don't think that's a good idea. We don't need to read this,' I tell her. 'Isn't that what people always say? Never to read the articles about you?'

'Yes. We do,' she shouts.

So I go on. I'd give back every penny of the Seven Rules money not to have to. But I do. *'Verity Francis, 28, attended the course with her husband, Noah Baker, also 28. "They acted*

SEVEN RULES FOR A PERFECT MARRIAGE

happy when they were in front of us," Verity says. "But they're not. Their marriage is on its last legs. He told me that they stay together for the brand, because they know they'll lose all their deals if they split up."'

'I didn't say that!' I yelp. Fucking hell, how could she have told them that? After I'd confided in her. She knew the stuff I told her was personal. The stuff she told me was too, and I'd never repeat that to anyone, not even Jessica. How could she have listened to me say all that stuff and then gone straight to the fucking press?

Jessica is sanguine again. Clinical, even. 'If you said anything even remotely close to it, then you're an idiot. By the time she went to the press, it was third-hand.'

'It's not what I said because it's not what I think—'

'It doesn't matter what you said. It matters what she heard. And what they've printed. I should have been more across this, I should have spoken to her when she seemed down at the end of the weekend – I should have—'

I shake my head, desperate to tell her that it's not her fault. 'It's not that, it's nothing that you did. She needed money, she wanted to leave Noah but she couldn't afford to.'

'How do you know that?'

When I was producing political radio, I would occasionally be in the gallery, running the sound and video output for a big meaty interview. And occasionally I would be working when a politician would make a massive cock-up, when they'd admit to having known something or done something which was illegal or at the very least going to tank their career. And I'd watch as they realised what they'd said and then tried to backtrack and correct their statement. There was always this same look of panic on their

faces, as it dawned on them. That's what's happening to me
right now.

'Jack?' Jessica repeats. 'How do you know that about
Verity?'

'After Clay turned up, all the stuff about not taking a
break ... I'd been planning to talk to you, I was going to say
that I wanted to go back to working on my own, I wanted
to write my book and go back the BBC. I had this
whole plan worked out about telling you that I've been
really struggling with it, and I kept telling myself that we
just had to finish the retreat, and then I was going to tell
you that I wanted to quit. But then Clay turned up and
started talking about America and you'd basically bought
us a brownstone before he'd finished his sentence and I just
felt so trapped ...'

I say nothing. She says nothing. It's silence. 'So I went
into the kitchen and she was in there, and I ended up
talking to her for a while. About us.'

Jessica slams her coffee cup down on the counter. 'You
told her this stuff? It came from *you*?'

I nod.

'You literally had one job,' she screams at me. 'All you
had to do was participate and smile. And instead, you found
the one person there who wanted their own marriage to
fail, told them all our dirtiest secrets and then let them tank
our entire fucking career. What were you thinking?'

'I don't know,' I say quietly.

'You need to read what else your "therapist" told them,'
she snaps.

'I'm not reading any more,' I say weakly. 'I don't want to
read any more.'

'Fine' she says, snatching the paper from the table. 'I'll read it to you then. *"I just think it's wrong," says Verity, who has been married to her husband for a decade, "that they're pretending to be so happy. It makes other people feel guilty when their marriages have struggles. Jack told me that he missed the version of Jessica who he fell in love with, when they were younger."'*

'Oh, this is a good bit,' she sort of yelps. *'Verity, who is nearly ten years younger than Jessica, says, "Jack told me that he and Jessica don't have much sex anymore, and that she's obsessed with getting pregnant, but that she can't relax and that he thinks that's why it's not happening for them."'*

She puts the paper down and looks at me, her face twisted with hurt. 'How could you say that to her?'

'I *didn't* say that,' I say, or shout. 'I didn't. Jess. You know I wouldn't say that.'

'I don't know what you would or wouldn't say,' she retorts, picking her handbag up. 'Honestly I don't think I know you at all.'

Rule Six

Your parents are your family and your responsibility

The Awkward Family Dinner

Jessica

When Jack asked me to marry him, I only had one worry – if we got engaged, we were going to have to put our families in one place at one time, or specifically, his parents, my father and my stepmother, Karen.

My mum has been dead for the better part of a decade so I shouldn't be a baby about having a stepmother, but there's a reason all the fairy tales make stepmothers seem like witches. She moved in the week that I moved out and redecorated the entire house, painting the wallpaper over with grey paint and putting thick grey carpets down over the wooden floorboards ('So much more cosy!'). Since her arrival, there's been no trace of my mum in the house. I tried to be good about it. I got a therapy app on my phone, read a book about learning to like your stepparents, and then decided to say fuck it and just let myself admit that she's a bitch. Her twins, Leila and Sammi, moved into the house and they've got a whole little life together with Dad. They go on cruises and to Disneyland. I make a big deal about hating mass-produced packaged travel so

*that when they don't invite me we can all pretend that's why.
Obviously the sensible part of me knows that it's really Dad's
fault. He could take trips with me, come to London to take me
to lunch, phone me once a week on a Sunday. He doesn't do any
of that and that has nothing to do with Karen. But it's easier
to blame her than to accept that he's slipped into being a boring
suburban dad who doesn't bother.*

*Anyway, all of that adds up to Jack and I being two weeks
pre-wedding, and our parents still not having met. Everyone
said that we had to introduce them before the day itself, so his
parents have taken a pre-booked off-peak train from Cambridge.
They're both tall, bony and wearing raincoats despite the fact
that it's not raining. I've met them lots of times before, obviously.
I've stayed at their house, with its high ceilings and antique
books, piles of papers everywhere and Radio 4 on in every room.
I went to their other sons' solemn Oxford University chapel
weddings (the only woman there in a push-up bra). They've
known me since I was about twenty-one, and I assume at some
point they gave Jack the thumbs up because my engagement ring
is a beautiful sparkly Victorian one from his mum's family. But
despite having spent a decent amount of time with them, we've
never progressed past small talk. They've tried occasionally, offering gambits about books they've enjoyed or plays they've seen,
but it's always been very clear very quickly that they think I'm
an intellectual lightweight.*

*I find them standing in the middle of the pub with an absent-
minded air. 'What can I get you to drink?' I ask his mum.
'Champagne, seeing as we're celebrating?'*

'I'll be fine with tap water, thank you. Gerald?'

*Jack's father nods that he'll have the same and I go to the
bar feeling scolded. I get two bottles of Hildon for them in an*

act of extravagant defiance, and order myself a very large glass of Sauvignon Blanc.

Jack escorts my family in from the car park, where I assume they'll have parked the huge gas-guzzling SUV they drive. I realise, to my horror, that it's not just Dad and Karen. I go to hug my father.

'I didn't realise you were all coming?' I say, totting up how much more this thing is going to cost us with two additional people, neither of whom look like they want to be here.

'Hello, babes,' Karen says, kissing me. 'This place is a bit dark, isn't it?'

'I didn't realise you guys were coming,' I say to Leila, who is messaging someone on her phone.

'Mum made us,' Sammi says, looking up from her own phone.

Obviously there is no reason why two eighteen-year-olds would want to come to a lunch full of people they don't know. They sit down at the shared table, where there now aren't enough chairs. Jack and I drag another two-person table and put it on the end, which means that Sammi and Leila are bisecting the table. Jack and I exchange glances and decide that all we can do is split the difference. He sits at the far end, and motions to Karen and my dad to join him. I swallow and then sit across from his mother and father. This is going worse than I had anticipated, and I've been dreading it more than I'd dread a sort of smear-test, bikini-wax, bra-fitting trifecta.

'How was the journey?' I ask Jack's parents brightly. I never thought I'd long to sit between my dad and Karen.

'Oh fine,' Gerald replies. 'Jane got a very good deal on the tickets.'

'That's good,' I say. 'I can't believe how expensive tickets are getting now. I was reading the other day that apparently they're

going to go up again next year as well, and then they'll just be even worse, and it's not like you're getting anything different, are you? It's the same train, and it's probably going to be late!'

They both look at me like I'm a burbling idiot. There's a very long silence which neither of them seem worried about filling. I look at Jane's hands, big and red. The gold ring on her wedding finger is the only jewellery I've ever seen her wear. No one says anything.

Silence is burning my skin. Jack says that his parents would go a couple of hours just moving around the house, cooking, sorting things out, without speaking to each other. This makes Karen's constant opinions about people on benefits, with a backdrop of Now That's What I Call the 80s, seem appealing.

'Have either of you read anything good recently?' I try, when the silence gets too much. Across the Berlin Wall that is the Twins, I can see Karen explaining to Jack why we need to stop all immigration and my father is looking at his watch.

'I enjoyed the latest Richard Flanagan,' Jane replies eventually.

'So did I!' I say with delight. Why have I done that? I don't know who Richard Flanagan is. I don't know what his book is about, or what it's called – with a gun to my head, I still couldn't tell you anything about it.

'Did you?' Gerald says, sounding pleased. 'I always forget that you're a reader.' Yes, Gerald, I want to say. I did the same degree as your son. At the same university. I actually got a 68.9 and he got a 67, so technically I'm more of a reader than your progeny.

They talk about the book for a while and I'm delighted for the distraction. The waiter comes and asks what we want.

Leila, not invited to go first, starts. 'For starters, can I get the chicken satay skewers but like without any of the satay sauce on it?'

'So just ... plain chicken?' the waiter asks.

'Yeah.'

He makes a note. Fucking great, now we're having starters, which absolutely no one wants. It's going to drag the meal out by another half an hour, maybe an hour, it's going to cost another hundred pounds, and they weren't even supposed to be here. I order the pâté and the burger because I'm starving and I don't care about being thin for the wedding anymore.

'No starter for me,' Jane says, 'I can't ever manage that much food. I'm not sure how you do it, Jessica. The plaice, please. Could you do a salad instead of the potatoes?'

This is not a slight. She is not talking about my body. She is not commenting on what I ordered. She does not have the girls' school complexity to say anything that passive-aggressive. She's a sensible, down-to-earth woman who likes plain food. She sees food as fuel, not as a way to punish or reward her body; she would be horrified to think that I'm upset by what she said. I know all of this. But none of it matters. And worst of all, like a monstrous stab in my stomach, I want my mum. I want someone sitting across from me chiding me gently for not eating enough, telling me that I need a nice lunch. I want someone to gently run their hand across my cheek and tell me that I'm going to be a beautiful bride. I've got two women who are both perfectly qualified to act like a mum to me, and it's not going to happen. Karen will tell me that she's not sure the dress was the place to save money and Jane will give me a curt nod and no one is going to tell me that they love me and they've been excited for this day since I was born.

I flame bright red, and obviously because I've got red hair, when I blush it's super obvious. Across the table, Jack catches my eye.

'What's wrong?' he says, as we pretend to order more drinks at the bar.

'Nothing,' I say. 'Just. You know. I miss my mum,' I say, trying to keep myself together. There's a break in my voice.

He wraps his body around mine and squeezes so hard that the ache in my chest temporarily subsides. 'I know,' he says. 'I know.'

This isn't the time to cry. 'How's it going at your end of the table?' I ask, knowing that the answer isn't going to be good. We've spent less time with my family, but every time we've been to stay, it's been fairly awful. My dad claps him on the back a lot and tells him that it's fine not to make much money, in a way which very clearly suggests it's really not okay. And Karen tells him endlessly that 'the media' is biased and brainwashing. Last time we stayed, he genuinely almost burst a tyre accelerating away when it was time to leave.

'Karen has told me I need to cover more stories about scammers who come over here and get on benefits,' he sighs, 'and your dad has said about four words. The twins are playing Candy Crush with the sound on. How's it going at yours?'

'Silence, a conversation about a book I pretended to have read, and some accidental food shaming from your mum.'

He looks shamefaced. 'I'm sorry about them.'

'I'm sorry about mine.'

'Let's swap seats,' he says, as the waiter hands us a bottle of wine in an ice bucket.

'We can't do that. It'll look so rude.'

'I don't care,' he says, steering me towards Dad's end of the table. 'Go and sit next to Martin, ignore Karen and get some time with him. And when he tries to pay the bill because I make a "pittance", smack his wallet out of his hand.'

I smile. We swap seats. And he is completely right. It's easier. Karen tells me a long story about this cream she's been using to make her cleavage less crepey, and actually it sounds quite good. I *say I want to get some and she says she'll pop some in the post, which is generous. She looks down the table at Jane. 'D'you think she wants some too?' she grins.*

I want to tell her not to be bitchy. But instead I laugh. 'No,' I say. 'I don't think that's her vibe.'

'Nice to see my girls getting on so well,' Dad says, coming back from the bathroom. 'It's going to be a top day.' He pats my shoulder, and I know he wants to say something about Mum, and I know he can't, and I'm sort of okay with that. At the other end of the table, the Rhodes clan are doing cryptic crossword, which Gerald has torn out of the paper and brought with him in his raincoat pocket. They're silent, and happy.

After what feels like a really, really long time and is actually only about an hour, everyone makes their excuses. Jack walks his parents to the station. I wave my father off, feeling like the most mature adult of all time for having refused his offer to pay. 'I know it's tough without her,' he says to me, gruffly, as he gets into the car. Then he presses some notes into my hand.

'Jack and I paid!' I say.

'Get yourselves something nice for dinner then,' he says. He looks guilty and sad and like he needs to spend some money to feel less guilty and less sad. And he can afford it.

When Jack reappears from dropping his parents off, I'm sitting outside the pub with a bottle of champagne.

'We're not going to be able to pay rent,' he says, on the approach.

'Sponsored by Martin. How was the walk?'

'Fine. They've found a museum of Roman life half an hour down the road from our wedding venue so now they're really excited about coming.'

I half laugh. 'Doesn't it make you sad? That they don't care about us getting married?'

'*No.*' *He smiles at me.* '*They don't care about anything which doesn't have a citation index. It's just how they are.*'

We sit in companionable silence for a few minutes.

'*I think maybe that's the way to play it, you know,*' *Jack says eventually, refilling our glasses.* '*I handle my family, you handle yours.*'

'*Isn't that the opposite of getting married? Aren't we supposed to like, unite our houses or whatever?*'

'*We both know neither set of our parents wants to be friends with the other. And we don't want to be anything like either of them. It'd be nice if we could have a big happy Mediterranean family all living under one roof, but it's not happening. You're better qualified to deal with your family's brand of mental and I'm better equipped to do mine. So let's do it that way.*'

'*It just sounds a bit selfish,*' *I counter, despite longing to agree to the deal.*

'*Not at all,*' *he says, looking quite pleased with himself.* '*It's prioritising each other's happiness. Handling our own business.*'

'*How would it work? If we're in Cambridge for Christmas, you're going to tell your dad that he has to let me watch the King's speech even though it's "monarchist propaganda"?*'

'*Exactly. And if we have to spend the weekend with Karen and Martin, you'll tell him that my terrible RSI means I can't play golf with him.*'

'*Don't you think we'll be upset if our kids do the same thing to us one day?*' *I ask him.*

'*We'll have to try not to be the kind of parents who require it.*'

I raise my glass to his and offer a little toast. '*Okay, it does sound like quite a good deal.*'

'*This marriage thing is a piece of piss.*'

'*We're not even married yet, you big show-off.*'

We clink glasses, and I look up at the clear blue sky. It's warm and light and the air smells of pollen. I hope it's like this two weeks today. But even if it isn't, it won't really matter. It's a little pub-and-registry-office wedding. I'm not doing it for the wedding bit, I'm doing it because I want to be Jack's wife.

Jessica

I stand on the street, shaking, and realise that I've forgotten my sunglasses. It's bright, cold early spring sunshine, so my eyes start streaming, or maybe I'm crying, I don't know anymore. There are tears pouring down my face either way. I'm still wearing my pyjamas under my coat, I've only got 23 per cent battery on my phone, and my career is over. All because my husband poured his heart out and told a load of massive secrets about me, about us, about our marriage, to a stranger. As I stand in the street, dithering, a man pulls up on a motorbike. He takes off his helmet to reveal a bald head, and then takes a huge long-lens camera out of his bag. He checks the door numbers and then angles himself outside my house. Surely not? They haven't sent a photographer to get pictures of us? I start walking before he can notice me, thanking my lucky stars that I'm only a tiny bit internet famous, and not any kind of actual celebrity. But the faster I walk, the more apparent it becomes that I don't know where to go.

When my mum died, one of the things I wished I had an answer to was when I'd stop wishing I had her around.

But actually I'm quite glad I didn't ask anyone, because I think they'd have told me the awful truth. It's never. You never stop wishing you had your mum. It still hits me at weird moments. When someone at work would get flu and go home to be looked after, when my friends have fights with their mums over lax grandparenting, and now apparently when you have the worst fight of your life with your husband and you don't know where to go. I could go to Dad's but I'd rather do almost anything else. I could go to Tom and Grace's, but they'll be getting their kids ready for school or nursery and I'd have to face them after they've clearly read the article. So the only place I can think of to go is Clay's flat. My phone is, obviously, blowing up. Producers for shows I've been on are asking me if I want to do a slot to tell 'my side' of the story. Various brands who work in the divorce space are asking me if I want to discuss branded work. Our account is full of people messaging to ask whether it's true, to tell me that they don't believe me, to say that they're disappointed, they're not surprised, they are surprised. My friends, who are mostly too cowardly to admit that they've seen it, are dropping 'Hey, how are you?' messages, some from people I haven't seen for literally years, who obviously don't give a shit about my welfare and just want to know what's really happening.

'Are you home?' I ask, when Clay picks up the phone.

'I will be in ten minutes. See you there,' he tells me, making it so that I don't have to ask. When my cab pulls up outside his flat, he's waiting on the doorstep, at the top of a little flight of stairs. I wanted stairs like that up to my front door but I decided we shouldn't buy a house like that because it would be a nightmare with a pram. But we still don't have a pram and maybe never will, so that was stupid, wasn't it?

'Darling girl,' says Clay, opening his arms. 'Come here.'

He ushers me inside and then hugs me for a moment. Then he pushes me through to the kitchen where he takes a bottle of vodka from the freezer and pours two little blue shot glasses.

'It's the middle of the morning,' I say.

'Yes,' he agrees. 'It is.' We both drink. 'But what a fucker of a morning you've had.'

He refills my glass but not his own. Then he gives me a bottle of very cold water from the fridge and steers me to the sofa, an enormous white marshmallow of a piece of furniture. It's comfortable but very difficult to maintain a dignified posture on.

'I would like you to turn your phone off,' he tells me. I look at my phone. I don't actually know how you turn this version off, I've never felt any need to. Silent in the theatre and airplane on a flight, but never actually off. I google for the instructions and then obediently hold the buttons down until it's no longer the thing which connects me to the whole of the rest of the world, and instead just a very expensive paperweight.

'Are you sure that's okay?' I ask.

'Ignoring it is the best thing you can possibly do. I say that as your manager, and your friend. And the publishers or anyone else should go through me anyway, so it's just one less thing for you to worry about.'

'Thanks,' I say.

'Do you want to talk about next steps?'

I nod. 'Are there next steps? I sort of assumed I'd need to put the house on the market and update my LinkedIn.'

He half laughs. 'Not yet. Is it true?'

I'm sort of surprised he has to ask. 'Of course it's not true!'

'You're not having problems?'

'Having problems doesn't mean you want to split up,' I say, twisting the bracelet around my wrist.

'*Are* you having problems?'

This is a trickier one to answer because it's direct. Because yes, if I'm properly honest, we are. But not the way Verity described them; she's made it sound like we're miserable and we're just staying together so we can make money by pretending to be happy, which is a cruel misrepresentation of what I've been trying to do.

Clay seems to have got bored of waiting for me to answer and starts making a complicated coffee. 'All right, easier question,' he says. 'Are you splitting up?'

'No,' I say, emphatically as I can muster. 'We're not.'

'All right. Well, at least that's easier. I won't lie to you, it isn't good. What this girl is saying is damning, and unless Jack can prove that he didn't say any of it to her—'

'He did.' I swallow. 'Not all of it. But he said some of it. I don't know how much.'

Clay takes a moment to compose himself. It's the first time I've ever seen him look shocked. 'Then there's not much we can do in terms of arguing that it's defamatory or libellous,' he says evenly.

'Okay.' I nod.

'So then I think it's going to be about image rehabil-
itation. Admitting that you've had a bit of a time of it,
that the bootcamp was as much about you and Jack working on your marriage as anything else. We do a post about
how you've never pretended not to have fights; we say that
your fertility situation is private and personal.' I wince at
his words. 'Which is entirely true,' he carries on. 'And we
distract with this Verity girl.'

'What do you mean?'

'We push that she came on the retreat, abused your
hospitality and trust; that her marriage is obviously in a
real state; that she was jealous of you and exploited some
admittedly real struggles that you're both having, and that
she took it public to try and promote herself, to make a
quick buck.'

'I don't think she was jealous,' I say weakly. 'I think she
just needed the money. She told Jack she wants a divorce
and she needs money to leave her husband and build a new
life for her and the kids.'

'Would you have done that? When you were really broke?'

'I don't know what I'd have done in her situation.'

'You're too bloody soft,' Clay says, ruffling my hair like
I'm his teenage child. 'You need to get a stomach for this
stuff. We're not going to make you as famous as I want you
to be without breaking a few eggs.'

'That's a very confusing metaphor,' I say, pulling a sofa
cushion to my chest. 'But we need to think of another
plan. I don't want to make Verity the villain.'

'Okay,' he says. 'Leave it with me. I'm going to leave you
to watch something while I do a proper damage assessment, and then I'm coming back. All right?'

SEVEN RULES FOR A PERFECT MARRIAGE

I want to resist because I'm in my thirties and don't need to be treated like a small child, but I'm too tired and sad and angry. 'All right.'

He hands me the remote control and doesn't even roll his eyes when I open Netflix and put the first series of *Gossip Girl* on. He disappears into his study and I lie on the sofa, watching the faces on the screen, wondering how long we can pay the mortgage for with what's in the bank, whether I will be able to keep seeing my lovely therapist, whether I can still have my gym membership, whether I'll still be able to pay for my dad to have his hip replaced privately. The list of things we need to pay for goes on, and on and on. Or maybe Clay will come back and say everything's over, and then the list will have to be cut short. I wish I could call my mum.

An hour later, when Blair and Serena are fully on the outs, Clay comes back. I jump up, like he's coming out of the operating theatre to tell me how the surgery on a loved one went.

'What?' I ask.

'Mixed,' Clay says. 'The publishers still want book two. They want to discuss acknowledging this in the book but we can come to that later.'

'What about the Americans?'

'They're not at their desks yet. You haven't signed any paperwork, worst luck, so they might try and reduce the amount they were offering, but I'll do my best.'

'Okay,' I say. 'What else?'

'The mental health app and the laundry people don't care, they want to keep working with you.'

I do some sums in my head. That means we can pay our tax bill for this year, and keep up our mortgage payments, but not much else.

'There's a couples' therapy brand who want to talk about a partnership, which is good.' He sees my expression. 'Okay, it's not good, but it's something.'

'What's the bad news?' I ask tentatively.

'The vitamins and supplements brand are pulling it; I think the fertility stuff is a worry for them.'

'Sure,' I say, trying to sound fine. 'Makes sense.'

'And your next appearance on *Morning Chat* has been cancelled. They said they'll pick up the discussion about a regular slot at some point.'

I sit up slightly. 'Well, that's good, I guess.'

Clay looks at me pityingly. 'That's showbiz for "you're dumped", I'm afraid.'

'Oh.'

'Yeah. So now we wait and see. It might be that other outlets follow, or *Morning Chat* might just be being over cautious because we're in the eye of the storm right now, and come crawling back next month. It could be either.'

'Okay. So it could be worse?'

'It could be so much worse. I'd still quite like to knock some sense into that husband of yours.'

'I know,' I say, trying not to think about Jack and what's waiting for me at home.

'There are also a lot of interview requests, from big podcasts, broadcast media, the usual. But I'm thinking that's too much of a risk. I think we keep control of all the content coming from you both and maybe just lay low for a few days. Agreed?'

'Agreed.'

When I get home that evening, I close the door behind me, quietly, and Jack doesn't ask where I've been. Maybe he assumes or feels that he doesn't have the right to ask after what he's done. I make the mistake of turning my phone back on and see people making videos about the story, posting their theories on all sorts of websites; there are newsletters and blog posts and think pieces. Some girl I knew at Bristol has done a self-indulgent column for one of the papers about how we were pressuring people to stay married. I didn't expect that from someone I once lent a spare pair of knickers to when she stayed over and slept with my housemate.

A couple of days pass with Jack and I barely speaking to each other. We sit through a painful council of war with Clay, the publishers, PR, and the crisis comms people they ended up hiring even though I don't think they said anything other than 'don't respond to any posts about you'. Everyone keeps saying the same thing – it will go away. People will lose interest. It won't matter this time next year. But we don't have a clean slate anymore. We're not blame-less or unassailable. Whenever we get a big brand deal or announce a new book, this is what they'll comment under-neath. We've joined the long list of influencers who have a chink in their armour, a top trump that someone else can literally always use to tell us that we're bad and wrong. And I guess maybe there's a power in that. I might be able to find some freedom in it, eventually, in the idea that the

thing I've been most afraid of came true and I survived it.
If I survive it.

And then it's time to put a post up from our own accounts.
Much like the times we have sex when I'm ovulating
even though neither of us really wants to, we've got to try
and perform something intimate to get the result that we
want. It's all very sexy. I pick a picture of us, on the retreat,
sitting next to each other in the snug, both talking to other
people. I go through dozens of drafts and eventually settle
on something which I think is pretty good. And then I go
to Jack's study, where he's been hibernating for the last two
days, mired in shame, and I knock on the open door. He
looks hollowed-out. I know how bad he feels. I've barely
said anything that I want to say to him because despite the
fact that we all know he's the cause of this problem, I hate
seeing him suffer and I absolutely can't be the person who
does that to him.

'Hey.'

'Hello,' he says, sitting upright. 'All okay?'

We're back to awkward housemates again; so much for
the progress of the retreat. 'Yeah. Fine. I wrote something.
For social.'

'Oh, great,' he says. I offer my phone and he takes it,
awkwardly, as if he's worried he's going to drop it. He reads
what I've written:

*Had a busy week? No, us neither. To be serious, we know that
we've been at the centre of a bit of drama this week. We've said
no to the interview requests and we haven't gone on any podcasts,
because we wanted to look at ourselves before we start talking*

about what happened. The piece about us was, at least in places, true. But it wasn't the whole truth. We have been struggling lately, and maybe we owed it to you guys to be more honest about that. Fertility, work, getting a bit older, it's all added up. We're a work in progress, and we need to keep talking about that. Thanks for bearing with us. J&J ♥

'Looks good,' Jack says, handing the phone back, barely looking at it. This is the man who rewrote the wording on our wedding invitation nine times, the man who personally checked every single credit for every radio show he produced, long after that was below his pay grade.

'Sure?'

He doesn't meet my eye. 'Yep.'

He goes back to his computer screen, where he seems to be reading about some cricketing controversy from the eighteen hundreds.

'You don't seem very interested,' I say.

'Do you actually want my feedback?'

'Of course I do. Why else would I have asked?'

'It's just a bit more of the same thing, isn't it? Aren't people going to see straight through it?'

'What? It's me being honest about the fact that we've had some struggles and apologising for not being transparent about it.'

'Okay, well firstly, why do we even need to apologise?' His face is open, he means this; I cannot believe he is asking this question.

'Because our management told us to.'

'But who do we owe this to? These people who follow us for free? Or the people who bought our book, which has good advice in it regardless of what we're doing in our personal life? Like, do people get pissed off with Jane Austen for writing romantic fiction and being a spinster?'

I'm really running out of patience now. 'Do you want me to post this or not?'

'You asked if I thought it was a good statement, I told you that I think it's more of the same toxic positivity bullshit – now you can do what you usually do and post it anyway.'

I blink at him, as if he's just hit me. Then I go to get my laptop, bring it back and smack it down on his desk. I open it, and find the spreadsheet where I track our finances. I make it as big as I can and then jab my finger at the words on the screen. 'Mortgage. Insurance. Heating. Electricity. Internet. Socialising. Gym membership. London Library membership. Ten different streaming platforms. The new sofa, the old sofa we're still paying off. Your credit card from when you were twenty-five. My credit card from when I was twenty-five. Student loan, student loan, student loan for your MA – are you looking at this?'

'Yes,' he says, though he's barely looking at it at all.

'How do you think we pay for all this?'

He swivels on his chair, like a truculent child. 'Jessica, I know how we pay for it.'

'So where do you get off being angry with me for trying to do damage limitation?'

'I'm sorry,' he says, getting to his feet. He picks up a stress ball, some stupid freebie we got at one of the first events we ever went to. Pushes it between his hands, worrying at it. 'I'm not angry with you,' he says. 'I'm angry with them.' He gestures at my phone. 'All these strangers in parasocial relationships with people on the internet, and our so-called management team who are making us prostrate ourselves for forgiveness when we haven't done anything wrong. They keep saying the word "accountable", over and over again, and I don't want to be accountable. I don't want to apologise to them because I didn't do anything to any of them!'

I say nothing. Jack says nothing. I leave the room and I post the picture. But it doesn't work. The next day Clay gets a call from the American publisher telling us that they love the book, but the timing isn't right. The contracts will not be drafted, the great American dream is dead. Jack tries very hard to pretend that he's sad about it, but I know the truth now. He hated our work together, and rather than telling me that, he sabotaged it. Subconsciously, I think. I don't think he's cruel enough to do anything like that on purpose. But the outcome is the same.

Jack

It feels a bit like someone has died. Everything feels wrong, and the atmosphere in the house has curdled. There's a sort of hush over it and I find myself in a weird kind of purgatory. Jessica isn't playing music on the speaker; the flat screen in the kitchen doesn't have reality TV on while she cooks. It's too quiet, and it's made me realise that it's everything she does that makes our house feel like a home. But despite the silence and the weird grief that hangs in the air, we still keep going about our daily routines. I don't know what else to do. I assume she doesn't either. Jessica goes to the gym, replies to work emails, and makes salads she barely eats. I go for long walks, read the papers and try to sort the garden out in an attempt to do something useful for once in my life. We hardly speak to each other. I realise she probably doesn't have anything nice to say to me at the moment, but I'd still prefer her shouting and screaming to politely freezing me out. She's stopped cooking for 'us', just making her own meals, so I wait until she's finished and then go and make myself something. I leave her to have the big TV in the living room, giving her space as I read in the study, pretty much living out of there so she can have the run of the rest of the house. I don't know how long it can go on like this, honestly. It's three days since the story broke, and everything about her is still a walking 'do not disturb' sign. She claimed in the crisis meeting with Clay, Suze and the team that she didn't blame 'anyone' for what happened. She was ostensibly reassuring Suze that she wasn't angry for the Verity story getting out, and me that she wasn't angry that I poured my heart out to a stranger, a stranger who happened to really need cash. But she didn't mean it. I know she didn't mean it. I don't blame her for not meaning it. She was in touching distance of having everything she'd ever wanted, and if I'd kept my mouth shut, she'd have it by now. When the news about the American deal falling apart came through, I realised that I'd never truly known the meaning of the word guilt before. Clay said loads of things in an attempt at reassurance, that it's better to start afresh with a different US publisher than to take a reduced deal from this one, that the news cycle is fast and people will forget about all of this, that our sales numbers are still strong and our career is not over. I don't think Jessica believed a word of it. I think she'd hoped that we'd put a post on our account and everyone would sort of get over it, but it hasn't worked. Clay commissioned a 'social listening report' which is basically a big document where they tell you what people don't like about you. Which means that we paid several thousand pounds to have a social media consultant tell us that people think we're 'fake and pretentious' because our apology sounded like an act. The worst part of the entire thing is that when the report came through, Jessica gave me this look of resignation. Like she was gearing up for me to gloat, to point out that I was right and the apology was pointless. I didn't want to say that. I didn't even think it. And I actively hated the idea that she believed I could watch her hurt and struggling and even dream of saying 'I told you so'.

Tonight's activity, as part of the 'pretending everything is normal in the hope that it might one day feel okay again' plan, is taking my parents to the opera. I'm getting changed into my smart suit because my mother likes that, and Jessica is sitting at her dressing table, applying a lipstick which is exactly the same colour as her actual lips. I go to kiss her goodbye. She doesn't pull away but she instantly tenses up when I touch her, which is much worse. She smells sweet and sharp, like blood orange.

'Remind me what you're doing this evening?' I ask, trying to make conversation.

'Quick drink with Clay and then dinner with Grace.' She dusts powder over her cheekbones.

She would usually offer to join us at the opera, and I would thank her but say that I didn't like to put her through it, but clearly we're not dancing that dance anymore. She did actually used to insist, years and years ago, before we came up with the 'your family are your responsibility' thing. Which was for the best. The four of us have always had a terrible time together, and it's only marginally better if my elder brothers are in attendance. Jessica gets defensive of me because everyone thinks I'm the family halfwit ever since the not-getting-into-Oxford thing. My parents think Jessica is sweet but 'unchallenging', which for them is on par with being a racist or a nonce. For her part, Jessica finds my parents judgemental and stressful, which again I can't fight her on. My parents have always seemed to regard her as flighty. Fluffy. A pretty girl lacking substance. Which makes absolutely no sense when you consider that we met at the same university on the same course where she got a better degree than me. Jessica isn't stupid. She's incredibly bright. She's just completely unconcerned about whether things are high- or lowbrow. She finds the Kardashians as interesting as she found the Borgias, and will talk about any of them in equally rapt detail. My parents have developed a charming tendency of pretending that they don't understand what we do for a living, which would be more convincing if they weren't both fluent in five languages and entirely abreast of current affairs.

We spent the pre-marriage years buying our families thoughtful Christmas presents (Jessica for my mother), feigning interest in investment portfolios (me for Jessica's father), and generally pandering to our parents' every whim, hoping it might make the whole thing work better. And it never did, so when we came up with the policy of handling our own parents, which would eventually become rule six, it was a staggering relief.

At exactly 6.45, I meet my parents outside the Royal Opera House. They've been seeing whatever opera was in during the autumn/winter season since I was a child, a treat that I was allowed to take part in once I turned eight, just as my brothers had been. Because what eight-year-old doesn't dream of seeing *Die Fledermaus*? Obviously, we go in November, because non-serious operagoers attend in December when 'tourists' turn up for a festive outing, whispering and rustling sweets.

It's not pretentiousness from my parents. They really just love this stuff. Their CDs of Tutti Van Whatsit have worn through. The car cassette of Verdi's *Macbeth* has had the spooling brown tape rewound more times than I can count. They can't imagine that anyone would turn up to watch an opera to show off, or to wear a smart outfit. My mother has worn the same navy blue dress, my father the same black jacket, for every one of these trips we've ever taken. The routine for these jaunts is always the same. An early supper beforehand, the opera, then a frantic Tube ride to the station where the only topic of conversation is missing the train, before a freezing twenty-minute wait on the station platform because we had allotted twice the requisite time to get there.

This year I decided to try and change it up, maybe even improve the age-old routine. I used my connections – or rather, connection singular, Clay – to get decent tickets. I figured given that he takes 15 per cent of our money, we might as well take advantage of the full 'service' that he claims to provide on his website. My parents' usual high-octane thrill comes from sitting in their specified seats for the first half, working out if there are any better unclaimed seats, and then grabbing them after the interval. This year I chose to ruin their fun by getting us a box. But as a result of this very generous arrangement, I now have to take pictures of myself in said box, because the nice people at the Royal Opera House would appreciate some content from me about our visit. We all know that my parents find my transition from reputable producer on a serious political programme to influencer distasteful at best, so why I have chosen to rub their noses in it is anyone's guess. I suppose on some level I'm hoping they might see the enormous privilege it affords us and think, *Fair play, why not make hay while the sun shines?* And, as it's increasingly looking like the only way to make things right with Jessica is to sign on to spend the next year salvaging 'the Brand', and writing another book, I'm keener than usual for their buy-in. The voice in my head which most vehemently looks down on our career has always been my parents', so perhaps if they understood it a bit better, I might judge myself less. Flimsy, I know. But I've got to try something.

What the opera house actually wanted in exchange for the best seats in the house was a picture of Jessica posing in the lobby, but she's not here, so I have to do it. Jessica has a skill for taking a large number of pictures discreetly so that we don't look like embarrassing tourists. My mother, on the other hand, can't find her glasses, or work my phone. She complains loudly about missing disposable cameras and I want to die. Then we (very slowly) make our way to the box, where I have to relive the horrors of the lobby by asking my mother to take yet more pictures of me, this time sitting in my seat. It's a very easy quid pro quo, and this is a very generous exchange, but I still feel like actually I would have paid basically all the money I have to avoid ever doing this again.

There are programmes on our seats and free drinks waiting on a small table in the box. My parents bear this odd scene with benevolent confusion and say all the right things about what a lovely treat it is.

'This is lovely, Jack,' says my mother as we settle into our seats. 'Aren't you generous?'

'I mean, I didn't pay for it,' I say, unable to just let this go. 'It was a press freebie.'

'Are you press?' my father asks, switching his everyday glasses for his watching-theatre glasses. He doesn't mean this to be a devastating put-down, he's just a nice man in his seventies who doesn't get it.

'No,' I say. 'I suppose not.'

The music starts and I've never been so glad to hear someone warming up an instrument.

We watch the opera. Or rather they watch it and I watch their faces, wondering if they're having fun, trying not to reflect on what a terrible idea this whole thing was. My mother is rapt by the performance in a way that she's never consumed by anything else. My father looks calmly content. The opera, if nothing else about the evening, is perfect to them. I scold myself for trying to improve on a routine they've had since they were students, when they used to take the bus down from Cambridge and queue up for return tickets on the off-chance they'd be able to catch the show. Thinking of them, queuing in their coats, two post-war babies who loved each other almost as much as they loved the silence of their libraries, makes me feel happy and sad in equally enormous measures. In the forty-five years they've been married, I am relatively sure that they've never had a real argument. They've gone blue murder over Kant or Keats. But nothing any closer to home.

As I try to focus on the stage, I notice in the half-light that my mother's hands, resting on her opera glasses, are red, presumably from the garden. She's had a bumper crop of cauliflower this year, she told me earlier with pride. My brother was also made a don at an Oxford college. She said that with a little less pride than the bit about the cauliflowers and a nasty part of me was pleased. It's reassuring to see that no matter what any of us do, we're never going to be able to compete with the joy of a really good vegetable harvest. I had therapy a year or so back, mostly out of interest. Jessica went, so I thought I should. We talked a bit about my parents and my relationship with them, and the therapist asked whether I'd ever considered telling my parents that their lack of approval hurt me. I didn't know how to explain to him that I don't need to. I know what they'd say. My mother would be sympathetic, of course. She'd be sad to hear that she had in any way hurt my feelings. But she would also be genuinely bemused that an adult man in his mid-thirties could possibly crave approval from his mother.

The show finishes and my parents applaud enthusiastically. Obviously this is the only correct time to express approval; they do not approve of people who clap between movements. We find our way through the crowds and out into the Covent Garden Piazza, where the air is crisp and cold. Someone's selling roast chestnuts, which is weird because I don't think anyone has ever wanted to buy any, but it makes the air smell like Bonfire Night, which is lovely.

'Would you like to go for a drink? I'm actually a member of a club nearby so it won't be too crowded or anything,' I offer. By 'club' I mean Soho House, because I secretly think it's quite impressive that I'm a member there, so despite knowing my parents as well as I do, on some level I want them to be impressed too. I made faces about the pretentious application process to join and rolled my eyes at the annual fee, but I love it there. I was, of course, utterly delighted when our membership cards arrived. I started suggesting it to friends instead of the pub. 'I know it's pretentious as fuck,' I'd say, as we drank expensive beers on the smoking terrace. 'But it's central and it stays open late?'

My parents both look at their watches. It's 9.30. 'We'd probably best be getting off,' my father says.

'The train—' my mother ventures.

I already know that this is a mistake, but I can't seem to stop myself. 'I've booked a car to drive you home.' If I'd said that I had booked them two places at a local orgy, they couldn't have looked more shocked. If I felt gauche earlier for getting them seats in a box, it's nothing to how I feel now. To my parsimonious parents, who darn socks until they're more darn than sock, and shop at Aldi ('like being in East Germany, darling, but very good quality'), taxis are sacrilege.

'Is it part of the opera house thing?' my mother asks, confused.

'Will they want a picture of you standing next to the taxi?' laughs my father.

'No,' I say, grazing the cobblestones with the tip of my shoe. 'I just thought it might be nice to have more time together. Have a drink afterwards. There's not a lot of time to chat, during an opera.'

Both parents can clearly see that despite being closer to forty than thirty, I am about three foot high right now. I briefly wonder if my jokes about influencer life might have made Jessica feel like I do right now.

My mother fixes an enthusiastic smile. 'Absolutely, darling. What a good idea.'

I walk in silence with my parents from Covent Garden to Soho House. Even though it's only fifteen minutes, I can feel myself losing the will to live. I try to tell myself that it'll be better when we're inside, but I know perfectly well this is only going to get better when their taxi arrives to whisk them home. Then, I'm struck with a genius idea. I look at my phone.

'Sorry, guys, this is a work call,' I say, pausing. They stand at the side of the street while I stride a few paces ahead and then dial the taxi company. I look back at my parents, giving them a wave and a smile as the taxi operator picks up. 'I've got a booking to collect my parents and take them back to Cambridge in an hour, and look, I'm going to level with you, I'm having a genuinely terrible time and I'm wondering if there's any chance you might come and pick them up early?' Another smile back at my parents, who are giving side-eye to the picture of a meaty man on the front of the sex shop I've left them next to.

The operator agrees to send someone ASAP and at last, I feel like things are starting to look up. I miss the door twice because I'm distracted, but eventually we head in and settle at a table. The magic I was praying for, the nearly Christmas miracle where they were bowled away by the tasteful interiors and celebrity clientele, does not happen. But because it's Saturday night, the music is blaring and it's too loud for them, which admittedly would have been the case if it were any decibel level above zero, but even I'm struggling. My parents ask for a single gin and tonic each. I ask for the same and then excuse myself to the loo, at which point I catch up with the waitress and ask her nicely to please make mine a generous double. She smiles. 'I'm the same when my parents visit,' she tells me.

My parents and I make small talk through one gin and tonic, and then the 'Hallelujah' chorus starts in my head as I get a text telling me that the taxi has arrived. God bless Mick in the bookings office. I see them into the taxi. My father gives me a handshake and my mother bumps her bony cheek against mine. Then, unusually for her, she takes my hands in hers.

'We're very glad that you're doing so well,' she says. She stops, searching for words, despite being one of the first women ever to get a PhD in ancient languages. 'Your happiness is paramount to me,' she adds. She seems satisfied with this and closes the door behind her. My father has said about five sentences all night. If I ever manage to get Jessica pregnant, then I'm absolutely resolute that I won't just allow silence to do the parenting for me. I get that they're clever people, they like subtext. But maybe when it's your kids, it's okay to put the 'I love you and I approve of your life choices' thing in clear, bold-lettered denotation. I watch the car disappear and then I decide to go back inside, not ready to face going home yet. I find another table, this time on the terrace so that I can smoke.

'Another G & T, please.' I gesture to the same blonde waitress as she passes the table.

'Double again?' She smiles. She's so painfully young. And it's also fairly painful that I'm at an age where I notice that people are young.

'Why not?' I ask.

I sit outside and inhale a cigarette almost in one breath – I bought a packet on my way out earlier tonight in the knowledge that my parents are the only people in the world who drive me back into the loving arms of nicotine, even though I officially quit years ago. I sit, looking up, trying to remind myself that my parents are further away with every passing second and that next year we can just get cheap tickets and have done with it. I check my phone. No missed calls, no messages. By instinct I go to Jessica's name, but hover my finger over it, unsure what to write. I want to tell her that if my snide attitude about the world of content creation has ever made her feel like I do right now, if I've ever behaved to her like my parents do to me when I talk about work, then I'm a piece of shit and I'm going to spend the rest of my natural-born life making it up to her.

It's good that she didn't come tonight. There's no reason she should have to be bored stiff at the opera and patronised by my dad. But I can't help wishing she was here, wishing that we were ploughing through a bottle of wine together, venting about my parents and maybe throwing in my siblings and the whole turgid lot of them for good measure. Maybe if I call her, maybe if she's still in central with Grace, we could both get in a taxi, we could tumble into the house and find our way into bed, or stay out and sing karaoke in a terrible bar, or walk all the way home like we used to when we were broke and wanted to save money on the Tube. I don't really care what we do. I just want to see her.

I tap my screen and the phone rings. Weirdly, I can hear a phone ringing behind me. You're not supposed to use your phone in here, though people do. I hear it ringing and crane my head. Jessica would have told me if she were here, surely? It's not exactly unusual, she comes here a lot. I get up, following the noise of the phone to the other side of the terrace. My eyes catch her shoes first, panning up her body, along her legs, up her torso, to her tight black dress, her beautiful red hair, to her cheeks slightly flushed, to her expression. Horrified expression. Presumably horrified because sitting next to her isn't Grace. It's Clay.

Jessica

'Hello, darling,' I say, getting to my feet and kissing Jack lightly on the lips, the same kiss we've done every time we've said hello or goodbye for the last however many years. Grace pointed out once, a few years ago, that at some point during a grown-up relationship you stop kissing with tongues, and I've always wondered if that's a meaningful moment, like it might hold the clue to whether a relationship will last. Anyway, this clearly doesn't look good, so I try to keep my tone as light as possible. 'How was the opera?'

'Hello,' Jack replies robotically. 'It was fine. Thank you.'

'I thought you'd still be with your parents. Weren't you going for a drink afterwards?'

'I thought you'd be with Grace. Because you told me that you were spending the evening with Grace.' He holds eye contact and the challenge is clear.

'Clay, pull up a chair for Jack,' I say. I gesture to the waiter for another wine glass, hoping Jack will just sit down and not cause a scene because that's the last thing we need right now, when we're still very much in damage limitation mode. You're not allowed to film or take pictures in here, but people tend to ignore that, and I'm sure we're not famous enough that anyone has clocked us yet, but it only takes one person, as we well know from recent experience. Clay returns with a stool from another table. It's much shorter than the other chairs, so if Jack sits on it he's going to look like a gnome. I take it instead, and then sit with my chest at table height, trying to keep it together.

'I was supposed to have dinner with Grace,' I explain, pouring a glass of wine for Jack, reaching upwards to the table. 'But there was some riot on the PTA – apparently one of the parents brought E-numbers to a bake sale and all the kids went mental. I don't know the details but it's big drama. So she cancelled.' I'm talking way too fast now, and it's making me sound suspicious even though I'm telling the truth. 'So Clay and I thought we'd have dinner.'

He and Clay are staring at each other across the table.

'I'm sorry about the American deal,' Clay says. He's polite, but I don't think he's stupid enough to think it's a good thing to say right now.

'Me too,' Jack retorts. 'Sorry to have lost you that fifteen per cent.'

Clay shrugs. 'I don't think I'm the one you need to apologise to.'

247

'Good, because I'm not apologising,' Jack says, getting to his feet. 'I am, however, leaving.'

Clay rolls his eyes. 'Going to throw another tantrum because you want to be writing your clever little nothing book instead of something which actually sells?'

I gasp. And in the seconds where I search for the right way to tell Clay that he's out of order, Jack picks up his jacket, puts one arm in the wrong hole, realises, clearly panics at how stupid this is going to look and grapples to put it on properly.

Clay sniggers and Jack looks like he wants to hit him. He won't hit him, obviously, Jack's never hit anyone. The only bad school report he ever got lamented his lack of aggression in rugby. But there's real hatred in his face when he looks at Clay.

'I'm going home,' he says.

I pick up my bag and turn to Clay. 'Put it on my tab. And don't talk to him like that again.'

'He's been a prick to you,' Clay protests. 'Someone needed to tell him.'

'It's my marriage,' I say over my shoulder, walking away. 'Stay the fuck out of it.'

Rule Seven

Always leave the party together

The Anniversary

Jessica

'Remind me why we're doing this again?' Jack calls, from our bedroom. It's still mostly not unpacked; there are cardboard boxes, bubble wrap in neat piles, a mirror and a handful of framed prints propped against the wall. It's surprising our stuff has made such a mess, given that our previous flat was like, five square metres, and this is a three-storey house. Honestly, I'd have been tempted to get rid of everything from that place, donate it to charity and start again. But obviously Jack would never have countenanced it.

'We're doing this,' I call back from our pristine en suite, newly painted the exact colour of the inside of a shell, 'because we barely even had a wedding last time.'

'I liked the first time,' Jack says defensively.

I loved our wedding too, but it wasn't what I would have chosen. We were broke, we wanted as little help from our parents as possible, and we were in our mid-twenties so we'd barely been to any weddings and had no idea how you were supposed to plan one. So in the end we had a little ceremony at a registry office on

Upper Street in Islington and then we rented out a pub with the lowest minimum spend we could find. We put cash behind the bar and ordered loads of pizza. The photographs were all taken by our friends, and someone Jack worked with at the BBC, a nice middle-aged dad in a Supergrass tribute band, did some songs for free because they liked the chance to practise. They played My Girl, fairly badly; everyone drank Punk IPA. I wore a dress I'd got on a mega discount and then tried to starve my way into, which never properly fit because I kept forgetting I was on a diet and eating crisps. All the pictures show me with chubby arms and a huge grin on my face, clinging on to Jack in his blue suit and shiny brown shoes. We look like teenagers going to prom.

So when the money from the book deal, the big fat sexy money, hit our bank account, I proposed that we do a party to celebrate our seventh wedding anniversary. And yes, a little part of me was thinking that it would make good content and that we could probably partner with, if not a champagne brand, then at least an English sparkling wine label, and that someone would probably lend me the kind of wedding dress I'd spent the last decade watching my friends wear for their own big days. Jack had rolled his eyes a bit, but more in a performance of being a typical man than anything else. He's not really the kind of blokey bloke to object to putting on a beautifully tailored suit and hosting our friends for an evening.

'Bloody hell,' he says, looking up from his chest of drawers, haphazardly unpacked, where he's searching for his aftershave. 'Look at you.'

I look in the mirror behind him. The dress is floor-length and almost white. There's the merest hint of ivory in a nod to the fact that I've been married for an age so if I'm still a virgin then things have gone pretty catastrophically wrong. It's got tiny lace edges and little straps, and I've had the best spray tan of my life so for once I'm not the colour of printer paper. My hair is slicked back and a make-up artist has applied gentle pink-gold make-up. I look nice. For the first time, possibly ever, I can't see anything in the mirror that I could improve. In fact, there's only one thing which is going to improve this moment and I can't quite believe I'm about to do it.

Jack goes back to putting cufflinks in, his back to me. I grab my phone and take a picture, his back, and in my hand a positive pregnancy test. The last photo ever taken of him before he learns he's going to be a father.

'Jack,' I say. 'Turn around.'

He looks at me for a moment, smiling, and then notices what's in my hand.

He bounds across the room and wraps his arms around me, smelling of the same spiced fragrance he's been wearing since we were students. 'Let me see!'

I hand him the test and watch as he drinks in the two lines, one very strong and dark, the other light but still very much there.

'It's light,' he says, 'that line, is that okay?'

I nod. 'That's normal, it just means it's really early. So we can't tell anyone.'

'Of course,' he agrees, clearly trying to fight the smile lighting up his face, trying to seem cautiously cool. 'But fuck me, Jess. We're having a baby.'

The car arrives and drives us to the venue, the top floor of an art gallery with panoramic views of London. Everyone is already there, milling around, drinking, chatting. My father and Karen have found seats and are probably complaining that the food is vegetarian. Jack's parents are talking to his brothers and their wives, all wearing the plain navy shift dresses they whack out for every single occasion. Our friends, our lovely friends, Tom and Grace holding hands, always so in love, Jack's work friends, the team from our agency and our publishers, everyone's here. We walk in, hand in hand, and the band I found after hours of scrolling start playing My Girl, just like at our real wedding.

The air smells like flowers and perfume; people are on the terrace smoking and looking at the haze over the city as the sun goes down. Dinner is served at long tables. It's all sharing plates and I insisted on catering for one hundred when we've only got seventy-five because I want everyone to eat as much as they want. It's perfect. I step outside on to the terrace to take a picture of the sunset, as everyone else is starting to sit down to eat.

'Jess.' Clay catches my arm. He looks worried. My stomach drops.

'What? What's wrong?'

'There's something on your dress.'

I look down at the front of my dress. It's pristine, I've been so careful. Then I look at Clay's expression and realise what he means. I run my hand down the back of the dress and my hand meets a sickening, sticky wetness.

'What do you want me to do?' he asks.

'Get Jack,' I whisper.

He's back with Jack within moments. One look at my face, at my stained dress, and he knows what's happening.

'What do you want to do?' he asks. Why does everyone keep asking me that? I take the champagne glass out of his hand and down it in one.

'I want to go home,' I say.

'I'll call an Uber,' Jack says, grappling with his phone, putting his passcode in wrong. His hand is shaking.

'No,' I say, 'I think maybe you should stay.'

They both look at me. 'What?' Jack asks. 'Why?'

'I don't want them to know. You can explain. Make an excuse.'

His face twists with worry; clearly he doesn't think this is a good idea. 'Are you sure?'

'Yes,' I say, resolute. I can't go home with him and feel the disappointment radiating from his skin.

'Okay,' Jack says, pulling himself up taller. 'Okay, I can do that. And then I'll come straight home. Do you need to go to hospital?'

I shake my head. I've had enough friends go through this to know that you don't need to go to hospital, that they can't do anything at this stage. You just ride it out and let it happen. I think there's a part of me that wants to believe I might still be pregnant. But I know I'm not. And right now my main concern is how I'm going to get out of here, and get home without anyone noticing that I'm bleeding, and without bleeding on some poor Uber driver's car.

'Okay. I can take her,' Clay says. 'You manage the situation here. Suze is around, she can give you some comms advice. I'll drive Jessica home.'

I look at Jack. Maybe this isn't what I want. Maybe I don't care what everyone thinks. Maybe I want Jack to take me home and hold me and make me chicken nuggets like he did before.

'Okay,' I say quietly.

Clay slips his jacket off and hands it to me. I put it on, and it's just long enough that it covers the back of the dress. He pauses outside the ladies' bathroom downstairs, without my needing to ask. I go inside. There was a part of me upstairs which was hoping that maybe it was a mistake. Maybe this wasn't really happening. I'm on the pregnancy forums, I've read the books, I know that spotting can be normal in early pregnancy. This is not that. The nude shapewear I wore, to conceal any evidence of having a body

253

under the dress, is soaked in blood. I stuff handfuls of tissue paper between my legs and then put the jacket back on. When we reach the car, I realise to my horror that his vintage sports car, the one I've taken the piss out of on various occasions, has light-tan leather seats. When I pause, he takes a navy tartan blanket from the back and chucks it down without saying anything.

We drive home in silence. I unlock my door. He hunts down a bottle of whiskey in the half-unpacked kitchen. Then he squeezes my arm. 'Do you want me to stay for a bit?'

I shake my head. 'I'm going to have a shower. And then I'm going to bed. Jack will be home soon.'

Clay nods. Clay leaves. I take the dress off, dropping it on the floor. I borrowed it from a brand. I was supposed to send it back. Obviously, I can't do that now. I run a shower the hottest it will go, sitting and watching the blood mix with the water. I'd like to cry, but I held it in for too long in the car and now I can't manage it.

I don't have any pads because I use tampons, but I remembered from when I had the abortion that you're not supposed to use tampons for this. Something about infection. I go to the study, the fourth bedroom in our huge new house. Ironically the one I'd earmarked for a nursery. I pull out boxes and boxes of free press samples I've been sent until I land on some eco sanitary-product PR box. Mercifully they've sent towels. I press a massive thick wadded one into my knickers, then put on a pair of pyjamas and get into bed.

When Jack gets home, he comes straight upstairs and crawls in next to me.

'I shouldn't have let you go home alone.'

'No,' I say into the darkness. 'You shouldn't.'

'I was in shock.'

I shrink away from him. 'Me too.'

There's a little pause.
'I'm sorry,' he says eventually.
'I know.'

Jack

We take a taxi back to the house in icy silence. The driver probably thinks we're two nervous singles who met in a bar and decided to make a night of it. That would explain the feeling of expectation hanging in the air. But it's not actually sexual tension. It's just horrible tension, like a headache pressing at the inside of my skull. I notice Jess pulling down her dress and can't help but sneer. I can't believe that she was spending the evening with Clay, probably having a great time bitching about how useless I am and being told she'd be better off without me. But they're not sleeping together. Obviously they're not sleeping together. Fuck, what am I going to do if it turns out that they're sleeping together?

It's a stupid question because I trust Jess. I love her, I know her, and I'd stake my life on the fact that neither of us have ever seriously considered for a moment that we might be with someone else. Our lives are too tightly bound, and we were too happy. Even while we've not been so happy, sleeping with someone else has never felt like it would help. Sure, I notice women. Occasionally I notice their bodies or their faces. But I've never had any meaningful desire to take one to a hotel room and ruin my marriage for a clumsy fuck. And I know Jess is the same. She likes a flirt at a party, but that's it. Which surely means that she was with Clay for something else. But is that actually any better? If she's off with him because she wants someone to talk to about what a shit I am – or worse, because he's the only person she thinks she can talk to about work stuff – then honestly, I think maybe I'd rather she *was* shagging him. Sex is one thing, it's just sex. But as I watch the lights of London on a Saturday night pass through the cab window, I think there's a very real prospect that it might be the big life shit that she's sharing with him and by rights I'm fairly sure that stuff is supposed to be mine.

We arrive back at the house, and I pay for the cab, giving him a ludicrously large tip in the hope that at least he has a nice night, and then follow Jess into the house. She stops to take off her coat but I don't bother and just stride through the house, into the kitchen, to pour myself a glass of wine.

Jess follows me and then stands in the doorway, silhouetted with her hands on her hips.

'Are you going to say something?' she asks, infuriatingly just as I was about to.

'Why didn't you tell me that you were going to have dinner with him?' I ask. I go to the fridge and take out a bottle of wine. I don't want a glass of wine, but I do want something to do with my hands while we talk about this, because at the moment I feel like I'm playing the role of Wronged Husband in a school play.

'I told you, I was going to have dinner with Grace then she had a PTA emergency so I hung out with Clay,' she explains, slowly and clearly as if I'm one of the E-number-addled kids in Raffy's primary school class.

'And you didn't think you should have mentioned it to me?' I ask.

'Honestly? No. I didn't. I thought you'd be vibrating with stress because you were with your parents, and I thought telling you would make things worse. You're weird about Clay. You always have been.'

She's not totally wrong, but I can't accept this. 'I'm not "weird" about him, I think he's an arsehole, and I don't really like that you spend personal time with someone who has ignored every suggestion I've ever made and clearly only values you as a source of income.'

'You know most men would be angry in this situation because they were jealous. Because they were worried that their wife was going to be unfaithful or at least enjoy getting pissed with a good-looking male friend. But you're too selfish to even be jealous. You don't like me spending time with Clay because you don't like him.'

This isn't entirely true but there's way too much nuance to explain, and I don't think I'd express it well enough. 'Does it matter why I'm angry?' I ask. 'You lied about seeing him because you knew I'd tell you I didn't want you to—'

'I understand that you don't like Clay, but in any relationship, you have to retain the right to have your own friends, our networks don't have to be—'

'Stop it.' I sigh.

'Stop what?'

'You're talking like you're writing another book,' I tell her.

'I'm not going to get to write another book, thanks to you.'

'How many times do you want me to say that I'm sorry?'

'But you're not sorry, are you? You're sorry that I'm upset, you're sorry that it got in the papers. You're not sorry that you destroyed my career because now you might get to write your tragic Martin Amis fan fiction.'

She has never, not in the entire time we've been together, said anything that mean to me.

'Jesus, Jess,' I say. 'It's nice to know what you really think. It's just a shame that all that honesty stuff at the retreat was clearly bollocks. A band-aid for a bullet hole.'

'Okay, let's have some real honesty, then. Let's stop this stupid "trying" thing, and tell the cold, hard, fucking truth.' She raises her voice.

'All right, if that's what you want.' I take a breath and look at her. My veins are twitching with the adrenaline of the fight. It's been a long time since we really lost it with each other. I'm scared to hear what she has to say, but I can't back down, and in some gruesome way I want to hear it.

'I miss you,' I say. 'I miss the version of you who would stay up till four a.m. drinking and talking shit. I miss how light and fun and mad you were. I miss you being creative and having ideas. All you talk about, think about, write about, is our bloody relationship. You turned our entire life upside down so that you could get what you want, so that you didn't have to be the girl with the job she hates in marketing. And you never once stopped to ask how I felt about it, about having to give up a job that was important to me and that I really fucking loved, all because it was a conflict of interest with your career, which consists mostly of posting photos of yourself on the internet all day.'

'You're right.' She doesn't seem to have heard anything I've said. 'I wasn't honest before. Because I knew if I was honest, I'd probably destroy our relationship and I didn't want that, because despite your very obvious disdain for me, I was trying desperately to make us happy. But I'll be honest with you, if that's really what you want. You're lazy and spoiled and entitled. You complain about a job that you hardly have to lift a finger for. I spent years working in shit jobs where people talked down to me for fuck-all money, and I did it with good grace. You've done eighteen months of this, so that we could buy a house, put some savings in the bank and maybe, sue me, buy a few nice things, and you've done it with the worst attitude possible because it doesn't meet your exacting standards. You're an intellectual snob who still needs his parents to think he's brilliant, and you've never got over not getting into some up-its-own-arse university when you were eighteen. You decided who I am, fourteen years ago, based on the fact that I had a topless tan, and not for a single fucking second since then have you considered that I might not be quite as carefree and childish as you want me to be.'

I'm not sure what hurts more: the fact that she clearly wants to upset me, or the fact that so much of what she's saying is – at least in part – right.

'That's not fair, and you know that it's not fair. You've changed.'

'People are supposed to change!' she shouts.

'Not this much – you were a joy, you were spontaneous, and free. Now you won't go anywhere unless you've packed the right vitamins. You came to our final English exam without a bloody pen—'

'Of course I had a fucking pen, Jack.'

There's silence in the kitchen now. 'What?' I ask.

'I had a pen. I'm not an idiot. I wouldn't have turned up to an exam without a pen. I just wanted an excuse to speak to you.'

'What?' I say, dazed.

'That's a good thing. It's a compliment. It's because I liked you, because I fancied you—'

'Sure,' I say, feeling a bit shell-shocked as I run my hands through my hair. It shouldn't matter. It doesn't matter, really. But that was our whole thing. It was in my wedding speech, it's the story we tell when someone asks how we met, it's our backstory, our, I don't know, *lore*. It was the first impression I ever had of Jessica and, she's right, the foundation stone for how I've read her over all these years. But apparently it wasn't real. 'I'm just slightly processing that you've been lying to me for the last fourteen years,' I say. It's supposed to sound dry, sarky but affectionate. It doesn't come out that way.

'Can you see how mad it is that you're mourning a story from over a decade ago, and not any of the stuff we're actually living through right now?' she snaps.

She looks at me for a moment with pure, white-hot anger, and then she draws a breath. And I know what's about to come is going to hurt.

'Can you see how "mad" it is that you tanked our entire career because you couldn't keep your mouth shut? Or that I've spent the last eighteen months trying to get pregnant with hormones and supplements and needles and all you've ever said on the topic is "it's going to happen"? Or that I finally found something I love doing as a career and you take every single opportunity you can find to make sure everyone knows that you think social media is beneath you?'

I sit down on one of the kitchen stools and decide that I actually really do want the glass of wine I poured and then left on the side. I take a big sip. It's not very cold and not very nice.

'Are you done?' I ask.

'No, I'm not done,' she says, her voice calm. 'When I told you I was on a press trip to Bath, I wasn't. I was with Clay.'

Jessica

The tension that crackled in the air when we were screaming at each other has dissipated. The air is thick and heavy now. I want to put the words back in my mouth, to unsay them. Everything feels brown and bitter.

'Why were you with Clay?'

I lean on the counter of the kitchen island, the marble cold under my forearms. It's a sort of barrier between us, me standing on one side, him sitting at the other. Like a boxing ring. Appropriate, I suppose.

'He took me to hospital.'

He looks surprised. 'Hospital? Why?'

I'm not deliberately eking out this information; I don't think this situation needs any more drama than it already has. I just can't work out how far back to go, or what to tell him. I take a long breath. I should have told him at the time. I know that. But every time I've ever tried to talk to him about fertility, he's told me that it's going to be fine, without a single word about how, or why, or when.

'I had a D & C.' I pause before explaining. 'That's a procedure where they try to clean out your womb. Usually after a miscarriage, it's supposed to make you—'

'I know what a D & C is,' he says. He's sitting and I'm standing, so in my heels I'm taller than his head height. He looks up at me and in this half-light, he looks so young.

I want to point out that I could be forgiven for thinking that he, a man, wouldn't know the details of a gynaecological procedure designed to improve fertility after pregnancy loss. The meanest part of me wants to ask whether he knows about it because he's done research into fertility issues, or whether he just happened to work on a programme for the BBC where it was mentioned.

'I had one done. And you have to bring someone with you because you're sedated.'

Jack looks like he might cry. 'You had a procedure under a general anaesthetic, and I didn't notice?'

'It was a routine day procedure and I had it done at a private hospital. Clay brought me home, you were out. I was okay the next day.'

Jack gets to his feet and walks across the kitchen, I sense with no purpose other than to move his legs in the hope that it'll help him process this information. 'Why didn't you tell me?'

'I don't know,' I say. Which is true. I don't really know. But that's not fair, and it isn't going to make this any better. 'I didn't want you to know. I thought you might be judgemental.'

'Why would I have been judgemental?'

'Because you're the most judgemental person I know' would be the obvious answer, but this isn't the moment.

'Because the clinic said it wasn't necessary. But there was a small chance that the D & C might help boost my fertility, so I wanted to do it.'

'And you think I'd have judged you for that?'

'You judge me for everything I do, all of the time!'

Jack sighs. 'I wouldn't have. I swear. I wouldn't.'

I don't think that's true, but we're reaching a calm impasse and I don't want to rock the boat. I go to where he's standing, looking out of the window at the garden and the orange windows of the houses opposite ours.

'Is there anything else?' he asks. 'With Clay, or anyone else?'

'No. Nothing,' I say, pleased that we're finally at the end of this horrible conversation.

'You've never spent time with him without telling me? Other than that?'

Why won't he drop this? 'I mean, not never, no. We went to an antiques market, we've had coffee before, I went to his house when the news broke. I needed someone to talk to, and he felt like the right person.'

'I was the right person,' he half shouts. 'You barely know Clay!'

Exasperated, I prise the heels off my feet and go to sit down on the little sofa at the far end of the kitchen. I admit, his reaction is surprising. I really did think that he was aware that Clay and I hung out. I've never hidden when he and I are WhatsApping, he's walked into the kitchen when we've been on the phone. I thought he might be ignoring it, or not engaging with it, but I was convinced he knew.

'Because we're close,' I say quietly, my arms around my knees. 'We've spent more time together than you realise.'

'Time together?'

I nod. 'I've needed someone to talk to. About how bad things are. Were.'

'With us?'

I nod again. 'I know it doesn't sound good. But I've been lonely, and I don't trust anyone else to keep it a secret. I thought talking to him was the safest way to make sure that it stayed private, that it didn't damage the brand.'

Jack rolls his eyes. 'Why is it always about the brand with you?'

'It's not always—' I argue.

'Yes, it is – why else would you have let Clay – who is basically just someone we work with – into something that should have been personal to us?'

And then I say the thing I didn't want to say. The thing I've spent months trying not to.

'Pretty rich from the man who let Clay drive me home from our anniversary party when I was having a miscarriage.'

There's another long, sharp silence. He's on the other side of the kitchen, miles of tiled floor between us.

'You told me to,' he says eventually. 'I wanted to take you home, and you said someone needed to handle the people at the party. That was what you wanted. I didn't want to stay, but I thought you deserved to decide what happened. I wanted to come with you.'

'Yeah,' I respond, suddenly overwhelmingly tired. 'Well, maybe I was having the worst day of my entire fucking life, and you should have stepped up and told me sod everyone we invited, I'm staying with you.'

He pauses for a moment. 'How was I supposed to know that that was the one moment of this whole new venture of yours where you didn't want me to prioritise your image over your feelings?'

'Oh fuck you,' I say, getting to my feet. 'Have you ever asked yourself why?'

'Yes,' he snaps. 'I ask myself that constantly. Why is it always about the job?'

'Because sometimes it feels like it's the only thing I've got.'

I'm done. I'm done being the driving force, the bad cop, living in a house with someone who thinks that I've sold my soul for cashmere and attention. It's not my fault that I – the less academically brilliant one of the two of us – happened to hit pay dirt on social media. I didn't start doing this because I wanted money, I started because I liked talking about relationships. And I've kept doing it because I still feel that way, and yes, it has brought in some money but I'm not sorry for that. No one else seems angry that I found something I was good at and I made us a life with it. But Jack, who used to see me as the most magical person on the face of the earth, now talks to me like I'm a disgraced politician. I don't want this anymore. I want to feel loved. I want him to see the best in me. I want him to like me.

And now that I've said everything I wanted to say, told him every nasty truth I'd been hiding, I'm quite sure that that ship has sailed. I don't like who I am when I'm around him, the way that I nag and scold and complain, the way that I'm always the adult, the demanding one, the one objecting and redirecting. All those words they only ever use to describe women – bossy, demanding, dramatic, diva – they swim around my head and they feel horribly, painfully true. I don't want him to be unhappy, and I don't want to be unhappy.

Neither of us says anything for a while. Then I get to my feet. Take a bottle of water from the fridge, and trudge slowly upstairs. Every time I hear a movement from outside the bedroom I freeze, thinking it might be him, coming to tell me that he loves me, that we can make this work. But he doesn't come upstairs, and eventually I hear the door to the spare room close. So I take a suitcase down from the top shelf of my wardrobe and very slowly, very sadly, I start to pack.

Jack

For the second time in a week, I don't know where Jessica is. She left the kitchen at the end of our argument, and when I woke up the next morning, she wasn't there. I don't exactly blame her. I said some horrible things last night, we both did. I fucked up by talking to Verity, and I think we've both known for a long time that I screwed up last year, at our anniversary party. So obviously, I feel guilty. But more than that, I feel angry. Angry that we were making progress, that we were doing better and getting better and it looked like we might actually be able to make things okay. We just needed a period of easy, gentle time, and we'd have been okay. And then all this shit – Verity, Clay, the American deal – came at us and the fragile peace we'd been building was crushed.

As soon as I woke up, I called her. Then messaged her. All the messages delivered but weren't opened or read. Her phone went straight to voicemail when I dialled. So I left it for a while, and then tried again an hour later. And then again, another hour later. And at this point, the terror has set in. She's never done this before. Even during Veritygate she was only gone for a short while to get the newspapers. In the entire time I've known her, she has never deliberately not replied to me. Back when we first finished university and went our separate ways, we used to email. I'd write to her first thing in the morning, from the college IT room. She'd reply last thing at night because her mornings were spent working at the local coffee shop and her afternoons were taken up with caring for her mum. I knew, without a moment's doubt, that when I logged on each morning I'd have a message from her. No playing hard to get. Getting together was hard enough, halfway across the country from each other. If we go much longer without her replying to me, we might reach a new record for the longest we've ever gone without speaking. This can't be right. I need to work out where she is.

If there's one way to find out if she's okay, it's going to be the Seven Rules account. So I go into the spare room that she uses for work, and turn on the massive great iMac. Jessica is not a safety-conscious person, she's too open-hearted for that. She didn't lock her doors at uni, she leaves her handbag on the back of her chair when we're out, lends people expensive clothes and expects to get them back. She's an optimist. Which is probably why she's also fairly lax with her computer security. The password to open her user is our wedding anniversary, as it is for basically everything, and anything which isn't that is ILOVEPONIES123. And once I enter that, her browser pops up, just exactly as it was when she closed it earlier. There are dozens of tabs, because she uses the computer in a cheerfully haphazard way which makes my teeth hurt. I shouldn't look. But I do. The first one is a men's jumper, and she's bookmarked it JACK BIRTHDAY. There's a handful of other tabs with similar labels.

On eBay she's watching a couple of first editions of Jeeves and Wooster books, despite the fact that I've already filled most of the shelf space in this house. She's a fantastic present buyer, constantly on the lookout for the perfect gift for people. Usually if she does spot something brilliant that one of our friends or family will love, she'll buy it on the spot and then won't be able to wait until their actual birthday or Christmas, handing it over immediately instead. One of the many things I've always teased her for. And loved her for.

Then there's a parenting forum. She's been posting in the fertility section. There's a tab: 'threads I've started'. I tell myself I'm not going to, and then I do it anyway. I want to know her. I want to know what she's been thinking and feeling and wrestling with. And oh God. She's started so many threads. So, so many. Asking about symptoms she might be experiencing, asking about supplements, sex positions, dietary improvements, clinics, experimental treatment. 'My husband isn't willing to try IVF yet,' she's written on one post. 'What's wrong with your husband?' some anonymous poster replied. 'Does he actually want a baby?'

There's another post titled 'D & C – DO I HAVE TO TAKE SOMEONE WITH ME?' in which she'd posted that she's having a voluntary D & C, because she's read that it can improve fertility after a miscarriage. 'Do I need someone to take me home or will the clinic discharge me?'

she'd asked. 'My husband isn't able to come with me.' Even on anonymous forums, she's lying to preserve a perfect image of us. Or maybe, I find myself thinking, because she's protecting me.

A nice fellow forum user has explained that she will definitely need someone with her because it's a brutal experience. I realise that, last night, when she told me that she'd been to hospital with Clay, I gave almost no thought at all to her being in pain, or her having something medical done, only the fact that she went with Clay. Fucking hell. I close the tab because I can't bring myself to read any more of it.

There, on our profile: 1.1 million followers. Down from the 1.25 we'd reached before I blew everything up and, as Clay's updates remind me, still falling. @Jack&Jessica. When her account about our relationship started to gain traction, she paid a couple in Texas, who barely posted, to buy the username. It cost her $150 and I thought she was absolutely mad for doing it. Shows how much I know.

Next to the inbox is the 'settings' icon. For some reason I click on it and then hover the mouse over 'delete account'.

All of our problems started with this account; we were happy before. Happy and kind and a team. Weren't we?

I think back to Jessica's Sunday night blues, coming out of the shower with an expression of condemned misery, hardly able to talk while we watched TV, insisting on another episode because going to bed meant going to sleep, and going to sleep meant waking up to another week of work. The emails she'd send me in the middle of the afternoon when she'd been talked down to and told off all day, no matter how hard she'd tried. It was years of that.

And it got progressively worse with every year she stayed. I remember it would take her weeks to amp herself up to apply for other jobs, and then when she got rejected, because she didn't have the right experience or there were too many people trying to get into social media and content creation, she'd pretend not to care but it would tear her up. And every rejection meant weeks before she could bring herself to try again. After months of it, she just stopped trying, and my cajoling only made things worse. But everything making us miserable now stems from this account.

While I'm hovering my mouse over the 'delete' button, dithering, the little message icon in the corner flashes red. Without thinking about it, I click. It's a message, in a long thread.

> *Thanks. It's a really good point. I think it's just the stigma of being the first of my friends to split, y'know? Like everyone is going to be saying I've failed.*

I read the conversation, and see that it goes back several weeks, in dribs and drabs. It's with a young woman in Kent who is thinking of leaving her husband, who has a gambling addiction. She's exchanged maybe thirty messages with Jessica, during which Jess has sent charity resources, offered advice, and reassured this girl that leaving her husband is a perfectly reasonable thing to do. And now I can't stop myself – I open the inbox and I scroll down. There are hundreds, if not thousands, of conversations.

Young women, older women, young men, middle-aged men, people in same-sex relationships, people with kids, people with fertility issues. Every one of them is asking Jessica's advice and she has replied to literally every single one. It can't have been easy, carrying all that emotional baggage for other people, listening to them talking about their horrors when she was having her own private ones. But her responses are brilliant and well considered. The advice is thoughtful, and reasoned and kind; it's even funny in places. Where there are suggestions of abuse, she's firmly directed people to the police, and in some cases it looks like she's even helped a couple of people to extricate themselves from horrible relationships. Time after time they apologise for not buying the book, or not being able to afford the book, and either she gives them advice anyway or she offers to post them a copy. She solves spats, advises on rifts, even sometimes helps out with things which have no bearing on marriage. I don't know how long I'm reading for; my back is aching by the time I look up from the bright white screen, into the darkness of the room around me, realising that I have catastrophically misjudged my wife.

The box room, the one I occasionally allow myself to fantasise about wallpapering with dinosaur paper, is home to all the free stuff we get sent, which Jessica clears out once a month by dropping a load of boxes at the refuge and the food bank. She hasn't done it for a while, so the products are piling up, and I know that somewhere in here I'll find what I need. Eventually I find a nice-looking notepad with a pale blue cover. I grab a Sharpie and I write 'RULES' on the front. Then I take a picture. Jessica makes this look easy, taking nice pictures. It's surprisingly difficult. But once I've got something passable, I open a draft post. Then I take a deep breath and start to type.

Jessica

I wake up, head on a crisp white pillow, to the feeling of a small child's soft hand stroking my cheek.

'Do you think she's dead?' Ada whispers.

'Probably,' Raffy says. I rush to sit up and open my eyes because I have a feeling I know how he's going to check whether I'm alive or not, but it's too late, and Raffy flings his entire body weight, which is quite a lot even though he's an average-sized five-year-old, at my sternum.

'Woah!' I yelp, sitting up.

'Yay!' Ada shouts. 'Not dead!'

After we throw some pillows around for a bit, and I've dodged Raffy's question about what death really means (because I can't remember what Tom and Grace decided about their kids and the topic of mortality), we go downstairs. Grace is standing at the kitchen counter in her leggings and a jumper which says HOT MAMA on the front.

'Sorry,' she says. 'I would have stopped them coming into your room, but when they're harassing you, they leave me alone, so ...' This is the most candid thing she's ever said to me, and I assume I've earned it by turning up tear-stained on her doorstep after the row with Jack last night.

'Not a problem,' I say. 'We had fun.'

Grace makes me a cup of coffee and we sit at her huge kitchen table. Some of the records, which were mounted in brackets on the walls, displaying their sleeves, have gone. The paint is a little darker in the squares they used to occupy, where the sun hasn't bleached it. I assume Tom has taken them to his new place. I feel a pull in my chest at the idea of him unpacking and putting things he loves on new walls. Another for Grace, who has to look at those empty squares every day.

'So what happened?' she asks. And it's a fair question. When I turned up last night, I was too sad to talk, and I knew she'd give me a bit of space, but she's a lawyer, she wants answers, and she'll get them out of me whether I like it or not.

After I left the house last night, I walked to the end of the street, once again hoping that Jack was going to follow me. He didn't, and so I opened my phone and started to call a taxi before realising that I didn't know where I'd be calling it to. Last time I went to Clay's, and I could have done that again. But it felt like if I did that, if I went to see the person we'd – in part – been arguing about, I'd be picking a side. And I didn't want that. I considered my dad's place, and yes, I could totally have gone there. It's not like he'd turn me away. But I reasoned that he'd want to know what was going on, and as he's been looking for a reason to dislike Jack since we met, this would provide exactly that. Maybe, I tell myself with a little twinge of hope, it's a good sign that I don't want to tell my dad about all this, that I want him to still approve of Jack. That I don't want this to be the end of us. I started to look for a hotel on the basis that paying for somewhere to stay would unquestionably be the best and most sensible thing to do, but the thought of it made me feel so achingly alone. So, I swallowed the pride which I had let get in the way of my friendships, and I dialled Grace's number.

'Get in a taxi,' she said, before I'd even finished my sentence.

And now we're sitting in her kitchen, drinking massive oat milk cappuccinos while her kids destroy the playroom, and I notice the rude nakedness of her left hand, from which her massive diamond wedding band, and even more massive diamond engagement ring, are conspicuously missing.

I tell her everything. About the fertility stuff, the Clay stuff, the American deal, the whole horrible, sticky mess. And eventually, once I've finished projectile talking at her, she considers me for a moment, and then asks, 'Do you think he's being unreasonable?'

I sigh. 'I don't know. It would be easier if I could say which one of us was capital W wrong. I know this isn't exactly what he wants to be doing, but it's setting us up for life. Once we've got a decent dent in the mortgage and some savings, and all our debt is paid off, he can write clever books all day long.'

'Have you told him that?' Grace asks. I shake my head. 'Out of interest,' she asks, 'why are you so averse to letting him do his own thing? To doing this influencer thing on your own?'

I don't like the question, but we're having a go at this honesty thing, so I tell her the truth. 'We're a brand. A team. A package deal.'

'Do you have to be?' she asks, cocking her head to one side.

'I tried to make a success of things on my own for years. Literally years. I applied for more jobs than he'll ever know. I tried blogging, I wrote short stories, I went to evening classes to learn how to write for TV, I even tried stand-up.' Grace laughs at this. 'And the only time I managed to succeed at anything,' I go on, 'was when he was doing it with me.'

Grace gives me a look, which I think is supposed to tell me that I am being insane. 'Look,' she tells me, getting up to wash the cups, which we've barely finished drinking from. Tom used to laugh about what a neat freak she is. I wonder how much of a journey it is from laughing to sneering. 'I don't know shit about fuck when it comes to being an influencer. But the market is predominantly women, right?'

'Yes.'

'And most of your audience is women?'

'Yes.'

'And you're doing most of the work for this joint account?'

'I don't know if "most" is fair ...' I trail off as she waves a hand at me.

'So you're smart, and funny, and attractive. You've got good clothes and good ideas. Have you never stopped to think that this huge, mostly female following is actually there because they like you? Like, specifically you?' she says, hands on hips.

I lay my head down on her dining table and moan dramatically. 'But if that's true then Jack and I have been having the worst fights of our life for no bloody reason.'

Grace laughs. 'Look, I know you guys have had a rough time, but I really don't think it's terminal. A decent therapist and a couple of rounds of IVF and you're golden.'

I know it's not that simple. It's the kind of flippant throwaway comment which means Grace gets sent to HR intermittently for being mean to the Gen-Zs at work. But

I like it. She makes it sound so straightforward; I almost believe her.

'Okay,' I say. 'I'm going to call him and say that.'

Only I can't find my phone. I had it last night, but when I woke up this morning, I was so distracted by the kids that I didn't look for it. And now it's totally disappeared. We hunt high and low, tipping out my handbag, my overnight bag, looking down the sides of the bed, and then suddenly Grace realises what might have happened. Flushed, we go back downstairs, and Grace summons the children into the kitchen.

'Did one of you take Jessica's phone?'

They both shake their heads.

'Are you sure?'

They both nod.

'If you can find Jessica's phone, I'll let you watch Peppa on the iPad.'

It transpires that Ada and Raffy do know where my phone is, and it appears within seconds. They're then given the iPad, which is a bit like a winning lottery ticket as far as they're concerned.

I take my phone off airplane mode and notifications start rolling in. Just like before when the Verity story came out.

'Fuck,' I say, opening it. 'Something's happened.'

Grace leaps into crisis management mode. 'What? Another article? Where are you seeing it?' She opens her phone and her work laptop and starts frantically googling. 'I can't see anything on any of the tabloids? Just the same article from before.'

'It's not that,' I say quietly, looking up from my phone. 'Jack has posted something. On our account.'

Grace takes a sharp intake of breath. 'Oh God. What now?'

Slowly, trying to keep myself composed, I open our profile. And there, in the top left-hand square, is a photograph. It's a different resolution from the ones I take, and it's not in the colour story my grid is currently adhering to. Have we been hacked?

It's a picture of a notebook, and in his handwriting, writing I've been looking at for nearly half my life, he's written: 'RULES'.

'I can't do it,' I say, looking away from my phone. 'You read it.'

'You'll have to read it at some point, you might as well rip the plaster off,' Grace says.

'At some point, sure, but not yet. Please. You just read it and tell me what it says.'

'Grow up.' Grace sighs.

I hold her gaze.

'Fine.' She sighs again. 'I'll read it to you.'

Anyone who follows us will know that I fucked up this week. And what you've read – the things I said – were partially true. But they were also only part of the story. We did write a list of rules for our perfect marriage, and we wrote them by living our lives. And for a long time, they worked. But we got older, and life did things to us: we struggled with infertility, money, career turbulence – all the normal, horrible stuff that makes a life a life. I told someone last week that our rules weren't working, and I was wrong to say that. They did work. They just aren't working for us right now. The truth is, there are no set rules for a marriage because a marriage isn't a set thing. It's a living, breathing organism and you've got to keep changing to keep up with it. It doesn't matter what your rules are, it matters that you're both still trying to make them.

I haven't been a great partner over the last few months. I broke Jess's trust, I hid the fact that I was struggling, and I wasn't there for her in moments when she needed me. And because of that, I damaged our marriage, and I damaged something she'd worked hard on: this community. She's had her flaws, too. Neither of us has been perfect. But some people now claim that because she and I are having trouble, our rules don't work. But those people are wrong. We know those rules work because they got us here, and they made us into a couple who want to keep trying to be happy together, whatever it takes.

There's no one set of rules which will last forever, and now it's time to make some new ones. And I'm very much hoping that Jess will make them with me.

Grace stops and looks at me. 'What do you think?'

'I think I need you to drive me somewhere.'

In films, when there's a mad chase to the airport, the protagonist usually runs towards a waiting taxi, or speeds her sports car down the road. She doesn't usually have to wait for her best friend to find two children each a pair of matching Zara trainers, and then strap them into their uber-safe rear-facing car seats. It takes nearly half an hour before we can slowly reverse out of the drive, with the *Moana* soundtrack vibrating through Grace's Chelsea trac- tor of a car.

'Hurry up!' I say. 'I need to tell him I've seen it and I love him.'

'You know that thing in your hand makes phone calls as well as posts photographs, right?' Grace says, driving directly over a mini roundabout.

'I don't want to call him, I want to turn up on the door- step. It's romantic.'

Grace rolls her eyes, then indicates.

'Nope,' I say, reaching over and cancelling the indicator. 'I need to make a stop before we go home.'

'Where now?' Grace asks.

'WHSmith's.' She takes corners worryingly quickly. 'I'd forgotten what a horrible driver you are,' I say, gripping on to the handle and understanding why they shelled out for the £500 car seats.

'You don't even have a licence!' Grace retorts, cutting someone else up and giving them the finger. My satnav takes us to the nearest branch of WHSmith's, where I buy every single pack of biros that I can find while Grace waits outside, double-parked in the enormous four-by-four, ignoring anyone who beeps at her. Then I run back to the car, arms full of packs of ballpoints.

'Now you can take me home, please,' I say.

Jack has rung me twice – presumably he's at home wondering whether I've seen his post and if I'm okay – but I'm tired of hiding behind my phone and want to talk to him in person.

Grace screeches to a halt outside our house, waves me good luck and then she's gone because the kids have a spin class or something. I ring the doorbell despite the fact that I've got keys, and stand, waiting for him. He takes a while, and eventually when he comes to the door, he's wearing pyjamas and the dressing gown he's had since uni.

'You came back,' he says, a big smile appearing on his face.

'I did.'

'You saw what I wrote?'

'Yes.'

'What did you think?'

I hold up my WHSmith's bag. 'I agree. I think we need some new rules. This time I brought a pen.'

Some hours later we are lying on the softly carpeted floor of our living room, surrounded by pens. I roll over and realise that one has been digging into my back. Jack laughs and takes out his phone. He takes a picture and shows me the perfect outline of a Bic in my skin. 'You should post that,' he laughs.

'Nope,' I say. 'This one's just for us.'

The Happy-ish Ever After

Jack

I know that Paris in the springtime gets great press, but I don't think you can beat London in the spring. It's the exact sort of late-March day that makes me want to jump for joy. I leave the office to realise that for the first time this year, I am leaving in the light. The sky is the kind of blue you find in children's storybooks. I decide that I will walk home. My hours are different from my first stint at the Beeb – more sociable, more conducive to a grown-up marriage. A little part of me misses roaming the Broadcasting House in the middle of the night, knowing that the only people listening are taxi drivers, drunks and insomniacs. But this is good too. It's a different show – a higher profile one. To my surprise, they offered me a better job, something I wouldn't have thought I was qualified for. Ironically they cited my 'incredible experience navigating the world of social media' as one of the reasons I was right for the role. Jessica was kind enough to laugh.

Her following is still growing at a rate of knots. She's been asked to contribute to some government investigation into how images can be marked for editing and 'unrealistic changes'. She talks about infertility sometimes. Not all the time. She turns down requests to talk about it publicly. She doesn't want to be a spokesperson for infertility because she doesn't want to be infertile. But she's not hiding it anymore. Not from them, and not from me. She invites me to doctor's appointments and I'm grateful to go with her. I sit in lobbies and listen when she explains what happened, and then when she's processed everything, I venture my opinion. I've learned that there's a middle ground between telling her everything I feel and expecting her to manage it for me, and shutting her out by telling her absolutely nothing.

Nearly at our house, I stop at the wine shop and pick up a bottle of their palest rosé to start the weekend. Then I turn my key in the door and find her sitting on the sofa, legs twisted underneath her, bashing away at her laptop.

'You're going to end up with a wizened spine if you work like that,' I say, going to get two wine glasses.

'Fuck off,' she says good-naturedly.

'Rosé?'

'Go on then.'

I bring her a glass and she stretches up to kiss me. 'Love you,' she says. 'How was your day?'

How was my day? Bloody marvellous, actually. I tell her about the interview we set up, about how Helen's questions didn't get approved but that I reworded one of them and it slipped through the net so she had one of the UK's most odious men twisting on the line. She laughs at my mean expression. Her fingers are so long and tanned on the stem of the wine glass, her arms dusted with fine rose-gold hairs which are somehow like sand on a beach.

'How was yours?' I ask. She tells me about her morning yoga and the fact that she wants to try something called 'oil pulling'. I laugh at her and she laughs along. She had a big essay deadline last week, so she's been taking things easier, but she's within touching distance of being qualified, a huge step on the road to becoming a bona fide therapist. And in the meantime, there's her next book. The one which doesn't have my name on. Pre-orders are better than anyone had hoped. I had always said that I wouldn't be jealous if she did this on her own, but I had no idea whether it would be true. I just knew that I didn't want to stop her from doing any of the incredible things she's capable of. To my relief, it turned out I am not jealous, just overwhelmingly proud. I love my normal nine-to-five life. I love shit office coffee and talking about *The Apprentice* with my colleagues. I love the Tube and Pret sandwiches just as much as Jessica loves the freedom to wake up when she feels like it, take a long walk in the middle of the day and work exactly as much as she deems necessary.

'Shall I cook?' I ask.

She considers me for a moment. 'No,' she says. 'Let's go to the pub. But let's be quick, I'm absolutely starving.'

Within minutes she's downstairs, wearing jeans and a white jumper. Her face is bare and there's a slight softness to her cheeks which she had lost for a while. She looks so much like she did when we first met that it catches in the back of my throat.

'Come on,' she says.

Months ago, when we were desperately trying to get ourselves back on track, Jessica said that she didn't know what to do anymore. I think at some point during this whole thing, we realised that there's actually only one rule either of us needed to understand: there aren't any universal rules for a happy marriage. Some days, total honesty is the best policy. Other days, discretion is the better part of valour. There are times when we need to stay up late to hash out the argument, and times when a good night's sleep – even in separate bedrooms – makes us more able to talk calmly to each other the next morning. There are weeks when we need a kick up the arse to make sex a priority and weeks when it's fine to just spoon instead, times to cheerlead for each other tempered by times to tell the other one they're pursuing a very bad idea.

In the end, we didn't fix our marriage because we followed the rules. We didn't 'fix' it at all because, happily, we discovered that it wasn't broken. We've realised that it's always going to be a work in progress. Week by week we make it better, by spending time together, by talking about things. By shouting and crying and shagging and by showing each other in a thousand tiny ways that we're in this forever.

After dinner we walk hand in hand down the road, stopping to look at the heavy blossom making the tree branches sag. I always thought that a happy ending would mean parenthood, and that hasn't happened yet. Perhaps this time next year we'll be doing the same thing with a pram, or we'll be in a hospital waiting room, about to hear a heartbeat on a scan. But even if we aren't, if it's just her hand in mine, even if there is never a third, smaller, sticky hand in ours, I know without any doubt: we're going to be okay. And sometimes – not all the time, but in moments like this one – we will be more than that. Occasionally, we will be perfect.

Acknowledgements

I started writing *Seven Rules for a Perfect Marriage* in September 2020, on Corsica Street, Highbury. Five years later, I went back to finish the final edit, sitting in a café across the road from the flat where it all started.

When I began the book, I was married, and trying to get pregnant. By the time it was finally done, I was half-way through a very complicated divorce, single mum to a two-and-a-half year old, living in South West London and in a relationship with a new partner. Arguably, out of getting pregnant, becoming a single mum and dating for the first time in over a decade, finishing the book was the hardest part.

Happily, I had some help along the way, from a cast of characters old and new. First up, the old guard: my agent Eve White, along with Ludo Cinelli and Steven Evans, who have represented me with unwavering support since I was a twenty-something baby author. Without Eve ringing me intermittently to remind me I actually should finish the book, I probably wouldn't have.

My parents, Tim and Charlotte, who stepped back into active parenting duty for both me and their granddaughter when my life fell apart, and my siblings Lucy and George and their divine partners Matt and Ellie, all of whom have created a better-than-normal non-nuclear family for my daughter.

I also couldn't write an acknowledgement without recognising the usual cohort of people who inspire me, share with me, read my writing, let me read theirs and provide a shoulder to cry on/come to my house with wine when I can't afford a babysitter. Ellen Scott, Miranda Larbi, Jessica Lindsay, Madeleine Spencer, Angelica Malin, Felicity McDonald, Stephanie Barrett and Hannah Connolly.

Then there's some new important people around – the post-divorce generation.

Charlotte Knight, my eternally stylish stage, screen and book-to-film agent, one of my favourite lunch and gossip companions, who took a gamble on my career when I was four months post-partum and mostly just cried all the time.

Nick Stylianou, my first ever male friend and now writing partner. I look forward to becoming an EGOT with you.

My boyfriend Mark O'Brien, who proved, despite all my protestations, that actually it was possible to fall in love again, and perhaps even stay in love. You have shown me that the cliché is true, and that love really is a verb. Workshopping, proofreading, daydreaming with you are some of the best ways to spend my life. I hope we have lots more fights about lots more novels.

Margot Persephone Iris, my daughter. It's impossible to know whether you'll ever read this, but if you do, then I suppose you'll know a little bit about what it was like trying to get pregnant with you, and all the different permeations of it I experienced along the way. It's a cliché, but it's entirely true that I am grateful for every single aspect of that journey because it produced you, and as far as I'm concerned, there would be very little point to the world without you in it.

Lastly, Darcy Nicholson. My first editor, and now my editor again, who plucked me out of low-grade Twitter journalism in my mid-twenties, taught me how to write a book and then took another punt on me seven years later, when God knows I needed it. Thank you for being the backbone of my writing career.

A Note on the Author

Rebecca Reid is a writer and former digital editor of *Grazia* who is obsessed with how people relate to each other. In addition to writing for outlets including *Daily Telegraph, Glamour*, and *Stylist*, and regularly contributing to *Good Morning Britain*, Jeremy Vine and BBC Radio, she is currently adapting 90s cult film *Single White Female* for the stage and is working on various TV pilots. Rebecca has previously written five books (four thrillers, one non-fiction) but after almost a decade of journalism about sex and relationships, not to mention the demise of her own marriage, she finally felt ready to pen a love story. She has an MA in Creative Writing from Royal Holloway and lives in South West London with her toddler.

A Note on the Type

The text of this book is set in Bembo, which was first used in 1495 by the Venetian printer Aldus Manutius for Cardinal Bembo's *De Aetna*. The original types were cut for Manutius by Francesco Griffo. Bembo was one of the types used by Claude Garamond (1480–1561) as a model for his Romain de l'Université, and so it was a forerunner of what became the standard European type for the following two centuries. Its modern form follows the original types and was designed for Monotype in 1929.